God's

Gambit

The Cosmic World of Olympus

Joseph Bell

Copyright © 2024 by Joseph Bell

All rights reserved. No part of this book may be used or reproduced in any form whatsoever without written permission except in the case of brief quotations in critical articles or reviews.

This book is a work of fiction. Names, characters, businesses, organizations, places, events and incidents either are the product of the author's imagination or are used fictitiously. Any resemblance to actual persons, living or dead, events, or locales is entirely coincidental.

Printed in the United States of America.

For more information, or to book an event, contact :
Email : TCWOlympus@gmail.com
Web: http://www.thecosmicworldofolympus.com

Book design by Joe Mansir
Cover design by Joseph Bell

ISBN - Paperback : 9798990153349
First Edition: December 7, 2024

Contents

CHAPTER ONE: KNOCKED DOWN, NOT OUT 2
CHAPTER TWO: INFORMANT 15
CHAPTER THREE: CHAINS OF FATE 29
CHAPTER FOUR: A HERO'S BURDEN......................................40
CHAPTER FIVE: THE MOTHER OF MONSTERS................60
CHAPTER SIX: THE BELLY OF THE BEAST 83
CHAPTER SEVEN: THE POWER OF UNITY..........................96
CHAPTER EIGHT: JUST THE BEGINNING 101
CHAPTER: NINE: THE UNDERWORLD 121
CHAPTER TEN: ATLANTIS 133
CHAPTER ELEVEN: A REALM BUILT FOR TITANS........143
CHAPTER TWELVE: FROM CHAOS TO ORDER..............154
CHAPTER THIRTEEN: A PROMISE KEPT 164
CHAPTER FOURTEEN: THE OLYMPIANS..........................184
CHAPTER FIFTEEN: TEMPTATION 200
CHAPTER SIXTEEN: TANGLED DESIRES 213
CHAPTER SEVENTEEN: SEEDS OF JEALOUSY 227
CHAPTER EIGHTEEN: SNAPPED 245
CHAPTER NINETEEN: THE WEIGHT OF DECEIT 251
About The Author 269
Acknowledgments 270

DEDICATION

To my mother, Cheryl Mansir, and Joe Mansir,
Your love and support have been the pillars of my journey, nurturing my dream and vision for the Cosmic World of Olympus. This book, and all that the brand encompasses, flourished under your guidance and belief in my aspirations. Thank you for being my steadfast cheerleaders, for every word written and every world built is a reflection of your unwavering faith in me.

To my beloved wife, Ivy, and our wonderful children, Ethan and Livia:
My love for you knows no bounds. You inspire me daily with your joy, curiosity, and boundless
love. Thank you for being the light of my life and the heart of my world.

Joseph Bell

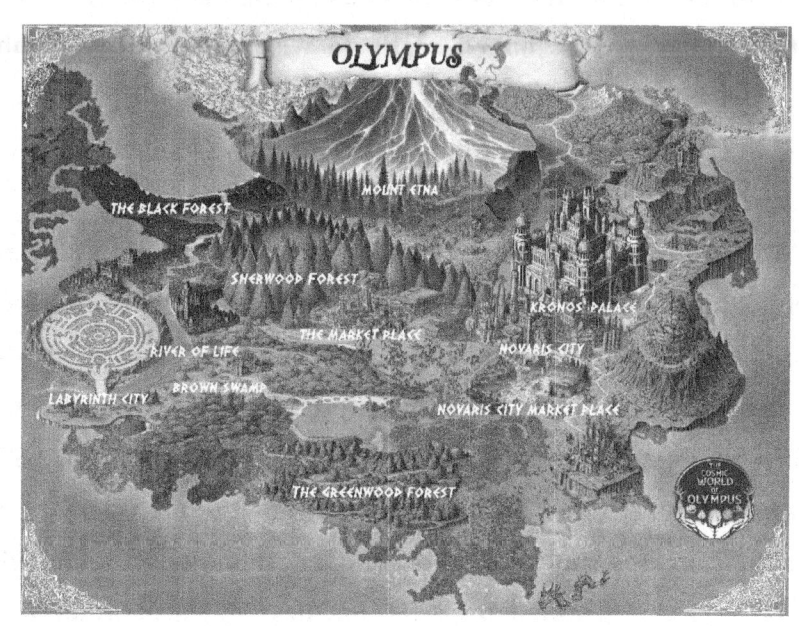

CHAPTER ONE: KNOCKED DOWN, NOT OUT

From shore, the island looked small and spare, barely more than a clump of dirt rising from the river. Inexpertly-built huts did little to shield their occupants from the inclement weather, and chickens had escaped their enclosure to run amok. The blue-green waters of the River of Life churned high at its shores, such that one good storm looked ready to wash the entire scrubby stretch away. No one who passed this island would ever have thought it capable of containing the remnants of an entire army, the last of the force that had been amassed to defeat a god.

But appearances can be deceiving, and those bold and pure in spirit and motive could cross a sudden shallow stretch of river, to find a much larger island than they had seen from shore. No less ramshackle, though. Horses clustered together in poorly built stables and most of the buildings were lean-tos. A few worked at plucking chickens or making bread, but most of the warriors sat like their horses, huddled and wearing their weary grief like blankets. They grouped together heedless of race: minotaurs, wizards, men and more, sharing bowls of a thick lentil stew, speaking little. Every so often someone glanced toward the largest of the island's structures, a long, single-story house that had been closed and quiet for some days now. Two women sat outside the house, watching four children as they played with sticks and stones. The grass around the house had sprung out of the mud overnight, and new ivy twined up one wall. The roof was fuzzed with moss. Whenever one of the soldiers caught the eye of Leda or Ivy, they smiled a weary smile; *soon,* their eyes seemed to say.

Soon, we will have news. Soon, we will have our plan. But when they glanced at each other, their expressions were full of worry.

Inside the house were three gods, two humans, and a Mother. Ethan and Raven stood at a table laden with uneaten food, holding hands. They were islands of calm in a flood of confusion. For the three boys — Hades, Poseidon and Zeus — stared at Gaia, the woman who once bore them and gave them away.

The woman who told them now that they shared a bond of brotherhood with the very tyrant they had tried to kill.

"That's impossible," Zeus spoke first. Through a haze of grief and confusion, Hades recognized his brother's tone. Such bravado usually meant he was uncertain and afraid. "We've seen Kronos and he's nothing like us."

Gaia tilted her elegant head and smiled a smile like cool waters. Her dress was moss-green, her skin as dark as the fertile ground of Olympus. As she moved, flowers folded and unfolded on her dress, white lilies to acknowledge the dead. "No one is like you, my youngest," she replied. "Each of my sons is unique."

Brother. The word was like a gong in the stillness of the room, shattering the fragile peace they'd put together in the aftermath of the battle. The orchestrator of Hades' every sorrow — the killer of his wife and brother, the commander of armies that had raided his home and sent his family into hiding, the shadow that had loomed over his entire life - was his own flesh and blood.

In a twisted way it made sense. Hades could see the similarities in the threads of power, the magic they drew on. They had no need of staffs or wands or complicated spells the way wizards did, and nor did Kronos. The way Gaia's power seeped from her was a reminder of their own abilities, and Kronos' powers were a dark mirror to their own.

Gaia stood and crossed her arms over her chest like a shield as she moved to the window. When sorrow fell over her face, a shadow passed over the sun as well, and the room became dim and cold. "I bore Kronos to be the leader of this world. I didn't understand how the power and the pressure would corrupt him. He moved free of my influence, and disdained both my wisdom and my love. When I realized he was headed down a dark path from which I could not move him, I knew I had to stop him some other way. That way was the four of you."

"Now the three of us," Poseidon murmured, putting a hand over his heart as if it physically pained him to say it. Their fourth brother Atlas had been Poseidon's twin, and his death at the hands of Kronos the tyrant had naturally hit Poseidon the hardest. Worse, Poseidon's own love, Diana, had been murdered by one of Kronos's hideous creations, Medusa, during the battle. Poseidon was perhaps the only other person in this room who truly understood what Hades was feeling right now.

"If you work together, you can defeat him," she said.

"And we would be kinslayers." Poseidon clenched his massive fists and looked at the ground, swallowing.

The kinslayer was accursed, a bad epithet to have put to one's name. Yet Hades forced himself to think past his grief and confusion. "Perhaps we would not be kinslayers, but heroes," he replied. "Few would mourn the death of Kronos. Who would wish to call us kinslayers and spit at our feet?"

Poseidon dragged his lips back in a humorless smile. "Oh, I

don't know. His armies? The people who work for him?"

"His armies are largely constructed of men who fear him too much to refuse their conscription," Ethan replied. "Or men who are opportunists and see the army as a place to advance their station and their wealth. They would abandon a battle they did not think they could win, and certainly none of them would dare to defy you if you could defeat a god of Olympus."

Zeus' golden head moved back and forth. "I can't believe it." He stared at Gaia resolutely, and Hades knew his brother was doing it to avoid looking at him. Guilt clung to him like cobwebs, and his fingers twitched. Hades stared at them, the hands that had cast the lightning that had killed Persephone.

Hades shook himself mentally. If he let his thoughts stray down that path, the only result would be the loss of another brother. Instead he cleared his throat and said, "We don't have much choice, do we?" All eyes turned to him. "Before the battle the world stood on the brink of annihilation. Nothing has changed that. Our initial plan has failed, and so we must find another." He stood, too, feeling the weight of all his father's teachings and expectations on his shoulders. It felt as though he carried the hope of the entire world.

Poseidon threw up his hands. "Just like that? After we lost–everything?" His voice cracked and he stopped, rubbing furiously at his eyes.

Hades put a heavy hand on his shoulder, squeezing gently. Well did he know his brother's grief. And yet — "Yes. Just like that," he said gently, and went outside.

###

Hades walked the perimeter of the island three times. After the first circuit he gave up on trying to think of a new strategy and let his mind wander. His thoughts swirled like the angry river around him, buffeted about by sorrow and anger, twisting and dividing only to braid together again. No matter how hard he tried, they always came back to her. Persephone, the light of his life, the only love he'd ever truly known. She should have lived. They should have won, then retired to somewhere very like this island for a long and happy and anonymous life. Hades couldn't help but think that his life would have been happier if he'd never tried to stand up to Kronos at all. For then Persephone would still be alive, and no matter how the tyrant ruined the world, Hades would have found happiness as long as she was by his side.

Now she was gone, and the world was without color. Part of him lived forever in that moment: he saw the glee on Kronos' skeletal face, the fury on Zeus' as he hurled his lightning. The deafening crack that signaled the end of his beloved's life and the end of *his* life, as he knew it.

On his fourth tour of the island, Hades knew that he had to transform this anguish. He had to turn it into something he could use. A rage that could be lit to destroy Kronos and ignite the fires of resistance once again, spreading them far and wide and inciting the rest of Olympus to rise against the tyrant. If anything could make the deaths of Persephone, of Atlas, of Diana of *all* the loved ones destroyed by Kronos' evil worth it - it was this. The destruction of Kronos and the evil he'd brought to the world.

Hades forced himself to bring that moment to bear again: the lightning bolt, the triumph of Kronos, the light leaving Persephone's eyes as her soul fled her body. He tried to focus on these things, but his mind's eye never let him forget his own brother, the wild rage of Zeus as he flung his lightning bolt. If Zeus had but thought for a moment, considered the consequences of his actions—

No. Hades could not blame his brother. Zeus had followed the plan, even as the plan had gone sideways. It was not Zeus who'd seized an innocent to take his place in death. It was not Zeus who'd truly killed Persephone. And the way Zeus wouldn't look at him, even now, reminded Hades that his brother acutely felt the guilt of her death. Hades would need to be forgiving. He didn't want this to come between him and Zeus for the rest of his life.

The air smelled suddenly of her: pomegranate flowers and spring. The rustling of the wind sounded like a whisper, and the hair at the front of his head lifted away as though drawn back by a caressing hand. He swallowed a sudden lump in his throat. "What am I to do?" he asked the wind in a hoarse whisper. "What are *we* to do?"

Only the wind answered, and it did not speak a language he knew.

###

Zeus went into the little room they shared and lay on his musty-smelling mattress. It was the only thing he could think to do; everywhere else had people, and he wanted to be alone. He didn't want to go out where the soldiers would be watching him with thinly veiled reproach, disappointment for failing them in so many ways. Or disgust, even, for killing one of their own. He didn't want to run into Hades, either. His brother would say all was forgiven, but Zeus wasn't an idiot. Hades had loved Persephone with a fire that another man could only envy. They were meant to grow old together and have a clutch of joyous children. They were the sort of people whose hearts lay with each other, not with any place or thing or vocation. Zeus knew that if their roles had been reversed — if Hades had killed Leda by accident — he would have destroyed the entire island and everyone on it in his rage.

And everyone else on this island had expected Zeus to destroy Kronos. To save them. To win the day. He was the most powerful of his brothers in battle, surely everyone could see that. With his lightning like arrows and the power of the storm at his fingertips, who could possibly have killed Kronos, if not him? Yet he'd failed. And if he'd failed, he did not see how anyone could succeed.

He could never throw lightning again. Not after seeing the destruction it could wreak.

The door creaked open. "Go away," he said morosely.

"No," said his wife, and shut the door behind her.

Zeus managed to lift his head from the mattress. He had the beginning of a pounding headache and all he wanted to do was sleep for the next hundred years. Waking up in a century sounded good - he could start over with everything.

But there was one thing he didn't want to start over with, and she was slipping under the blanket next to him, laying her body flat along his and her head on his shoulder. She'd tied her black hair behind her head and changed her hunter's garb for a green linen dress. "Where's Hercules?" he asked.

"Ivy's watching him. Zeus, what are you doing?"

"I'm thinking," he grumbled, shifting against the mattress. The straw tick.

"You're feeling sorry for yourself," Leda told him. She leaned above him, watching him with shining eyes. Her dark skin shone, too, with some inner light that always took Zeus' breath away. "My love, you don't have time for that."

"I'm not feeling sorry for myself," he protested, but they both knew he was. He scooted over to make a little more room for her on the mattress. "Besides, who's going to want to include me in the planning now? I can't be trusted." He'd been goaded into attacking at the wrong moment. He'd let his fury and his need for revenge cloud his better judgment, and many had paid the price for that. Ethan had taught him better. And the longer Zeus sat at that suffocating table, the more he could feel the eyes of his father upon him, judging. The eyes of his brothers, trying not to despise him. It was better to lie here.

"This is not the man of action I fell in love with," Leda reminded him.

"Well, you fell in love with a fool," Zeus replied.

Her lips pursed and her eyes swam with amusement. "Yes, I did."

"Hey!" She wasn't supposed to agree with him.

Leda sighed, and the amusement was gone, and that made

him even sorrier. "You are a fool to think you're not valued and not needed. I spoke with your father, and no man can take your place in the coming battle. You have a grand destiny."

"A grand destiny to mess things up," he said.

"A grand destiny to save the world for your son," Leda replied, with iron in her voice. "Or have you forgotten that he depends upon you? As we all do?"

Zeus sat up to face her, running a hand through his hair to get some of the straw out. The weariness of the battle, the guilt of his actions, the longing that he could be anywhere else, doing anything else — it made electricity flare in his eyes, and he clenched his fist to keep from singing the mattress with a little lightning bolt. "Maybe I'm sick of being depended on. Who chose this great destiny for me? Because it wasn't me."

"And who is the man who runs from it now?" she retorted. "Because that isn't you, either."

Zeus took a deep breath and drew the energy back into his body. Her words were cold and half furious, and they were right. Leda was always right. He'd always run toward this grand destiny. The problem was, he never thought he'd fail.

"I don't know what I am anymore," he confessed quietly.

The door opened again and Poseidon poked his tan head in. "You're our brother," he said. "We can all hear you, by the way. Come out, the war meeting's on again."

###

Hades took his place next to Gaia at the circular table and

forced himself to eat a bit of bread that tasted like mud and ash. A fiery tear still leaked from his eye, turning cool in the river island air and flaking off. Ethan and Raven stood as Poseidon brought Zeus, somewhat unwillingly, to the table. His brother still wouldn't look at him. Hades would have to rectify that. But right now they didn't have time for one of Zeus' sulks. They had to regroup, to figure out who was still with them and what they could do. He closed his eyes and swallowed his bread and forced himself to think of Kronos again, that triumphant expression as Persephone lay clutched against his chest, and used the resulting heat to fire his determination. They *would* make Kronos pay.

"We have to discuss our options," he said. "Leda, how does the army look?"

Leda had been trying to slip out the front door. She startled at her name, then straightened and put her hands behind her back, tilting her chin up. "Tired," she replied. "Defeated, which shouldn't surprise anyone. A little hopeless and without direction."

The words were meant as a challenge, and Hades took them that way, nodding to her. "It's time to give them direction. Whether that direction is to go home and give up arms, or to sally forth for another try."

"We can't possibly attack again," Poseidon said. Ethan was nodding. "We couldn't defeat Kronos with a fresh army at full strength, even though we had the element of surprise. Telling them to attack again would be like telling them to commit suicide. Unless you have some sort of plan...?" he raised a brow at Hades.

Hades shook his head. He didn't have a plan - not a plan of

direct attack, anyway.

He agreed with Poseidon's assessment, and Ethan and Raven obviously did as well. But he needed to make a point, so he turned to his youngest brother. "What do you think about it?" he asked.

Zeus' eyes went to the table. Never had Hades seen his brother timid. He'd hardly ever seen Zeus guilty, for that matter. "Everyone's exhausted," he said finally, in a tone so neutral it sounded like someone Hades didn't even know. Zeus was never neutral about anything. "Kronos' army has the advantage of numbers, and now they know what we're — capable of." He had to force himself to say that last part. "I don't think the faction leaders would join you if they didn't think we had a chance of winning. And, well, we don't." He took a deep breath but set his face resolutely.

"I agree," said Hades gently, and he was rewarded when Zeus' eyes flickered up in surprise. "Another full battle would be imprudent."

"So we've lost," muttered Zeus.

"We can't surrender," Hades said. That had become clear to him on his long walk. "Kronos won't forgive anyone who dared to defy him, not the lowliest footsoldier."

"Which means going on the run. Again." Poseidon made a fist and propped his head on it. His nostrils flared and outside the window Hades heard the roar of the river intensify. "How long will that work for us? How long before someone turns us in, or has our whereabouts tortured out of them? Kronos knows now that the Cross of the Iron Phoenix is spread across Olympus. His men will be working harder than ever to stamp it out."

Hades nodded. This was true, too. His brothers were wise in the ways of war. They would understand, therefore, what needed to be done. So it was with a sense of relief that he said, "What if one of us gave the others time? Time to escape, to assume new identities, to regroup?"

There was a brief and uneasy silence. Then Ethan said, "What exactly are you proposing, my son?" His jaw was twitching.

"I'm going to give myself up to Kronos," Hades replied.

Everyone started talking at once.

"Hades," Gaia began in her measured voice.

"You can't!" Raven half-gasped.

"Absolutely not," said Poseidon.

"If anyone does that, it should be me," Zeus said, loud enough to silence the rest of them. Color had risen in his cheeks, and once more he dared to raise his eyes to meet his brother's. Anguish swam there. "I was the one who failed. I was the one who brought this on you — on all of us. Father taught us to take responsibility for our mistakes, didn't he? So I should take responsibility for this. I can give Kronos another run for his money while the rest of you disappear."

"You shouldn't be condemned to death for a mistake," Hades said.

"Even though my mistake caused the death of someone else?"

Hades' heart wrenched. Unbidden, the memory of Zeus' face, twisted in fury, flashed in his mind. The raised lightning bolt, ready to fly. Hades closed his eyes for a moment, unable to let the pain shine out.

When he opened them again, he focused on the dark figure standing by the door. Leda, stricken, staring at her husband in shock.

It was her face that gave him the courage he needed to be gentle. "You didn't kill my wife, brother. Kronos did, and only Kronos. You have much to live for. What do I have?"

"A son?" Ethan reminded him tersely.

Yes. Little Achilles, the last remaining tether between Hades and Persephone. And yet — "I know that he would be in good hands." For how could Hades face raising his son alone, seeing the boy who was so like his mother?

Gaia put her hands on the table, and lilies sprung up around her fingers. "I do not like to involve myself in the wars of men," she said. "But this grief has been brought about by me. I bore four sons because your destiny was to defeat your brother together. One of you already took it upon himself to face Kronos alone, and the consequences have been dire. Do not repeat this mistake, son of fire." She fixed Hades with her grass-green stare, so luminous it reminded him of the forests of home.

"She's right." Poseidon said. "If we try to defeat him one at a time, he'll pick us off. And then what hope will there be for Olympus? We must do it together."

Hades felt frustration building in him. "But there's no way," he said. Why couldn't they let him do this? Sacrifice himself for the greater good? What more could he do, now that his plan had failed? As a leader he was evidently ill-equipped to plan a rebellion. Better for him to step aside and give someone else the time they needed to plan a successful one.

"We're not getting anywhere with this," Ethan said. "I think what we need is time." As Poseidon opened his mouth to protest, Ethan held up a hand. "Do you think the Cross never faced setbacks before? We have to regroup, to think of what worked and what didn't. It's true that this setback is...more substantial than most, but now we know things about the enemy that we didn't know before. We need to consider these and incorporate them into our strategy. Even now, scouts who weren't part of the battle are reporting back to me about the aftermath with Kronos' army. He didn't get out of this unscathed. Now we must be patient, and gather what information we can."

The brothers looked at each other, united for the first time since the battle in their confusion. "But...how long can we afford to wait?" Hades asked.

Ethan gave him a tight smile. "That is the true question."

CHAPTER TWO: INFORMANT

And so the ramshackle camp on the island disassembled. People took their chickens and pigs and horses and went home in groups of six or seven, with Poseidon pulling the river aside for them to cross. Merlin's son Harry Ambrose conjured a dense mist around the island to mask the activity, and so the days were wet and cold and rather dismal. Everything smelled of damp, and Hades' clothes took on a sour note. Those who stayed — the brothers and their families, and a few others — were strung like bows, almost vibrating from the tension. An army could descend on them at any moment, if their wards of protection and concealment failed. And likewise, at any moment, a strategy could reveal itself, a plan to overcome the tyrant at last. Yet the days continued, and the sun rose and cast a watery light over their camp, and nothing happened. Time stretched out so long it felt nearly meaningless, and Hades grew tired of looking at the sundials and the water clocks and anything at all that might tell the hour. The rest of his life was only taking him further into a lonely existence and farther from his last moments with her.

He started training again with the sword and a bident staff. At first he attacked a straw dummy, one of the remnants of the practice grounds from before the battle. He liked the bident staff, the way it could catch a weapon or a wrist between its two prongs. Once he'd mastered its basic forms he took turns sparring with Poseidon and Leda. They didn't try to talk, and he appreciated that. Poseidon was using training as a way to keep his own grief at bay and together, they could forget the outside world and all its ills as their weapons tapped relentlessly against each other. Hades trained until he was too tired to even think about what was next, until he could barely drag himself to his bed and collapse.

But when he did think about what might be next, his certainty grew. If there was only one way to save his family, he would take it. If Ethan and Raven couldn't find another way to Kronos, he would give himself up.

Whether he had the permission of the rest of his family or not.

But his plan never came to fruition. One day, as he was trading blows with Poseidon in the yard, the mist around them swirled away and a bright circle of light flashed off to the side of the training ground.

Hades and Poseidon whirled in tandem, bringing their weapons up. Poseidon raised an open hand and the river around them swelled, funnels rising from its surface.

"Relax," called an old and cantankerous voice. "It's me."

Hades lowered his staff. "You've got to stop doing that," he said to the old man with the waist-length white beard and blue robe who shimmered into existence before them. A moment later his red-haired son Harry popped into existence as well, smoothing down the front of his own brown robe.

Merlin had a staff of his own, and he spent a moment wiping off a speck of dust before regarding Hades. "Young fellow, I will do exactly as I please. As I have done for far longer than you've been alive. Especially when I bring you important news, for which you should be thanking me."

He raised his eyebrows expectantly. Poseidon exchanged an

irritated look with Hades. Neither of them really wanted to be facing this, Hades suspected. He'd certainly rather be hitting his brother as hard as he could, forgetting everything about the outside world. "We're not going to thank you before we even know what it is," Poseidon said when the silence stretched into awkwardness.

"Your father will hear of your rudeness," Merlin replied, and strode toward the house.

"Sorry," muttered Harry Ambrose as he trotted after his father, his face as red as his hair.

They stared at the little house for a moment after the door had shut. Finally Poseidon said, "I don't really want to go in. Do you?"

"No," Hades replied in relief. And so they went back to it.

It was at least an hour before the door opened again. By then they had grown tired of practice and were sitting on the ground, eating small sour apples in silence. Ivy had appeared with the children; she was teaching them how to string bows. Achilles had already begun learning to shoot, while little Hercules was mostly wrapping his string around the bow and singing to himself. The door opened and Ethan poked his head out. "Generals," he said, fixing Hades and Poseidon with equally stern looks.

Generals they might be, but they were also sons, and every son knew when to listen for his father's tone. Hades got to his feet, wiped his hands on his trousers, and headed inside.

Zeus sat within, looking more confident than Hades had seen him in some time. Of course, he hadn't seen much of Zeus, truly, since the battle. His brother was still avoiding him, and Hades found that he lacked the energy to reach out. He had enough on his mind, with a son to take care of and a wife to mourn and an impending imprisonment and torture to look forward to. Yet he would have sparred with Zeus, had his younger brother offered.

"We've got a lead, and a plan," Ethan said.

"Thanks to me." Merlin sat back and accepted the cup of tea Raven offered him.

"Kronos has returned to his palace and increased the wards and guard," Ethan said.

"So he's even harder to get to." Poseidon heaved a sigh. "Great."

"It is good," Ethan replied. "It means he's scared. Rattled. He's still looking for you, but he does think you can harm him. Instead of seeking you personally, he's been sending out his agents. And one of his top agents is —"

"My son," said Merlin. His mouth twisted bitterly. "Still."

Tom Ambrose. Hades felt a dull fire within him that was his anger rearing its head through the fog of his fatigue. Tom had been Atlas' friend, his confidant. And Tom had betrayed their brother to keep his place as Kronos' right hand man.

"Tom's actions in the battle and the, er, preceding troubles have cemented him as part of Kronos' inner circle. Kronos relies on him, and has tasked him with finding the three of you. It is an assignment that will bring him much fame and many accolades should he achieve it. Should he fail, the consequences would be dire. Tom is therefore operating in an interesting duality: on the one hand, he's nearly invincible, protected as he is by his status and his power. On the other, he's desperate to succeed — or rather, he's desperate not to fail."

"Aren't those the same thing?" Zeus said with a wrinkled brow.

Ethan warned him to be silent with a motion of his hand, and took over. "Tom, frequents the market in the center of Novaris every day, under different disguises. He's seeking information on the three of you." He turned to Hades. "My son, are you still interested in being captured?"

###

"How do I look?" Zeus turned and bowed to his brothers with an extra flourish.

Hades and Poseidon stared. "It's like you're a completely different person," Poseidon said.

"Even your voice," Hades agreed.

Zeus felt a flush of pleasure. Once they'd worked out the details of their plan, they'd broken down the rest of the camp and left the island, instead taking up residence on the outskirts of Novaris. In a few dingy rooms — the only apartment they could afford to rent — they'd sent scouts to monitor Tom's movement as he went through the market, tracking his steps, tracing the pattern. He walked the market every day, visiting in various disguises that the brothers would never have been able to detect but for the genius of Harry Ambrose. Tom's twin was as adept with magic as Tom was himself, but he also had a technical genius that, according to Merlin, had been the source of much of Tom's envy toward Harry. Harry had constructed a device that could trace the magic Tom used to disguise himself, and it was usually the work of half an hour to find the man himself and trail him discreetly through the market's winding streets.

Tom never went to the same stall twice in two days. He circulated the market, sometimes looking stern, and sometimes chatty. Sometimes he bought enough goods for the entire palace, and sometimes he never bought a thing. He seemed to revel in his ability to switch personas so completely; he walked the market for hours each day. It was a wonder he had nothing better to do — yet this *was* high stakes for him. He was tasked with finding the brothers or suffering at the hands of Kronos. And he was so confident of his success that he was getting careless. Once, as he'd picked up a kumquat and examined it for blemishes, he'd asked the fruit seller: "And where do these lovely items come from?"

"Right outside Labyrinth City," the fruit seller had said, all smiles and good business.

"Home of the Minotaurs. Frequented by the famous rebel Atlas," Tom replied conversationally, and Zeus had quickly pretended to be interested in an apple. "I heard he was something to behold. You ever meet him?"

"No, good sir." The fruit seller's expression closed off, becoming completely professional. "Why don't you try the kumquat? Only way to assess the quality."

Tom was never visibly disappointed by dead ends. He cheerfully moved on, as though he really had been making conversation. And he didn't always look for the brothers themselves. Sometimes he had a fake message to deliver to 'my sister's husband,' a man who looked exactly like Harper

O'Donovan, the leader of the Sherwood Outlaws and Hades' best friend. Sometimes he tried to trade contraband goods that would be attractive to anyone who wanted to fight Kronos. Sometimes he tried to pass himself off as a rebel, looking for the army that would bring Kronos to his knees.

Ethan and Hades had been too clever to have their men disperse in Novaris, the capital and center of Kronos' power. They'd been sent to the far reaches of Olympus, where Kronos' reach was less secure and the warriors could spend time constructing new identities. They would come back once their chances of being arrested were smaller, but right now the only men in the capitol were the brothers themselves, protected by the twin powers of Merlin and Harry. And with disguises like this, Zeus reflected as he stroked his long white beard, they were practically invisible anyway.

He nodded to his brothers. Today was the day. "Good luck," said Hades solemnly. He was always solemn now.

Zeus tried to lighten the mood with an easy smile. "Don't need it," he said, harnessing the confidence that had always come so naturally to him.

He picked up the heavy basket of artifacts that Merlin and Harry had prepared for him, groaning as he slipped the woven straps around his shoulders and secured it to his back. Whatever Merlin had found to pique Tom's interest, it was *heavy*. But it would capture Tom's attention, he'd assured Zeus. And Tom would know that only one man could have found such an artifact.

The market stretched like a maze across the middle of the city, with the best high-end goods and most fragrant, expensive spices in the middle. Then clothes, carpets, woodworking and toys surrounding that. Then the smiths and repairmen, men who did hard but necessary labor. And at last, the butchers and tanners, the men whose jobs were smelly and disgusting, but valuable.

That was the end of the official market. But wind through a couple of alleys, past a few moldering fruit stalls whose owners couldn't get a permit closer to the center, and you'd find something more. Stalls that had no permits to sell, and their goods were of a less than legal nature. Stalls that sold illegal spices that caused hallucinations, or books that Kronos had banned. Stalls that sold little charms meant to befuddle someone, or make them fall in love with you, or even kill them slowly through magic.

It was a slightly dangerous proposition to set up a table here, in the hidden parts of the marketplace. Kronos' guard could come at any moment and tear the whole thing down, and of course Tom could decide on a whim to capture any of the sellers to whom he spoke. Zeus found both of these outcomes unlikely though. He had to pay a couple of burly men at the entrance to the secret market a not-so-small sum to be allowed through to set up his wares, and that sum would go toward bribing the guard if they swung this way. He'd seen Tom come through here a few times, too, seeking information, and Zeus doubted Tom would risk driving off the seedy merchants here if he thought they might have information valuable to him.

And today he was scheduled to come back.

Zeus paid the men their gold, complaining like an old man about how much things cost back in his day and how extortionate they'd become, then hobbled into a dingy square with just one other exit, through a high-walled alley that led to a canal and the start of the marketplace proper. He resisted the urge to go over to the alley. Poseidon lay beyond it, ready to bend the canal to his will. Hades lurked in the chaos of the market proper, ready to act when the time came.

Zeus rolled out a threadbare carpet and carefully laid out his goods. He had a brass lamp, a golden flute, a pile of pages that Merlin had called a grimoire, and several fake wands. "Every merchant of your sort has fake along with genuine. Tom would be suspicious if you sat in a market like that with only goods of the highest quality." The merchants with the best stranglehold on illegal goods had their own shop fronts, after all.

There wasn't much. Zeus looked over at another merchant, a woman sitting at her own mat and eyeing him warily. She had a small case, propped open to show little paintings. One of them had maroon eyes, but otherwise they looked nothing like the three brothers. She was pretty, in a defiant sort of way, which was Zeus' favorite way. Zeus offered her a comforting smile, but she glared at him suspiciously and pulled her hood over her head, then folded her hands and sat in repose. Zeus sighed inwardly as he turned back to his own goods. *No talking to the other merchants,* he thought.

The sun was already warm. He wished he'd thought to bring water and a snack. One of the other merchants was selling something a man could drink; he saw a couple of cloaked figures come by and pay good gold for it. One of them even took a swig right in front of the seller. From the smirk on the seller's face, Zeus decided he'd have to be a lot more desperate to buy something to drink here.

It felt like hours before Ambrose came. Zeus had let his thoughts drift: to Leda and little Hercules, to his unmarred and simple childhood in Sherwood forest, to anywhere but that moment on the mountain when he'd ruined everything. He came back to himself only when he saw a middle-aged man bending over his wares, eyes fastened on the loose sheafs of paper that made up Merlin's grimoire.

"And what's all this?" the man said, and from his tone Zeus knew it was Tom Ambrose. Despite his disguise he still managed to look like Harry: auburn hair with streaks of white shooting through it like tiny lightning bolts. His face bore a few wrinkles but was still fairly fresh, with a pointed nose and chin and eyes that were a little too wide, making him look as though he were permanently surprised. He wore a fine gray suit with a white cravat, the sort of suit you'd wear when going to the fine center of the market, the sort of suit that told people you had money. It wasn't the sort of suit you wore down here. Out of the corner of his eye, Zeus saw the pretty girl close up her case of paintings and slip away.

Zeus made a show of checking the time on the modified pocket-watch Harry had turned into a detection device. The device glowed purple briefly, confirming that this was indeed Tom. Snapping it shut, he waved a hand turned gnarled and liver-spotted by his magic. "The highest quality artifacts of... black magic," he said in a dramatic whisper. "The wands have captured denizens of the deepest fiery pits of the netherworld."

Tom scoffed. "The wands are junk, old man. I'll warn you

once: don't waste my time." He flashed his coat, and on the orange silk interior Zeus spotted an embroidered book and wand, with a winged snake beneath them. It was the symbol of the Honorable Gentleman Wizard's Club, a club for which Tom Ambrose was a top member. It was the club through which Atlas and Tom had met, in fact. Zeus tried to smother his predatory smile. He'd destroy that club brick by brick for the role it had played in his brother's death. And he'd enjoy it.

Now he bowed his head obsequiously. "My lord, forgive me. I didn't realize we had a true practitioner among us."

"Which would have been easy to discern if you were any sort of practitioner yourself," Tom sneered.

Zeus felt sweat slipping down the back of his collar and tried not to shift uncomfortably. He lifted the brass lamp. It had a minor demon trapped inside it, the sort that could work petty spells for a man with much grumbling. "A distinguished gentleman such as yourself should have a familiar," he suggested.

Tom waved him off. "Familiars are more trouble than they're worth," he said. "What's this?" He pointed to the flute, but as Zeus explained how it could enchant anyone who heard it and make him a master musician, he could tell that Tom was listening with only half an ear.

"And this?" At last Tom pointed to the object that had captured his attention from the start. The grimoire.

Zeus spread his hands. "Nothing. Just some papers I stole from an old wizard's bag."

They'd concocted the story together, and carefully — a ragtag army on the road, sleeping off the battle, and an opportunistic man with his donkey who sold them a bit of bread and fruit. Zeus pretended he'd seen great magic from the wizard, and that night had returned to the camp to pilfer what goods he could. But the wizard had woken as Zeus reached for his bag, and these few scrap pages were all he could run with.

Ambrose fixed him with an intense stare for the duration of his story. When he was finished Zeus fought the urge to swallow, or look down, or appear dishonest in any way. What if Tom didn't believe him? What if he realized the grimoire was a plant?

"This old man," he said slowly. "What was his name?"

"He never gave it to me himself," said Zeus, scratching his beard. "But I heard someone call him Marzin."

Far from Merlin's most famous moniker, but one used in the South — one Tom should know.

"I see. And where was the army going?" Tom asked. His fingers drummed on his belt.

"Sounded like they were going every which way. Some were coming back to the city, taking up residence in the capitol like they were before they left. Others were headed to the black swamp and Sherwood. Some said they had business on Etna, though I don't know who wants to be hanging about there except for traitors and thieves." He examined his fingernails, as if to say that other petty thieves were far below him.

"And *Marzin*?" Avarice had lit a bright light in Tom's eyes. "Where was he going?"

Zeus shrugged. "He had some business to take care of, but he didn't say where. But I did get hired by a few of the gents to make a weekly delivery of goods. Like they didn't want to be seen out and about." He pretended to think as he rubbed his nose. "They were funny, those gents. One had maroon eyes. Where do you see that these days?" Then he pretended to come back to himself. "Here, you going to buy that or what?"

Ambrose fingered the purse at his belt. "What are you asking for it?"

"Three gold," Zeus said. It was an outrageous sum, yet Tom would know it was worth it if he could procure a few pages of his father's grimoire. Zeus saw the drink-seller in the opposite corner of the dingy square choke on the apple he was eating.

Tom considered him for a moment. "I have a proposition," he said at last. "I won't bargain you down, and in exchange you'll sell me the grimoire and take me to the house to which you make your deliveries. Deal?"

"Deal," said Zeus, holding out his hand to shake. As Tom took it he added, "I don't walk so well, though, so it'll take a little while." He handed over the grimoire and began laboriously packing his goods away.

Tom's face twisted into a faint, bitter sneer. "No matter," he replied. "I have nowhere else to be."

Zeus got to his feet, picked up his walking stick, and ambledout of secret market square with Tom in tow.

They came out into the part of the marketplace that sold decent fruit and bread — good enough for most of the people of Novaris, but far from the finest and whitest bread or the fanciest imported fruits a man could buy here. This part of the market was the most crowded as well. It was good for anyone who wanted to slip into obscurity, followed by a guard intent on catching sellers of contraband. It was also good for creating a diversion.

"Hm," said Zeus, stopping among the colorful stalls. "This way." He headed toward a cart with a bright pink canopy that sold cucumbers and peppers of every kind. As he went by he knocked his stick against the pole that held up the canopy, making it billow as it fell.

"Hey!" shouted the seller as he was enveloped in coarse, brightly colored canvas. It was the signal Poseidon and Hades had been waiting for.

Even Zeus didn't know where they were hidden, exactly. It was better that way, in case Tom caught on to Zeus' identity and managed to capture him. From seemingly nowhere — but in reality mustered from the canal around the corner — mist gathered on the ground, growing thicker and higher. All around them people gasped in exclamation and alarm. Tom stopped, eyes narrowing. A moment later the mist nearly swallowed him from view, for all that he was standing not a foot from Zeus.

"It's Kronos!" shouted Hades from somewhere in the mist, pitching his voice low.

At that, the alarm turned to outright panic. All along the alley shops slammed their canopies down and Zeus heard the trample of feet as people rushed to scatter. His job was simple in principle: keep Tom Ambrose in his sights at all times. That way, if Hades had miscalculated, Tom wouldn't get away.

But Hades didn't miscalculate. A tall form appeared from the fog as Ambrose turned around.

"You," Ambrose said, eyes widening. His eyes flickered between Zeus and Hades, finally realizing the trap.

"Me," said Hades, and did the best thing one could do when faced with an all-powerful wizard: he knocked him out with a fist to the head.

CHAPTER THREE: CHAINS OF FATE

Hades slung Ambrose's lanky body over his shoulder as it changed shape, becoming thinner and younger and, somehow, heavier. Poseidon kept the mist thick as they hurried home, ducking into alleys whenever they heard voices or footsteps. "We should've thought this part of the plan through more," Poseidon grumbled.

"You can think a plan to death. At some point, you have to act," Hades replied grimly. They were his father's words. No plan survived contact with reality anyway, though this one had done as well as a plan could, really. "Remember, every moment we hesitate, innocent people suffer." And no matter how half-baked their plans ended up being, anything that helped free this world from the tyranny of Kronos was worth it.

"I'm just saying, we could have brought the cart," Poseidon said. "Said our friend was drunk and we were wheeling him home."

"All this complaining from the man who's carrying nothing," Zeus scoffed. There was a red mark on each of his shoulders where the straps of the wicker basket dug into his skin. "I'm getting a cramp in my back."

"I'm carrying an entire canal full of water, thanks," Poseidon retorted.

"No one's having any fun with this," Hades reminded them. "Let's get home."

When they returned to their ramshackle apartment, they didn't even go inside. Ethan had procured a cart for them, with two large, confused goats strapped to the front and a false bottom into which they rolled Tom. Hades leaned over him and poured a dribble of sleeping draught on his lips. That ought to keep him out until they reached their next hideout — or at least through the gate and any checkpoints they might meet on the main road. It would be terribly awkward for the wizard to wake up and start banging on the floor of the cart as they got their papers checked on the way out of the city.

Leda had packed the brothers' few belongings and now she loaded them into the cart. Zeus, however, carried a rucksack on his back and held a walking staff in his hand. He nodded to each of his brothers and stuck his free hand out. "See you in the Black forest," he said.

Poseidon rolled his eyes. "Don't be ridiculous. Get on the cart."

"You know you're safer if it's just the two of you. Leda and I will make our way." Zeus flashed a smile that didn't reach his eyes. "Don't start the interrogation without us."

Poseidon looked as though he wanted to object some more, but Hades put a hand on his brother's arm. He knew what Zeus truly wanted. "You and Leda take the cart. I'll walk."

"Alone?" Zeus said.

"I've traveled alone plenty of times before," Hades said.

"Not when you were the most wanted man on Olympus," Poseidon pointed out. "You know father would never allow it." His lips thinned. "Why can't we all get in the cart?"

"I said we'd be fine." There was an edge to Zeus's voice now.

Hades moved in to embrace his brother in a brief hug. Zeus

went stiff. He'd been uncomfortable with physical affection ever since the battle. But Hades took the opportunity to murmur in his ear, "Think of your wife and son."

He pulled back. Zeus glanced at Leda; she narrowed her eyes. "What did you say to him?" she asked, putting a hand on her hip. She was ready to travel, in leather pants and a vest, and Hercules strapped to her back. She'd be the first to call herself tough, but walking all the way to the Black Forest would be hard for a child Hercules' age and the mother tasked with caring for him.

"All right," Zeus said. "Let's all go."

He sounded so grudging. Hades waved him off. "I'd like the time to think," he said.

Zeus' eyes clouded over, and the mist thickened and charged with electricity. Hades realized he'd said the wrong thing. Zeus would surely assume that he wanted to think about Persephone, about how it was Zeus' fault that she was gone. It didn't matter how many times Hades tried to tell him, or show him that he put no portion of the blame on Zeus' door. Nothing seemed to stick.

"Father would eviscerate me if he let you wander around by yourself," sighed Poseidon, but he gave up on arguing. "We'll both stay."

"Don't start the interrogation without us," Hades said with a brief smile. Not for the first time, he wished for simpler times.

"Don't be late," Zeus replied.

Hades nodded then turned to Leda, giving her a half hug. "Don't let him get into trouble," he told her.

"I wish I could stop him," she said.

Hades kissed Hercules on the cheek from where he sat

strapped to his mother's back. Then he stood back as Zeus and Leda climbed up into the cart. The road to the Black Forest was long, and putting off the trip wouldn't make it any shorter. They would head down to the south gate, which was in the worst repair and manned by the laziest guards, then onto the road. The Black Forest was a poisonous, dangerous place, but the Cross had kept a stronghold there for many years and even Kronos' fiercest underlings feared the place.

As the cart rattled out of sight, Poseidon's brow furrowed. "Why didn't you want to go with them?"

"Aside from the awkward prospect of three days on the road with a brother who thinks I hate him?" Hades replied.

"He won't think it any less now."

True, that. But what Hades had told Zeus was true, too. "I need time to think. And I think I need one last night in the city."

He couldn't put his finger on it, but something was here that he didn't want to leave behind.

He just had to figure out what before they left in the morning.

###

It was folly to walk around Novaris even in disguise. A curfew was in place, and though Hades could darken his skin to the gray of shadow and slip past the guard with little effort, he knew it was a risk his parents would have frowned upon. Why did he feel as though something was here? Some part of his soul? His whole soul belonged to Persephone, and she wasn't anywhere…was she?

The wind rustled in the night. It tugged at the cuff of his shirt as though trying to take his hand, and he followed where it pushed him. The city was still damp from the day of inexplicable mist. Cold seeped through his woolen cloak and clung to the inside of his shirt. The city smelled like dirt and wet garbage, with the occasional smell of baking bread or roasting meat as Hades passed a kitchen door. His boots slipped on the cobblestones as he made his way through quarter after quarter: the merchants' quarter, the workers' quarter, the aristocrats' quarter and even past the guards' quarter. He walked past the Honorable Gentleman Wizard's club, looking up at the ornately carved building where Atlas had spent some of his final days. Perhaps it was here; perhaps what drew him forward was some piece of his brother, trapped somehow in the club.

Hades put a hand on the stone and closed his eyes, sending out a question. He received no reply. And so he kept walking.

He wasn't sure what he was looking for until he came to the gates of the palace.

It rose harsh and unyielding in the night. Its black towers stabbed at the sky like knives. The processional road stretched, a horror of stone figures locked in their tortuous last moments. Hades flinched. Why had his steps drawn him here? He had no desire to look upon those he had failed, to remember that he was not only up against Kronos, but his monstrous creations as well.

Old training took over and he ran a critical eye over the palace's defenses. Odd that the procession road wasn't guarded. Perhaps Kronos was trying to lure him in. Perhaps he hadn't been drawn here by any good force or intuition, but by some sinister force. He frowned at the walls, trying to see who manned them at such a distance.

Then a shadow at the edge of the procession road began to unfurl, and Hades realized why there were no guards. No human guards, at any rate. The gate was guarded by a dog the size of a dragon.

Hades had heard of Kronos' newest chimera, the three-headed hound that could grow smaller or larger at will. The dog was entirely feral and would attack anyone who came near enough — even Kronos himself. It could tear the arm off a man and move like lightning. Kronos needed no palace guard here — no one would dare try to cross the hound known as Cerberus.

Cerberus sat up, looking down the processional road with glowing red eyes. Its three heads twitched, and it growled, mostly to itself. Its fur was silver in the moonlight, sleek and long and shining — *beautiful,* thought Hades in surprise. The hound's six pointed ears were all pricked, swiveling this way and that, and its long snouts were elegantly tapered and slightly open, revealing teeth as long as Hades' hand that gleamed like swords. A chain was wound around each neck, and Hades could feel the weight of power within it. No ordinary chains could hold a magnificent creature such as this one. They chafed at the hound's chest, too: Hades could see a patch of skin where the hair had been rubbed off, and he felt a pang of sympathy.

He had never felt sympathy for a chimera before. After all, they were created for cruelty and subjugation. They were not creatures created for Olympus, but for Kronos' twisted ends. And at first glance Cerberus was no different. His claws dug deep gouges into the stones in front of him and his red eyes blazed with hate.

Yet Hades did feel sorry for him. No creature should be chained forever. Was he not trying to free this entire world from chains? Could he do that, and allow the dog to remain in captivity?

His rational mind struggled to make sense of what he was feeling. Perhaps he could free the dog and create another massive diversion that would help them escape the city while the guard was engaged in putting it down. It was outside the purview of their mission, but missions, like plans, rarely survived contact with reality. Hades took a step forward without thinking.

But allowing the dog to be killed so that he and Poseidon would have an easy escape…how could he condone that? Yes, he was at war, and yes, sacrifices had to be made. But he shouldn't make such decisions callously, even those that involved the creations of the tyrant.

Besides, it didn't explain why he'd been so driven to stay behind in the first place.

The dog's ear twitched. Its head swiveled. Two red eyes fixed on him.

The head on the right opened its mouth to howl, but the head on the left growled in warning and it cut off with a small whine instead. Cerberus turned his body so that the left-hand head could look at him straight on.

Anguish. That was what Hades saw in those eyes. He wasn't even sure how he could tell, but it sent a tremor through his heart that threatened to open a chasm. Cerberus might be a chimera, a monster, but he was a creature in pain, too.

"You need freedom too," he whispered.

The dog cocked its heads. It said nothing, but lowered its massive chest to the ground. In any other dog, that would have been a gesture of submission. To Hades it seemed like an invitation. *Come closer.*

He took a step. "I'm trusting you not to make me your dinner," he said, grateful that his brother hadn't insisted on joining him for this walk. Poseidon wouldn't have let him get closer. It went against all rules of common sense, and Hades was usually so sensible. As he drew nearer he inhaled the thick scent of wet fur and raw meat that had been Cerberus' dinner. When he was close enough, he extended an arm. An arm that could be ripped off with a twist of the hound's head.

Cerberus' nostrils flared as the dog took his scent. He studied Hades. In those blazing eyes Hades saw not hate, but pain. And a plea for help.

Gently, the middle head lowered its nose against Hades' hand. The fur there was fuzzy and thin, the skin warm. And at the touch of finger to snout, Hades both understood, and became more confused than ever before.

Cerberus was in constant pain. His three heads were always battling each other — one remembering the pain of its past, its creation and training; one focused on its duties of the present, on the hunger that constantly rumbled in its belly, and one focused on the future, the unfolding destiny of Olympus as seen through the eyes of a hound. At a mere touch Hades saw all of this, and understood.

"Forget your past," he urged the dog in a low, calm voice.

"Forget your present. Come with me now, and let us focus on a different future. One we can make where both of us will be free."

The dog blinked at him, and though Hades did not see a new future unfolding in front of his minds' eye, he knew that Cerberus did. The future head was strangely still for a moment. Then it tilted toward the others. The present head bent in toward Hades, butting him with a force that sent him stumbling back. The past head licked him with a velvety tongue. He surprised himself with a laugh, the first genuine laugh he'd managed since Persephone had died.

It wasn't so unlike the day he'd met her, he realized as the past head yipped, puppy-like. He'd been drawn to the market, drawn to *her*, knowing that something about that day was special. Now he'd met a new companion, one that would be with him for the next chapter of his life, whatever that may be. Yet the choice had to be the dog's. So many choices had been taken away from him already.

Hades moved toward the thick chain that lay coiled at Cerberus's feet. It was wound around a thick iron ring at the palace gates, too thick to break and too thick to saw. But Hades had no need for strength or the tools of man. It was risky, yes, but some things were simply worth the risk.

He called power to his hands, and he wrapped them around a link.

The iron sizzled and melted. He pulled the link apart like taffy. He tossed both sides to the ground, then dismissed the lava with a quick brush of his palms against one another. Ash flaked into the air.

Cerberus put his head to the ground. Hades heaved on the chains and pulled them over the dog's head. This was harder work, and though it took but a few excruciating minutes, sweat soaked the back of his neck and under his arms when he was finished.

"You're free now," he panted as he stepped away. "You can go where you wish. Do what you like. I only ask that you forget the brutal ways of your old master."

Cerberus' tail came up. He leapt to his feet and suddenly he was much smaller. He came up to Hades' shoulder now. His tail wagged, and Hades reached out to scratch him behind the ears. The dog butted his head into Hades' chest again. Hades laughed. "You are welcome to join me," he said, feeling the stone-cold feeling around his heart crack a little. "But you can always make your own path, whenever you wish. Remember that."

He turned and walked back down the processional road, and his hound followed.

###

"What. Is that."

Poseidon stood in the door of their rented rooms with two rucksacks and two staffs — a bident and a trident. His golden muscles rippled as he crossed the trident in front of himself, and his aqua eyes flashed.

"It's Cerberus." Hades patted the dog on his middle head and was rewarded by a tail thumping against his leg. "Ready to go?"

"Is this why you wanted to stay an extra night? To free this monster?" Cerberus growled and Poseidon recoiled.

"He's no monster," Hades admonished his brother. "He's a creature of Olympus. Like all of us." He scratched Cerberus behind one pointed ear. The dog's three heads all turned toward him, whining. *It's all right,* he thought, and smiled.

"Technically he's a creature of Kronos." Poseidon edged out the door, then turned and locked it tight. "Do you really think it was a good idea to set him loose? What if he follows us? Can he even understand us?" He looked from Hades to the dog.

"He's a clever boy, he's got three brains to work with. And he is a dog who is free to choose his own master now." Hades found he was smiling. It felt good to be tied to someone again. He could almost see it — little Achilles playing in the forest with Cerberus, throwing three balls and laughing as the dog deliberated over which one to chase. "And I do expect he'll follow us. He's our newest recruit."

Poseidon groaned. "You can't be serious."

Hades took the bident staff and a rucksack and started to walk. The staff tapped comfortably on the cobbles, and next to it Cerberus' claws scratched on the stones. He took a deep breath of city air. It still stank like wet garbage, but it also carried the smell of possibility.

"Think this through, brother." Poseidon strode after him, hissing so as not to wake the whole street. "How are we going to get him past the gate? Someone's going to notice that there's but one three-headed dog in this city, and he's not where he's supposed to be."

Hades cocked his head and looked sideways at the hound.

Cerberus turned his past head to look back. He hadn't given much thought to how they'd smuggle the dog out, especially now that they were missing their cart. But a plan was nipping at the edges of his mind, a plan that was foolish and daring and something his father would have told him never to do. "Oh," he said. "They'll notice."

Ten minutes later the alarm bells blared over the walls of the city. The guards at the south gate shouted in panic: "*Hideous — what is that thing —*" as a dark three-headed shape knocked down the gate with a singular crash and bounded down the road, two men straddling its back. The hound streaked into the dim light of dawn and was lost to the road before anyone thought to follow.

CHAPTER FOUR: A HERO'S BURDEN

The Black Forest sat southwest of Mount Etna, which rose proud and fiery, while to the south Labyrinth City cut deep into its own mountain, in a series of passageways that went both up to the peak and down into its core. Within this famous duality resided both men and Minotaurs, bull-headed beasts who lived in the night and, it was said, thrived on lost travelers who descended too far into the bowels of the labyrinth.

Hades and Poseidon had dismounted Cerberus when they came to the edge of the marketplace. He'd shrunk to the size of a normal dog, just tall enough for Hades to scratch his head without having to lean down. Poseidon's eyes had bugged out of his head when he first saw the hound grow, but he'd had to admit (grumblingly) that Cerberus' size-changing abilities were fairly useful. "But now Kronos will know we've been in Novaris," he said as they walked up a thin stream to disguise their tracks. "He'll connect us to the disappearance of Tom Ambrose."

"And he'll be enraged," Hades replied. "Hopefully enraged enough to make a mistake."

The road branched at the marketplace, leading to Sherwood, Centennial City and Solara, and countless towns and hamlets in between. There was no way for Kronos' forces to be certain where they were going without the gigantic paws of the hound to track, and they couldn't send men everywhere.

Still, he wished it was less of a walk. Or that he had his cart.

They walked for a day and a half, sleeping under the open sky and eating without stopping, before they came to the edge of the Black Forest.

Sherwood was old, grand and imposing from the first step into its leafy realm. The edge of the Black Forest, on the other hand, was deceiving: slim birch trees, so unlike the oaks and yews of Sherwood that grew vast and strong and green. The birch painted a pretty picture in gray and black and white and looked like any other wood as they continued upstream. The air grew colder and crisper as they went, smelling of moss and grass and dirt and all the things Hades remembered from his childhood. He closed his eyes, enjoying the scent, detecting a hint of pine that Sherwood didn't have. Next to him, Cerberus splashed joyfully, chasing sunbeams and tiny black fish.

The change was gradual. The birch trees were less white and more gray, then less gray and more black. The moss that slicked the stones in the river turned to a dark green, and the stones themselves resembled obsidian. Even the leaves that shrouded them were darker in color. The trunks became wider and the trees themselves twisted, weighed down by black branches and black leaves and even tiny black flowers. Black birds and bats flitted above their heads, singing and screeching. Eventually the canopy became so thick that Hades had to conjure a bright ball of fire to help light their way. Cerberus whined and stuck close to him.

They finally left the stream when Posiedon spotted a tiny iron cross hanging from the branch of a tree. He pulled the cross free and pocketed it, and they splashed up to the bank onto the narrow footpath that wound between spidery roots. As they made their way deeper into the forest the trees grew yet more, and the roots grew with them, so great that they pulled from the ground and created grottos and shelters, dark as caves and about as dank. The roots impeded on the path and soon it was less like walking and more like climbing a mountain, scrambling over tough roots and balancing as they hopped from one to the next. "Wonder how Zeus fared with the cart," Hades said, and Poseidon chuckled. Every so often they found another hanging cross, a sign that they were going the right way.

At last they scrambled up a root that rose as tall as a house, and from there they saw a wide black lake, still as a mirror. All around it the trees rose, so tall that their crowns were obscured by the clouds. Cerberus' ears pricked forward. "We're here," Poseidon said. Hades nodded.

Poseidon waded into the lake first, parting it with ease, and they made their way to the other side. It was a good ten minute's walk; the lake was wide indeed. On the other side they made their way to the edges of the roots and clambered up to the shelter beneath them.

The grotto wound around the trunk of the largest tree Hades had ever seen. Hades had grown up in a house fit for four raucous boys, but this tree could have contained his home tree in Sherwood at least three times over. He and Poseidon greeted the watcher, who stared at the dog with wide eyes and didn't even ask for the password. Then they went through a curtain of smaller hanging roots and into a well-lit space beyond. Lanterns had been fixed to the side of the tree and gave the grotto a warm and cozy look, even though it still smelled of dirt. Someone had been hard at work bundling roots together to make a very bulbous table, while others had hauled in branches and stumps to make chairs and other bits of furniture. There weren't many members of the Order here — a couple of Minotaurs who had preferred to stay out of the confining depths of Labyrinth City, a few members of the Cross who had nowhere else to go. And Ethan and Raven, of course.

Raven sat over a small fire, brewing a pot of herbal tea. She rose as the boys approached and embraced them both, a smile crinkling at the corners of her eyes. She always had a smile for them, Hades thought fondly, even when she was somewhat dismayed — as she was now. She took a step back from Cerberus. "Boys," she said reproachfully. "I know you always wanted a pet, but do you remember what we said about the life of a revolutionary?"

"It's no life for a helpless animal. See?" Poseidon spread his arms beseechingly and said to their mother, "I told him not to bring it."

"Ceberus is his own creature." Hades stroked the future head. He wasn't sure how to explain it — that he was so sure they belonged together, that theirs was a companionship that was somehow meant to be. But he did know what would make his mother accept the decision, so he met her gaze with a wry smile. "I couldn't leave him chained up. You taught me too well for that."

Raven laughed, pulling her gray-streaked black hair into a ponytail. "So I'm to blame? All right. Go back and see your father. He's been waiting for you."

Hades nodded. "Perhaps you should stay here," he told the

dog. Cerberus sat, though a whine escaped him and his tail wagged anxiously.

"We'll see what sort of snacks we can drum up for a dog, hmm?" Raven extended a fist for Cerberus to sniff, then went over to a sack and started to rummage around.

Through another curtain, this one woven of springy twigs, Hades and Poseidon found Ethan, Zeus and Leda. They sat at a table, playing dice; Ethan got up with a grimace as they came in while Zeus leapt to his feet.

Ethan hugged them as fiercely as Raven had. "We heard your voices," he said. "Good timing. Tom Ambrose is awake, and he's none too happy."

"The sleeping draught worked," Zeus said. "He didn't wake up until we were already here and he was contained."

"And who contained him?" Hades asked. He'd have expected Merlin or Harry to be here, but he hadn't yet seen them.

"I did," Zeus said, sounding a little defiant. As though he expected Hades to scoff or be incredulous. But Hades merely said, "Good work," and nodded to all of them. "Should we begin?" He didn't much feel like resting at the moment. He wanted justice, and he wanted a new plan. Energy thrummed through his veins, the energy of Olympus itself. He could feel it rumbling beneath him, ready to explode at his command.

The men nodded, and in they went.

Tom had been tied to a trunk so wide it served as a bed. Electric bolts crackled at his wrists and ankles and spread over his chest. In the blue light he looked almost ghostly. He also looked determined, and terrified.

"I'll never tell you what you want to know," he said, lips twisting. "You think you can torture me?"

"Who said anything about torture?" Ethan asked. The older man took a seat on a much smaller stump and leaned forward, putting his hands on his knees. He surveyed Tom with no pleasure, just compassion. It astonished Hades, in fact, that his father could have such an emotion for the man who'd delivered Atlas to his fate. "Who tortures you at home?"

"No one," said Tom, too quickly. "You'll learn nothing from me."

"I presume it's Kronos." Ethan nodded to himself. "It must be lonely up there at the top, one of the only men who must constantly bear his wrath."

"I share his power," spat Tom. "I am one of his most trusted advisors. He values me."

"Yet I wonder if he values you enough to try and rescue you," Ethan said. At this, Tom was silent. His adam's apple bobbed as he swallowed. His dark brown hair was stiff with dirt and sweat, Hades realized, a far cry from the fine and polished gentleman he'd always appeared to be before. "No. I expect he's already written you off as a traitor. You could come back to Novaris with us in chains behind you, and he'd have you murdered in your sleep, in case you spilled some of his precious secrets."

"That's not true," Tom spat, but there was fear in his near-black eyes. He worked his jaw. "I am a loyal servant. The most loyal."

"May I ask you something?" Hades said.

He spoke gently, but Tom flinched as though he'd struck him.

To be fair, Hades *had* struck him in the past so perhaps Tom's instincts were correct. "Will it make a difference if I say no?" Tom asked sullenly.

That was a fair point. "Why is it, exactly, that you are so loyal?"

Tom laughed. It was a croaking sound that quickly degenerated into a cough, and Ethan hastened to hold a waterskin to his mouth. Tom drank greedily, then let his head fall back. "You all sound like my father. *But why, Tom?*" he mimicked in a high voice. "I told you, Kronos has power. And that's the only thing that means anything in this world. He who has the power makes the rules."

"Is that so?" Ethan asked pleasantly. He picked up a cup of cold tea and took a sip, as if this were a normal conversation between friends and not a chat between a man and his electricity-bound prisoner. "Then why is it that with all your power, you're dancing to Kronos' tune? Why aren't you making any rules of your own?"

"I'm making plenty," Tom scoffed.

"Not rules that matter. Kronos sends you out on a mission and you obey. You cannot fail, because the price is death. Succeed, and you get the next, harder mission. And the price for failing *that* is death. Eventually he will kill you because you cannot rise any higher — or because you pose a threat to him."

"Trust me, I don't need to worry about that," Tom laughed. "Once he's finished with you, the sort of power I have will be nothing to him." His mouth drew into a thin line, suddenly, and the laugh cut off. "The whole world will be nothing to him. He'll stamp out anyone who opposes him with the barest movement of his foot. He'll have complete control over the world." His voice began to rise. "And that's why I have to be loyal, don't you idiots see? Because once he's finished with you, no one will be beneath his notice. No one will be too valuable to dispose of. It will only be those who are loyal, and those who are dead."

"And one day, you'll slip up. Make some mistake, think for yourself, enjoy your life. Argue with the wrong chimera, maybe. And then you'll be dead, same as the rest of us." Ethan leaned back. "If I'm going to be executed for disloyalty, I'd rather be disloyal as a matter of principle. Or, rather, loyal to Olympus. To the people who need freedom from this tyranny."

"What is Kronos planning to do?" Hades asked softly.

Tom shook his head, gulping.

Zeus threw up his hands and stormed out. Rubbing his forehead, Ethan shot Hades and Poseidon a look before following.

Out in the antechamber, Zeus was pacing back and forth. Electricity crackled over his body as a testament to his rage. "Why are we letting that pompous windbag talk and talk?" he snapped as soon as Hades let the curtain fall behind him. "We need to know Kronos' plan, and we need to know it now. If it's as big as he's hinting, we'll need all the time we can get to prepare."

"*He* needs time to understand that his master won't help him," Ethan said.

"We can't spare that," Zeus replied.

"So what are you suggesting, exactly?" Hades wished he had some of his mother's calming tea. Maybe Zeus should try a cup himself. Even Leda was nervous to go near him; she leaned against the wall, arms crossed.

Zeus flopped down and stared at the little lamp on the table, eyes dark in the gloom of their lair. "We get the information out of him however we can."

"We don't torture people," Ethan said sharply. "We're better than that."

"Is it better to stick to our morals and die because of it, or break them for one man and save the world?" Zeus looked to Hades and Poseidon for support.

Poseidon's brow was furrowed. He looked uncertain. Hades could sympathize. Atlas had been his twin, and as much pain as the other brothers felt at the man's death, for Poseidon it was worse. But Hades put a hand on Zeus' shoulder, squatting so that he could look his brother in the eye. Zeus's eyes flashed with all the colors of the storm: deep gray, blue and black, the flickering white of lightning. "If we succeed by employing Kronos' methods, we'll only become him, in the end," he said softly. "Our birth mother created us to be his antithesis, and that's what we have to be. It's hard. But we have no other choice."

Zeus stared at him for a long moment. "No other choice," he repeated at last, but Hades knew his brother wasn't convinced.

"Let's take a walk," Poseidon advised, pulling Zeus to his feet. Together the two of them headed through the next curtain and out toward the lake. Hades watched them go. A moment later Raven came in, bearing three steaming cups on a tray. She set the tray on the table and handed a cup each to Hades, Ethan and Leda. The cup smelled of soil and moss, but the tea was sharp and fresh: peppermint, rose leaves and some herb Hades couldn't quite place.

For a few moments they sipped their tea in silence, sitting on the floor or on some stump, watching the flame dance in their lantern. Then Leda said, "He's changed."

"The ordeal changed all of us," Hades replied, swallowing the sudden lump in his throat.

"But now he is desperate to win in a way he wasn't before. It's not about the fate of the world." Leda looked toward the curtain and her husband. The firelight painted her cheek in gold, giving her a proud profile. She'd always been a warrior, with a warrior's confidence. It was strange to see her worried. "It's about justifying himself. Overwriting, perhaps, the sins of his past. If we win now, he'll be remembered as a hero and no one will think of the things that happened along the way. If we lose, he'll be remembered for…well." She sent Hades a knowing look.

"No one thinks of him that way," Hades said with a little too much vehemence.

Leda smiled sadly at him. "We know you are trying," she told him, and she didn't need to say more.

###

They tried again the next day. Tom was stubborn, unwilling to talk. Ethan let him sit up and spoon fed him gruel, which he complained about bitterly. Tom even got to go for a walk, flanked by the brothers and still shackled by his electric bolts.

"I can't betray him," he said as they forced him back on his makeshift bed. "I can't throw in my lot with you."

"Why not?" Ethan asked patiently, like had every other time.

"He'll destroy me," Tom whispered. A tear slipped from his eye and trailed down the side of his head.

"From here, it looks like you're destroyed either way," Ethan told him conversationally, offering him another drink of water. "Throw in with us and you'll at least clear your conscience. And if we do defeat him, you can be a hero instead of a man on the run."

Poseidon rolled his eyes. "Why not tell us? If he's so powerful it doesn't matter, what's the difference? Maybe you can strike terror into our hearts with the news." He wiggled his fingers, the way he did when he was telling a spooky story to the children.

Tom set his ragged gaze on Poseidon. "You mock my master, but you would not if you knew." He let out a rusty chuckle. "All right then. Let me up, and hear my story."

He was an odd one, Hades thought as Ethan helped him up. He knew what he was doing was wrong, yet he seemed to think he was in too deep to change things.

They brought him out of his cell and into the main room. Raven and Ivy should hear this, too. The children were asleep in the next room, having spent a long day chasing each other and Cerberus among the vast roots. Ethan found the most comfortable chair they had, a stump that had been carved with a back and arms and softened with mats of woven bark. He gestured for the rest of the cell to gather close and keep silent. Then he nodded to Tom. "Speak."

Tom swallowed and looked from face to face. "You might have been able to defeat Kronos on that mountain if he hadn't destroyed your brother first," he admitted.

Hades clenched a fist. They could go over this again and again, but it made no difference.

"As it was, Kronos absorbed Atlas' power. Took it into himself." Tom shuddered. "It was like nothing I'd ever seen. He was practically fizzing with it. He needed more. I only saved myself because I had been the one to deliver the news of Atlas to Kronos. I promised I could do it again." He swallowed. "I promised I could deliver all of you."

Hades glanced uneasily at his brothers. In the corner, Cerberus growled softly at the mention of his old master's name.

"I know you lost the battle, but we did not win it. Kronos was furious with me. He would have killed me, but I managed to convince him that I was still the best shot at finding you. As long as I was looking for you, I was safe. And once I deliver you to him, I'll be elevated."

Hades didn't miss his use of words. Tom somehow still thought he was going to get out of this on top. What sorts of tricks did he have up his sleeve?

"You're the biggest threat Kronos has ever faced. You're also...gods. Or similar to whatever he is. Kronos thinks that if he absorbs your powers, he'll become unstoppable in truth. So he's going to do that. Trap you, imprison you, and —" he gulped.

When more was not forthcoming, Zeus slammed his hand on the ground. "And what?"

"Enough," said Ethan with an iron look. He crossed to Tom and offered him more water. Tom drank eagerly, then nodded his thanks as he pulled away. Water dribbled down his chin and sparked off the electric shackles that still bound his hands.

"He'll use his power to grow to an enormous size. You see what the dog can do?" Tom jerked his head at Cerberus, who bared his teeth from where he sat next to Hades. "Kronos can do the same. But he doesn't just get as big as a dragon. He gets *enormous.* Large enough to swallow a man with one bite." He looked from Hades to Poseidon to Zeus, raising his brows. Willing them to understand.

"Are you saying he wants to *eat* us?" Poseidon's nose wrinkled in disgust.

"You would be imprisoned in his body for as long as he lived. Which — who knows? It could be forever. He could draw your power into himself from there. As long as he lived, you would live, eternally trapped inside him."

Unease rippled through the cell. Faces paled. "I thought my brother couldn't get any worse. It turns out he's a cannibal," muttered Poseidon.

"Why did you choose to tell us this now?" Hades asked from his place off to the side, putting a hand on Cerberus' silver back.

Tom's eyes met his. Behind their cold black Hades could still see fear, but not fear of him. Tom had never been afraid of him. Tom had always been afraid of one man, and one man only. "Because there are some fates worse than death," he replied. "And you deserve to know them. And because Kronos planned to move on Centennial City yesterday evening. Every moment you're out of his grasp, he takes it out on more innocents. There's only one way you can try to save them." He grinned, humorlessly, the shadows of the dancing lantern licking over his sunken face.

###

The next morning Hades joined his brothers for tea on the edge of the lake. The sun had already burned off the mist, slanting down to warm the black bark of the trees and line the leaves with gold. The warmth of it kissed Hades' skin and brought out the scent of wildflowers from around the forest. In the lake Achilles, Ivy and Leda were teaching Hercules, Maia and Perseus to swim while Cerberus splashed in the shallows. He tried to focus on the moment, on the shrieks of laughter as the children bobbed up and down and Poseidon sent gentle waves to cradle them and make sure they wouldn't hurt themselves. Moments like this were always bittersweet, always missing Persephone and Diana to round out their happiness. Yet he also knew that each of these moments might be the last he shared with his family. He should take them for what they were instead of wishing for more. As Cerberus plunged eagerly into deeper waters he took a deep breath. "I...may have a plan."

"It's not sacrificing yourself again, is it?" Poseidon asked, flicking a finger and sending the children gently bobbing toward the center of the lake. "Because it turns out that plan would have been a disaster."

Hades winced. "Well..." Zeus zapped him with a lightning bolt. "Ow!"

"I can't believe Dad made you the head of the resistance. Your ideas are the worst."

Hades couldn't help grinning. Zeus was almost acting like his old self again.

"Hades, what are you thinking? Really?" Poseidon asked.

"What if we did it? Gave ourselves up?"

"And…made Kronos all-powerful?" Zeus folded his arms. He looked on the verge of bursting into laughter. Or a fiery ball of rage. It was hard to tell with Zeus these days.

"Make him think he's won. We fight, make it hard for him. Make him think he got us legitimately. But maybe we could take him down from the inside."

Zeus flopped back against a root. "I'm sorry, but that is *ridiculous.*"

Hades grimaced. He'd been thinking the plan through all night, but now that the time came to explain himself he faltered. "But Tom said Kronos had no plans to kill us. He wants to capture us. Keep us imprisoned. Draw on our power constantly. And that means that once we're inside him, we're together. And we're where we need to be." He cracked a smile. "In the belly of the beast, as it were."

Zeus sat up suddenly. "And unwatched…" he added, narrowing his eyes.

"Able to work freely and in tandem."

"And what if Kronos decides to just kill us?" Poseidon asked. "Or we die by accident?"

"The same thing that would happen anyway," Hades said. "Utter subjugation of Olympus."

For a moment the brothers were silent, watching their children splash in the water. Leda kept looking over at them, her expression calculating. She knew they were discussing something serious, and she kept herding the children further toward the center of the lake. No one worried about drowning here, with Poseidon controlling the water.

"If we falter, we'll be the instruments through which the entire world is destroyed," Poseidon said softly. "Our children will inherit a legacy of failure and darkness."

"And if we succeed, we can end this nightmare forever," Hades countered, just as softly.

It rested on the slimmest strand of hope. If fortune did not favor them, their sacrifice would be for nothing, and they would usher in the darkest times of Olympus.

Yet doing nothing would spell disaster for thousands of innocents, and would it truly change the outcome?

"We should let Tom capture us," Poseidon said, and Hades smiled grimly at his brother. "It will make the deception all the more convincing."

"But do you think Ambrose can play the loyal servant to Kronos?" Zeus arched an eyebrow. "He's betrayed his master now."

"He had a small crisis of conscience," Hades agreed. "But I suspect he'll go crawling back to Kronos the moment we set him free. Maybe his gambit was to let us think he was on our side. He still thinks we cannot defeat the tyrant, and he is obsessed with keeping power. And his life."

"You can't fault him for that," Poseidon said.

"Yes I can," Zeus muttered.

"But the important thing is, Tom's found us now. He wants to make sure he's in his master's good graces, and if he brings us to Kronos he can explain his absence without having to reveal that he was captured, or explain how he escaped."

His brothers were silent, and his words fell into a little well of peace. Out in the lake Achilles laughed and dove after something at the bottom of the lake. His kicks sent ripples of water out to the shore, small actions that reverberated and rippled in a wider radius.

Every action Hades had ever taken had led him to this point, this opportunity to disturb the motion of the world. He imagined the ripple that Kronos' death would cause: people rallying to free themselves from the tyranny of his cronies from town to town, from city to city all across Olympus. He could not fail. He could die, but he could not fail.

"So we do this?" he said.

"We do this," Zeus affirmed. His brother's eyes were alight with an intensity he'd missed. Zeus needed a cause, needed heroism. It was good to be united again in a plan.

"We do this," Poseidon propped his arms on his knees and stared out over the lake. "For the children, and the ones who are left."

"For the children," Hades agreed softly, past the sudden lump in his throat.

###

The heart of Labyrinth City was a difficult place to go. The maze of streets wound *around* it, never to it, and only small, overlooked passages could lead to the very center of the town on the mountain. Most people needed a guide to get there, and even Kronos' lackeys had been unable to get to it when they marched into the city and set it to the torch, two days after the lost battle. As a result, in a city of ruin and wreckage the center was nearly pristine. A small market had been set up to hand out goods to whoever snuck in to procure their fruit and bread.

Someone had also put up a statue of Atlas. Standing tall, defiant, not hunched and agonized beneath the weight of the world. He held a globe on one shoulder and stood, staring out over the high walls of the alleys and streets of Labyrinth. His statue was such a colossus that it was visible from many streets away; Kronos' men had fired upon it with belly-bows and pots filled with fire, but nothing had yet brought the statue down.

Hades paid his guide well, then slipped into the square and made his way to the base of the statue. Small offerings of flowers and dirt lay there, and he thought of the way Atlas used to grow large bouquets of wildflowers and pluck them for Ivy every day.

Hades hesitated, then put a hand on his brother's large bronze foot. It was twilight, and most people were headed home — Labyrinth City's curfew had only become harsher since the failed rebellion. A chill wind brought the smell of ashes and smoke to him, the new smells of the city. "You know what it is to carry the weight of the world," he said to the statue, and he wondered if anyone else could have understood what he felt. When he'd put forward their plan to the rest of their family, things had not gone smoothly. Raven had put her hands to her mouth. Leda had looked furious and demanded to know why Zeus had seen fit to make such a decision without her. Ethan had stroked his beard, considering, then asked simply, "What do you think are your chances of success?"

The three brothers had looked at each other. The truth was, none of them knew. "If this plan is the most likely to succeed, then we are duty-bound to try it. What is your strategy? How will you work together to defeat Kronos, exactly?" Ethan pressed.

"Until we understand the conditions, it will be difficult…" Hades began uncomfortably.

"That answer is not good enough. You must be prepared for anything. Everything. You know better than to place all your hopes for victory upon having the right idea at the right time. You must run through scenarios. Think of likelihoods. Compare what you know of Kronos to what you know of your own abilities. Think of why *now*, of all times, is the best time to strike."

"Because every moment we wait, more people die?" Zeus said bitterly.

"But your failure means the death of Olympus itself. Your death means you will never see your son again." Ethan raised his brows as he looked from brother to brother. "We do this so that our children might inherit a better world than we lived in. You have the best chance of anyone to make this so. Don't waste it. Return when your plan is solid."

And so the brothers had sat down to strategize. They'd done as their father asked and discussed Kronos' weaknesses, of which he had few. His largest was his arrogance — his utter belief that no one could defeat him, not even the three brothers. That, combined with his need for more power, had to be exploited. And, of course, he wouldn't do anything to dampen the three gods' powers, either, for he wanted that power inside him and unfettered.

They'd put together a plan for their capture, for the way they would escape their chains, for their eventual defeat and even consumption. The others had already left the Black Forest, setting Tom free after he'd tearfully confessed that he'd like to repent and join the Cross. Hades and Cerberus were last, clearing their hideout and making it appear as though no one had been there in years. Hades ought to have made his way out of the forest while it was still light, but he'd been drawn to one last pilgrimage. Who knew when he'd be able to see Atlas again, even as a statue?

"In battle, there is a certain honor," he said, leaning against the statue. The bronze had captured the heat of the sun and now, as the night grew cooler, radiated it back as though it were warm and alive. "You give your all and no one questions your resolve. But this plan…a willing surrender, a calculated gamble, a deadly deception…it's a different battlefield. It's a chess game that can't be solved through military prowess. And nothing short of everything is the prize. Our legacy, the memory we leave behind…it's all at stake. A burning question. A fork in the road. Will we succeed, and make a brighter tomorrow for everyone? Or will I fail, and leave my boy an orphan?"

He hadn't asked this question of anyone before, not even himself. Admitting that he even had it sent a lance of pain through his heart. But Hades couldn't run from the possibility anymore. Achilles had lost his mother, and may well lose his father. And, shameful as it was, even before Hades had come up with this plan he'd struggled to be the right father to the boy. Grief over the loss of Persephone, the obsession with bringing Kronos down, had taken him away from his fatherly duties. And if he failed Achilles would have nothing to remember him by, nothing but shame. Somehow that, more than anything, made him ache to succeed.

He thought about what Atlas would say, if his brother were here. *You could give it all up, of course.* Said with a sly, sidelong look, an open laugh as he swept his swords through the air or did a one-handed pushup. Giving up had never been in Hades' nature. He was a warrior. A warrior who fought for love, for his people, for those who had no power and no voice to shout about the world's injustices. He'd never suffered the way Tom suffered, from an absence of conviction, and he was proud of that.

The best thing you can do for Achilles is to succeed for him, he imagined Atlas saying. *And the best chance of success is this, the plan. The second best thing you can do for Achilles is to make sure he is hidden and safe.* For Kronos *would* pursue the children, to absorb any power they might have inherited from their parents.

"I wish you were here, brother," Hades murmured, patting the statue's leg. Atlas had no reply to that, of course. Then he whistled softly to Cerberus, who was nosing around in a corner at the other end of the square, and he slipped away from the statue.

CHAPTER FIVE: THE MOTHER OF MONSTERS

Hades avoided the River of Life, choked with checkpoints and petty officials looking to wring a bribe out of any boatman who could give them information about the rebellion. He and Cerberus made their way through the Brown Swamp, with Hades slathering mud on them both to drive off the mosquitos. The paths in the swamp had flooded, which meant a slog back to Sherwood, but it was ultimately good. Kronos' men would have a hard time getting there, and the family would be safe for a little while longer. All the same, he breathed a sigh of relief when the reeds and cattails and mud of the swamp gave way to firmer ground and springy green grass. Hades bathed in the first stream he found, then set off on the stone paths of Sherwood towards his family home.

Sherwood forest felt — not peaceful, not exactly. It felt *abandoned*. There was a quiet here that had nothing to do with lazy mornings in the sunshine, though the sun sprayed through the leaves like rain and the bees droned happily among early blooming flowers. Hades thought of the way Sherwood had been terrorized by Medusa and avoided the town square. It was a small wonder that the people of the town had opted to flee instead of walking past the horrified visages of their loved ones day after day. He didn't even have the first idea of what he should do with all of Medusa's victims. He watched Cerberus chase frogs, laughing as each head sought a separate quarry, and tried not to think of how strangely his voice echoed in the silence.

Avoiding the square meant taking the back way to Ethan and

Raven's home, but at last he stood, with his pack and his dog and his hair mostly dry in the sun, before the house of his youth. The tree was older, grander; the door had been newly painted from red to blue. And here, at last, signs of life: chickens scratching in the yard, a target pinned to a tree, boots lined up outside the door. He raised his fist to knock on the door, but hesitated; a moment later he opened it, intending to slip inside.

He had no opportunity for stealth. As soon as he opened the door Cerberus was through it like a shot, scrambling up the stairs toward the sound of children's voices. Hades shook his head ruefully as he removed his shoes and stacked them up beside Achilles' red boots.

He walked past the bedroom of his youth and into the living room, where Achilles, Perseus, Maia and Hercules wrestled with Cerberus. The dog had grown to the size of the dining table and they each held on to one pointed ear, laughing as he shook his heads this way and that and hoisted them off the ground.

"You're here," said Raven with a sigh of obvious relief. A moment later the relief was replaced with a scowl. "And your dog is destroying my clean floor."

Hades winced at the clumps of mud Cerberus had sprayed around the room in his haste. But Raven couldn't keep up the ruse; she laughed as he embraced her. He turned to his father next, then his brothers. Even Zeus gave him a proper hug now, meeting his eyes with warmth and recognition. Perhaps they truly had put the death of Persephone behind them now that they had a new common vision. "How was the journey?" Zeus asked.

"Disgusting," Hades admitted. "I should have gone straight

from the Black Forest like the rest of you."

"My spies report that the flooding of the Swamp has been nothing but good for us, though," Ethan remarked as he took a loaf of bread, breaking off a piece and offering it to Hades. Hades had missed that constant scent of fresh-baked bread. "Typhon still styles himself the lord of this place, but he has no interest in getting his carriages and carts full of bullies stuck in the swamp."

"What does that mean for us?" Hades asked.

His father's sharp eyes widened a little. "You? Oh, nothing. I'm certain our new 'ally' will find a covert way to get here."

They didn't have much time, Hades knew. A day, two at most. Now that he was here they could start preparing for the next step: sending the children away. But that was something best discussed after bedtime. For now, Hades had a few more precious hours with his son.

They went for a walk together, talking about the herbs and fruits and animals of Sherwood. Hades told Achilles of his exploits as a young one — his poorly thought-out plans with Harper, the head of the Sherwood Outlaws, the first time he saw Persephone, the hours of secret training in the meadow.

"I want to be an Outlaw, too," Achilles said. He had a high, clear voice, still the voice of a child, but somehow serious. And why shouldn't it be? He'd seen so much already, experienced things a boy shouldn't experience.

Hades laughed, though a weight settled on his heart. "With any luck, you won't need to be an Outlaw. Maybe, by then, we won't have outlaws so much as…protectors." People who did what the guard were supposed to do. Assist those in need instead of taking from them.

He should tell Achilles now. But he couldn't bear it.

Cerberus gamboled among the flowers, snapping at passing bumblebees. Achilles proudly showed his father how well he could shoot, threw three sticks for Cerberus at once, and talked of learning to bake bread with his grandmother. Hades drank in his son's words, reveling in his voice, his enthusiasm, his seriousness about everything. He didn't want to stop the moment, to break it with his news. And when Maia came tearing out of the house to challenge Achilles to a wrestling match, the moment passed. He laughed at the little girl, so like her father in defiance and mirth — and in wrestling, too, for she took down the taller and older boy with a feral yell that made several branches shake loose their leaves.

Ivy came out to join them in the yard. She looked tired, her red hair hastily tied back and her cheeks sunken. "I don't suppose you've reconsidered," she said softly as she took up a seat next to Hades on the wooden fence. "For his sake."

"It's for his sake that I do it," Hades replied.

"Are you sure?" she asked sharply. "Or are you doing it for the glory?"

Hades felt a swell of warm anger, but forced himself to turn it back like a tide of magma. It was natural for Ivy to act out. She'd lost so much, and she'd done so much for them. "You know I'm not," he told her, keeping his voice even and measured, as reassuring as he could.

Her gaze dropped. As the sun descended, the trees of Sherwood were starting to take on their characteristic glow, and it framed her hair like a halo of fire. Tears glittered at the edges of her eyes. "I know," she said. "But I wonder about your brothers."

And one brother in particular, he'd wager. "We've been raised to this," he reassured her. "We'll see it through."

"If you can." She looked up again, dashing at her eyes as though they'd betrayed her. "If you can't, what becomes of them?" She nodded to the children. Perseus and Hercules had come out into the yard now, Hercules toddling on chubby legs. They started up a game of tag with Cerberus.

"I guess that's not a conversation we can put off any longer," Hades acknowledged, and felt a hole open in his heart. This one, like the one he bore for Persephone, would never go away.

###

Twilight turned to darkness, and by the light of the glowing golden trees they had a fine meal: roast chicken, boiled potatoes, plenty of gravy and good bread. The children exhausted themselves with games and wrestling, and at last begged to be put to bed. Hades sat with Achilles until his son's furtive rustling subsided and he breathed the deep, peaceful breaths of sleep. Then he snuck out of his childhood bedroom — the bedroom of his own child, for the moment — and went into the sitting room where his brothers now sat.

"Where's everyone else?" he said as he took his place.

"Ivy's putting Maia to bed, Leda Hercules. Perseus is already down," Poseidon said.

"And Mom and Dad felt we could use this time to talk," Zeus added.

Talk. Hades grappled momentarily within himself. The day had been so perfect, and was the very thing his child needed. He could find some other forest, some other home, and let these days stretch out before him. But…until when? They'd set their plans in motion. His past would catch up with him no matter what. When he looked up from the table to meet his brothers' eyes, they held the same determination. Poseidon poured him a cup of tea and pushed it toward him.

"Does this gamble afford us the greatest chance of triumphing over Kronos?" Zeus asked in his usual blunt manner.

Hades studied the tea. They couldn't predict the future, whether there would be a better moment in five or ten or fifteen years. That was the true gamble.

"If your answer is yes, then I stand by your side to the very end," Zeus added quietly.

Hades looked to Poseidon. Poseidon nodded.

"This is our sole path." There was no time for hesitation now. Life was full of regret, but it was also full of purpose. He couldn't think of missed days with his son now. He had to look ahead. "This is our solitary opportunity."

For a moment they were all silent. The trees outside rustled in a gentle breeze, and the animals of the night chirped and sang. Then Zeus cracked a smile and tilted his head, resolved. "Then I suppose we'll follow you into the jaws of a tyrant."

Hades took Zeus' hand in his left, and Poseidon's in his right. Together they formed an unbreakable bond. Together they had power that could overcome anything, even a god. So their birth mother had told them, and so they must believe.

"Together, brothers," he said. "Let's go through the plan one more time."

###

"My spies noted a party crossing the Brown Swamp," Ethan said to them late the next morning. They'd spent most of the day sparring, working on new magical tactics that they could hopefully employ against Kronos and brainstorming how their powers could work together. "It's Ambrose."

"You're sure?" Hades said. His heart was suddenly in his throat.

"They were dressed as a party of merchants. And let's be honest, merchants don't come to Sherwood anymore." Ethan gave him a bleak smile. The fact served to remind them of everything they'd lost.

"Then it's time," Poseidon said, putting a hand on Hades' shoulder. "They'll be another day at most."

Hades met his father's eye. He'd struggled with this moment since he'd come up with the plan. But Achilles needed guidance and family and love. A life of constant running was no life for him.

Perseus and Maia were practically twins, having been born a few days apart, and Ivy had proposed to Poseidon that she take in the boy. He wouldn't have to lose his playmate that way, she'd explained, and she was capable of taking care of two children, especially ones who were such friends. Poseidon had agreed immediately. "He calls her Mama, sometimes," he'd told Hades the previous night, tears swimming in his eyes as he drank his tea. "He forgets."

"He'll never truly forget his mother," Hades had sought to reassure him, all the while hoping that Achilles would feel the same.

Leda was ready to slip into anonymity with Hercules. She was a capable hunter and could live in forest, swamp or waste for years at a time. It was for the best, she'd told Zeus: instead of hiding and relying on people not to realize who Hercules was, she could teach him everything she knew in relative safety. But she had extended no such offer to Achilles, and having one little boy was hard enough.

Hades couldn't imagine asking Ethan and Raven to care for him. They'd already done the work of raising four sons, and their age was catching up to them: Ethan had never fully recovered from Atlas' death and walked only with the aid of a staff, while Hades caught Raven napping sometimes at night. They lacked the energy to keep up with a growing boy.

"Promise me you'll find someone," he said to his father now. "A good man, like you were. A family that can raise him like one of their own, and teach him to be honorable and kind. I want him..." He swallowed. He didn't want Achilles to be a warrior, or a leader, or a man burdened the way he was burdened himself. In more ways than one, what he wanted most for Achilles was a life of anonymity, the sort of life he'd never got to have. "I want him to become an honorable man. A kind man. The sort of man who is strong but understands how to use his strength. Do you know someone who can teach him to be these things?"

Ethan put a hand on Hades' shoulder. "I know just the man and woman," he said. His voice was soft, his eyes clear. He understood Hades perfectly. "The raising of a child is the most important work a man can do in this world. Except, perhaps, saving it." He offered Hades a brief smile of reprieve. Hades smiled back, grateful.

###

Ethan, Raven, Ivy, Leda and the children left that night. Maia and Perseus were sleepy and confused, while Achilles stood somberly in the door, being parted from his father for the last time. Little Hercules slept fast on his mother's chest.

Ethan looked at the whitewashed walls of the treehouse, the glorious and well-worn spiral staircase that took them up to level after level. The house still smelled faintly of good food, and if Hades listened carefully he thought he could hear the echoes of laughter from decades past. "You're going to destroy my house, aren't you?" Ethan said sorrowfully. "I don't suppose I'll be back here again."

"We'll do our best not to bring down the tree," Poseidon tried to reassure him.

Zeus shrugged. "We're supposed to make it look convincing, aren't we?"

Ethan laughed. Behind him, Raven stifled a sob. They were both doing what they could to keep the children from catching on, but the truth was painful. For they would all die together, or all rise triumphant together.

"You must go," Hades said gently. As bad as it was to say goodbye, things would be much worse if Tom Ambrose and his party caught them here.

Ivy and Leda raised their hands one last time, then turned and led their children out of the gate. They would travel together for a time before splitting up; they'd been careful not to tell the brothers where they were going, in case it was something Kronos might be able to divine when he absorbed them.

Ethan opened his mouth, looking a little stricken. Hades thought he recognized that look. It was the same look he was giving his own son now, the look that meant there were too many things to say and not enough time in which to say them.

Finally Ethan leaned in and embraced him. "I have taught you to be stronger than me, and better than me," he whispered. "No matter what happens next, I am proud beyond measure."

Hades' throat closed up. Tears welled behind his eyes. He couldn't reply; he nodded in thanks and swallowed hard, coughing once or twice before kneeling before his son. Golden light edged Achilles' face, and his wide brown eyes were shadowed in their sockets. "I will do everything in my power to make sure we see each other again," he promised.

Achilles nodded. "Take good care of your new family," Hades told him. "And remember that this is not my choice. I love you, my son."

"Love you, Dad," he whispered.

Hades allowed himself one hug, then forced his arms to part, to watch his child slip from his grasp and walk down the golden

73

path. Into safety, and out of Hades' life forever.

Poseidon helped him to his feet and together they watched their children, their parents, their loves walk around a bend and disappear from sight. Hades thought he could sense an entire future unraveling, changing.

"What now?" Zeus asked in a hoarse voice.

"Now?" Hades found himself again. "Now, we get to work."

###

Getting to work meant setting up fake wards, magic that they had discussed at length. They were part real, part elaborate illusion — Tom had to think the gods were protecting themselves, or he might suspect a trap. They also set up two moats: one of lava, and one of water. They surrounded the tree house and ripped up the road to either side of it, but it wasn't as though anyone was around to care. Zeus set thin strands of lightning between the trees around them to act as a sort of fence. They put up an obvious but complicated intruder alert spell, then retreated into the house to wait.

"Are you certain it'll be tonight?" Zeus asked as they found their beds again and lay there, contemplating the ceiling.

"No," Hades said. "Try to get some sleep."

He struggled to follow his own advice. His thoughts raced from point to point, remembering all the nights he'd spent staring at this very ceiling as a boy. And every time a songbird so much as chirped outside their window, he jumped and listened out for the telltale cracking of branches, susurration of voices breaking down their wards. What if Ethan's spies were wrong and this truly was a band of merchants? *Believe in the Cross,* he told himself, and tried not to think of what Achilles was doing right now.

He lay there until the sky grew light, and never fell into more than a half-sleep. "That went well," Poseidon grumbled. "Anyone get any rest?"

"Nope," said Zeus.

"No." Hades sat up. "At least they left us with plenty of provisions." No matter how long they waited, they wouldn't starve.

They drank some cold tea left over from the night before and finished off the last of the bread Raven had baked. Then they went out to check their wards, Zeus snagging an apple from a barrel by the front door as they went.

The wards hadn't been touched. But someone had been right up to the edge of them. The footprint was human and matched Tom's in shape and size, to the best of Hades' recollection. So the information given by the *Cross* had been correct after all. Tom had done his best to scuff out his footprints, but he'd missed one.

"He's waiting for his moment," Poseidon assessed when Hades showed the others.

"Which is what, exactly? When better to attack than when we're all asleep?" Zeus said.

"Maybe the wards are stronger than we thought. Or maybe he can't get over the lava or water moat, for some reason." Poseidon furrowed his brow and scratched at the back of his neck.

"Or maybe he's with someone — or something — that can't,"

Hades added.

"This isn't a great start to the plan," Poseidon said.

He was right. Things were already going wrong. Hades started to pace the perimeter, trying to look as though he were taking a stroll instead of thinking hard. "It could be that they're monitoring our movements. Trying to assess the best place to capture us."

"So we get to stick around here until they decide to strike?" Zeus' lip curled as he looked around. "I was hoping for action a little sooner. Or at least the chance to blow off some steam."

"If it's a fight you're itching for, I'm happy to knock you on your butt," Poseidon offered.

"As if you could," Zeus scoffed.

"What would we do today if we didn't think they'd come?" Hades interrupted them, glaring. How could his brothers bicker in the midst of the most important battle of their lives?

"Poseidon would fail to knock me on my butt," Zeus replied.

Poseidon spread his hands in a conciliatory gesture. "We would strengthen our defenses. Forage and increase our supplies. Spar."

"Then that's what we'll do. Act as if nothing is amiss." Hades looked out over the lava moat, glowing in the morning sun. It was out of place in the forest; the grass around it had dried and crisped. "We should split up," he decided quietly. Poseidon and Zeus raised their brows in question. "Ambrose will be bolder, act sooner if he thinks he can catch us alone. We feign surprise, we fight —"

"But not too hard," put in Poseidon.

"But not so little they know it's a ruse." Zeus ran a hand through his hair.

"Hey." Hades smiled. "Did Dad ever say that saving the world would be easy?"

"I don't think he ever said anything about this much acting, either." Zeus spun a lightning bolt in his hand like a dagger. "It was never my strong suit, you know?"

Hades wasn't sure about that. They'd been raised to engage in lies and duplicity, which were tools useful in any rebellion. This was just another sort of lie. "We can do this." He met Zeus' eye and nodded. "We can't fail."

He meant it to be encouraging, but Zeus' pale cheeks turned pink and he looked down. It was hard for each of them to forget their own part in their previous failure, and it was a failure they could not repeat.

Hades cleared his throat. "Zeus, since you're so intent on stabbing something, why don't you try to hunt us some dinner? Poseidon and I can forage and do a perimeter walk from opposing sides."

Poseidon nodded and went inside to grab his cloak and staff.

"Wait." Zeus bent down and scooped up a handful of pebbles. "We should be able to signal to each other. In case we're captured."

He selected two pebbles and held them between his fingers. A moment later a white-blue string crackled over them. He handed the stones to his brothers. Taking it made all the hairs on Hades' hand rise.

Poseidon took two more pebbles from Zeus' hand and

imbued them with the cooling power of water. Hades took two more, and Zeus let the rest clatter to the ground. "We may not be able to get to the stones," Hades warned as he imbued his two stones with the heat of the magma. "So we all meet back here for dinner. If one of us is missing by sundown, we'll know."

The others nodded their assent, and they parted ways. "You stay," Hades ordered Cerberus as he set off. He didn't think he could bear it if the dog ended up chained at the front of the procession road again. Or worse, executed for abandoning his old master.

Cerberus' future head whined urgently.

"I know." Hades scratched between his ears. "But that's the idea."

###

Perimeter work had never exactly been interesting, but Hades usually liked it. It helped him to herd his thoughts, to turn over problems in his mind and come up with solutions. Today he found it anything but restful. Every noise — every screech of a bird, crack of a branch on the ground, rustle in the underbrush — everything set him on edge. He was so busy worrying about whether he was about to be attacked from behind that he didn't pay attention to where his feet took him until he was in the town square.

He stopped, muscles freezing at the sight of the twisted and burned sacred tree at the center of the square. He'd married Persephone under that tree, and attended his brothers' weddings here. The last time he'd seen the stage in front of the tree, it had been ringed with terrifying visages, all the statues of Sherwood that Medusa had created. They were gone now; small mercy. Had Kronos ordered them shipped back to Novaris and his palace, or had the people of Sherwood removed the statues themselves?

It must be some plot of Kronos, Hades thought, clenching his fists. After all, there was no one left in Sherwood. All the same, he felt an uneasy tugging in his gut. As he walked through the center of town, past the ruins of houses and rotting spars of wood and threads of cloth that had once been vibrant stalls, there was a growing sense of *wrongness* that pulled at the edges of his mind. It could be a trick, he thought, and put his hand on the bident strapped to his back. He put his other hand in his pocket and sought out his brother's stones. He listened keenly for the sounds of feet shifting on the grass, a breath let out a touch too loudly.

Hades let his feet guide him away from the square. The paths here had become overgrown with grass that came up to his ankle. Good for hiding snakes and other traps, he thought. The trees here were stranger than he remembered, too. Their bark was darker, their branches more twisted. The leaves that splayed from them smelled bitter, and little poisonous berries clustered in them. A sickness had taken over the forest without anyone here to care for it. He followed the winding path, following the warning toll in his mind, realizing only belatedly where he was going. This was the way to the sacred grove, the ancient heart of Sherwood where the trees formed a circle that was, according to local legends, the first grove in the forest. The trees were bowed with age, their trunks thick and their leaves broad. Hades was struck with a sudden fear. If the sacred trees of Sherwood were corrupted, what did that mean for the whole forest?

A feeling of malevolence permeated the air as he approached the grove, and his stomach plummeted. He took his hand off the bident staff and put it on the nearest trunk, as if contact could help him divine the problem. But that had never been his magic. Atlas had known how to understand and manipulate trees and dirt and flowers.

The sky was suddenly darker than it had been this morning. He looked up. Storm clouds rumbled above him. The sudden change in temperature had brought on a mist — or perhaps it was some dark magic. Two figures appeared opposite the grove and Hades' hand was back on his bident staff before he had time to register the movement. But something stayed his hand. He *recognized* these silhouettes.

They resolved into Zeus and Poseidon.

"Brothers." Hades was half relieved for a moment. But his brothers were not. And a moment later, he understood why. For if they had all been drawn here by that same feeling of malevolence, it could only mean one thing.

"Ambush," breathed Poseidon, a moment before the grove around them lit like fire.

Hades' bident flew around to his front, guided by his hand. From the corner of his eye he spotted a flash of light and he turned the staff to intercept it. The ribbon of light glanced off the bident, wrenching at Hades' arm. Then it wrapped around Poseidon.

The big man flexed and heaved on the ribbon. From beyond the grove they heard a satisfying cry of pain. "Show yourself,"

Poseidon snarled.

"With pleasure," said a voice far too deep to be Tom Ambrose.

Typhon stepped through the fire. His eyes were glowing embers, and he ran a red tongue over his sharp teeth in anticipation. He looked different than the last time Hades had seen him: he'd capped his horns in steel that ended in claw-sharp tips, and the gray scales that rippled over his body were polished to a shine like armor. The knobs on his arms were sharpened to spikes. The half-beast had always contended for Sherwood, and as his eyes lit on Hades a special hatred kindled there. He'd been waiting for a rematch since Hades had humiliated him in the Sherwood market years ago. Well, if it was a rematch he desired...

Poseidon flicked the glowing ribbon like a whip. It lashed out, and Typhon took a step back to avoid it. He laughed as it flew back toward Poseidon, wrapping around his wrist. Poseidon brought his hand up to summon a whip of water, but his power fizzled in his hands and died out. He growled in frustration.

"Struggling with your little powers?" Typhon mocked. "Perhaps they're not so useful after all."

The ribbon of light was trying to attach itself to Poseidon's other hand now, working as rope to bind him. He flipped up his trident and severed the ribbon neatly. The ribbon recoiled as if in pain, but continued to wind up his arms — both of his arms. "Lucky for me, I don't need magic to destroy you." He swung the trident. It sang through the air and Typhon blocked it with one scaly, knobbled arm. He grunted with the effort, though, and when he tried to snatch the trident away Poseidon withdrew it so fast that it left nothing behind but the soft ring of its movement. Poseidon thrust, again so fast that his trident was nothing more than a blur of glowing light. It struck Typhon's scaly chest with a clang.

Typhon laughed again. "Do you know the last time I took a blow? Neither do I. Is this the best you can do?"

"No. Because he's got me." Zeus leapt, lightning spraying from his fingers —

And straight into a trap. Hades gasped at the elegance of it; the net had not been there before, but as Zeus touched it it shimmered into existence. Even though they were supposed to be captured he couldn't help shouting, "No!" as he sprang forward, just as he would have if they'd truly intended to win.

The magical net was neatly made. Hades would have liked to study it if he weren't busy springing a trap of his own. The more power Zeus pushed into it, the stronger it seemed to become.

Hades pushed the prongs of his bident staff between two lines of the net. Power sizzled down the length of the staff, jolting along his skin, making his teeth ache and the hair on his arms curl and stink. Hades gritted his teeth and twisted the staff, flushing it with power of his own. The net split and Zeus dropped to the ground.

"My thanks, brother," he said, grimacing as he stood.

Poseidon cried out.

They whirled around. Their brother was nearly encased in the magical ribbons. The more he slashed, the more they multiplied. As Hades neared to help Poseidon, he was slammed by a great brown and gray mass. They hit the ground hard, and sharp claws encased Hades' throat. Typhon leaned down. "Oh, how I've looked forward to this," he growled in Hades' ear. His breath stank of rotting meat and death. Hades tried not to gag. Summoning his power, he put his hand flat against Typhon's chest and let the magma roar. Light flared around his hand and Typhon screamed, scrambling back. Now the stench of charred scale was added to the smell of electricity and mist and burnt hair. Hades' stomach was churning, his mind spinning.

Typhon was between Hades and his brothers. Poseidon scrambled to undo the ribbons and Zeus fought a shadowy figure on his other side. "Tell me," the beast growled, baring his sharp teeth. "Will Kronos reward me for bringing him your head? Or will he punish me for taking it off your neck before he could have the pleasure? And more importantly, is the punishment worth the satisfaction?"

A figure appeared beside him. "You." Hades imbued the word with venom, as if he hadn't expected it.

"You can't kill him. Our Lord wants him alive." Tom Ambrose was pale, and wouldn't look at Hades.

Typhon growled in frustration. "Let me rip his legs off, at least."

"You're welcome to try. There's no one ordering me to spare you," Hades spat.

"Kronos wants him at full strength." Tom blinked, and raised a hand. Hades saw spells spinning against his palm. He swung his bident staff and knocked the spell from the air as Tom tried to discharge it. Tom swore and ducked as the spell exploded. Typhon wasn't so lucky: the spell caught him in the chest and sent him flying.

Hades and Tom circled each other, Hades with his staff at the ready and Tom with his hands out. Hades let his anger guide him, lend an air of truth to his performance. "I thought you felt remorse," he said, curling his lip. The contempt he felt for Tom was real, even if he'd never believed in the man's change of heart. "I thought you wanted to make the world a better place."

"There's a lot you think that's not true," Tom replied. Hades struck out first, and Tom dodged to the side, flicking a little spell that increased the mist around them. His shape disappeared in the mist and Hades spun, growling softly.

"For example." Tom's voice sounded right next to his ear. Hades whirled and his staff struck thin air, parting the mist and making it swirl. "You think there's hope. You persist in thinking you *can* kill Kronos, when that hope is nothing more than an illusion."

Lightning flashed from above, and Tom was right in front of him. He pushed Hades by the shoulder and Hades felt something latch there, something with teeth. He staggered back and tried to pull the spell off his shoulder, but no luck. And when he looked up again, Ambrose had disappeared.

The spell was making him feel dizzy. It was some sort of magic that leeched his strength. He tried to pour more power into his bident staff, but his hands shook and refused to cooperate. In the air around him he sensed them — figures, stalking, biding their time. Waiting for him to fail. He swiped the air uselessly with the staff. "Zeus!" he called. Could his brother not call up a storm to dispel this mist?

Zeus said nothing in reply, however. A chill drew over Hades like a coat.

"You always fight like this," came Tom's voice, this time from the other side. Hades turned again. He used more caution now, seeking out the air with his staff rather than swinging it uselessly. "Striking out in fury without thinking of whether you could ever possibly succeed. After all, what hope do you have against the master himself when you cannot best even three of his men?"

Three? Hades thought. Then a rough hand grabbed his arm. Typhon reared out of the gloom, muzzle bloody from some blow dealt by one of his brothers, eyes blazing with rage. He twisted Hades' arm until his fingers released the bident, then kicked it away. Hades was lifted into the air, then slammed on his back. All oxygen left him. Black spots bloomed over his vision. He tried to make his hands hot again, but the spell on his shoulder lapped up his power as he summoned it. It was growing heavy, fat off its meal, making it hard for him to get up. Typhon drew back a fist and slammed it into Hades' jaw. Nausea washed over him. The beast drew his fist back again, and Hades knew with utter certainty that if the blow landed, Typhon wouldn't stop until he'd killed him.

The panic gave him the surge of power he needed. He kicked Typhon as hard as he could. Typhon fell on his backside and Hades rolled away, scrambling to his feet. Dizziness threatened to take over, and he was still missing his weapon and unable to summon his power. But he tried to think. What would he do if he were truly trying to win? What would he do to turn the tide?

He reached not for his power, but for the power lurking far beneath the surface of Olympus.

He could feel the heat flowing. *Come to me,* he thought, and it bubbled in response. *Come now.* The ground began to shift.

"He's going to kill us all," growled Typhon.

"I don't understand — the spell should be working —" Tom sounded panicked.

"Cast it again," Typhon said

"I can't! I don't have the strength —"

"Enough of all this. Clear this infernal mist away."

That voice was new. Hades focused on it. Had he ever heard it before?

The thick cloud cover swirled over the ground, then receded, leaving behind ripped up patches of grass and mud, tangled roots that had been disrupted by the miniature quake Hades had summoned. His bident staff lay on the other side of the clearing, prongs-first in the grass. At the edge of the grove, up against the sacred trees, Zeus and Poseidon lay captured. A shimmering net covered both of them and they lay frozen, as if Tom Ambrose had stopped time around them. Zeus' eyes were wide with shock, Poseidon's with fury.

Hades started toward them before he noticed the woman.

She stood next to the brothers, dressed in practical city clothing: loose and comfortable trousers, which were now splattered in mud up to her calves. A shirt and coat that buttoned up to the collar. The coat was long-sleeved and pale, too. Her hair was pulled back in a practical bun, and her pale features were severe: a mouth drawn into a thin line, green eyes narrowed in concentration. Cheekbones that could cut glass. Right now she held something that resembled a belly-bow up to her shoulder — only it was much more streamlined than a belly-bow, and obviously had no need of being against her belly. It was long and fitted with a bolt like a harpoon, but the bolt was made of light, not steel, and Hades couldn't see where the bow drew back to fire it. Nevertheless she did have her finger on a trigger.

Their eyes met. She smiled. "Clear shot," she said, and pulled the trigger.

The bolt pierced Hades' free shoulder. Pain spread over him like fire and he screamed. He started to fall back, but was jerked forward, causing a fresh wave of pain that nearly brought his breakfast back up. He couldn't resist stumbling toward the woman. She drew on a thin rope of magic, attached to the bolt, pulling him inexorably closer to her. When he realized what was happening he tried to plant his feet, tried to pull away — but she only smiled, and pulled harder.

His hand went to his other shoulder. He could pull this spell free. It was a slippery little thing, but he had strength in his fingers yet. If he pulled it free he could snap the bolt, summon a wall of fire to push out Typhon and Tom and this newcomer. It took all his strength to succumb to the pain instead. *Remember your part,* he told himself. He was a warrior, but today he had to lose his fight.

Rough hands shoved him to his knees before the woman. She patted her weapon fondly. "I knew it'd work," she said. "Thank you for giving me the chance to try it, Tom."

"Don't forget to tell Kronos who made the magic bolt." Tom

sounded sulky.

"Naturally. I wouldn't dream of leaving anything out of my report. *No.*" This she said to Typhon, who'd put his claws around Hades' throat. Typhon withdrew, snarling. Hades had enough intelligence left in him to be surprised. Typhon never let anyone speak to him as though he were a simple beast. Who held that sort of power over him, aside from his tyrant master?

The answer came in a flash as Tom spun the net over Hades and Typhon hoisted the three gods, grumbling. *Echidna.* The alchemist who had created Typhon, and Medusa. The maker of chimeras. The mother of monsters.

"He's...using...you," he tried to croak at Echidna from his place on Typhon's shoulder.

The woman looked up from where she was cleaning out her weapon. "Who? Kronos?" She smiled and flicked a hand in dismissal. "So what? He lets me do as I like. Am I not therefore also using him?"

"How?" he whispered, but pretended he lacked the strength to finish it. *How could the world have people like you in it?*

Soon enough. Soon enough Kronos would be defeated, and all the evil Echidna had brought to the world would be vanquished. And Echidna herself — well, perhaps the brothers could find a suitable punishment for her.

CHAPTER SIX: THE BELLY OF THE BEAST

The brothers were tossed into the back of a cart. As Poseidon's head cracked against the bottom, he started to see through the spell. The cart was much larger than it appeared from the outside, and iron bars surrounded them, crackling with more spells to keep them contained. As they drove the cart toward Solara, Poseidon quickly realized that one of those spells kept the world from seeing them at all.

"I think we should organize a procession," Typhon rumbled as they splashed over a muddy part of the path. Solara, like the Brown Swamp, had flooded with the season, and most travelers were staying away. Ambrose sat next to him in the driver's box, concentrating on casting spells that would dry the road out and make it stable enough for their heavy wagon to cross. "Bring the prisoners to their doom in style."

"And risk being assassinated on the road? Do you know the rewards Kronos would heap upon the ones who brought him his brothers? No. We'll travel in secrecy until we've reached the palace," Tom snapped.

Typhon laughed. "Come come, little man. Who would dare try to assassinate *us*?"

"Or they might have some misguided allies trying to free them." Tom slapped at a mosquito that had become quite enamored of his ear. "Don't make a big scene out of this."

"Back me up," Typhon said to Echidna, who perched atop the carriage. She was staring down at the gods, head cocked, making notes in a little book with a scrap of charcoal pencil.

"I don't care how we get there, as long as we get there," she replied absent-mindedly. "Their eyes really are fascinating."

The intensity of her gaze made Poseidon want to *shut* his eyes. Actually, he'd really like to give her a rude gesture, but the ribbons that had ensnared him were pulled so tight he couldn't move his arms. He was pretty sure he'd lost all feeling in them some hours back.

He was starting to think that this whole 'get eaten' plan was a bad idea.

The things that are worth it are never easy, he thought. It was something Diana used to say, especially when she was out helping to deliver babies. Thinking of her opened up the deep well of sorrow that he'd been trying to cover for the sake of his son, for the sake of his brothers, for the sake of the cause. And the woman ultimately responsible for her death — the woman who had created the terrible gorgon Medusa — that woman sat right above his head, looking at him as though he were nothing more than an interesting specimen she was preparing to dissect.

He flexed his arms, tempted to break these pathetic chains, but felt a kick on the back of his calf. A warning from Hades. This was all part of the plan. *Except the part where I come face to face with my wife's killer.* Did Echidna know what destruction she had wrought? She had to. Yet she didn't care. He wanted to show her, to force her eyes open as he took her to every statue Medusa had created, as he showed her the homes and livelihoods that had been ruined by Typhon and his men. He wanted her to understand anguish the way he understood it, the missing of a mother and wife, the hole that could never be filled for either him or his son.

He'd been asked to risk his life for this gambit. He hadn't thought he'd be asked to risk his revenge — or given the chance to take it.

He wondered what Ethan would tell him in this moment. *Revenge is poison,* he'd probably say. *Think ahead, to the work that will make lives better.*

It will do nothing but hurt you in the end, Raven's voice whispered to him, a soft caress.

It is not the way to remember me, sighed Diana.

Poseidon knew all these voices spoke the truth. But they didn't tell him what he wanted to hear the most.

His brothers might understand. Hades would probably tell him to focus on the mission, that defeating Kronos would be enough. Perhaps he was right. After all, Medusa was a product of Echidna's twisted mind, and Echidna had only designed her because Kronos had allowed it — willed it — to be so. Destroying Kronos would take the fang out of her.

On the other hand, Zeus would tell him to make her pay. Zeus had never been good at letting go of grudges. Perhaps if they succeeded in this, Zeus and Poseidon would bring Echidna to justice together.

It felt like a faraway dream, lying here as he was with the hot marshy sun blazing on him and ropes of magic twisting his body into agonizing positions. But it was enough to hold on to, enough to allow Poseidon to meet Echidna's gaze without fear, or anger. *You will pay,* he thought at her. *I will make certain of it.*

Echidna merely continued taking her notes.

###

Passage through Solara took two days. Two days of aching limbs, baking heat, and only a little water splashed through the bars of their cage. No food. Hades drew into himself in a sort of meditative state, breathing slowly, conserving his energy, trying to shed the discomfort of the world. He felt it when they reached the edge of the marshland and began to make their way over paved roads, felt the air grow warmer and staler and smokier as they moved from the hinterlands toward the city. Soon he saw other travelers on the road, too, merchants Typhon stopped for 'surprise inspection.' The wagon began to wind up, then, past houses that became larger and more jagged. Places for the cronies of Kronos to have their homes and make their schemes. Beyond these things, Hades could feel it warping space, pulling happiness from the air: Kronos' palace. It pulled on him, too, but he ignored the temptation to give in to despair. Instead he renewed his determination: they would do this. They would wipe the blot of this palace from the very world.

He smelled smoke at the edge of the city. People were shouting and he caught the unmistakable clang of steel. Typhon turned to grin through the bars of the cage. "You hear that?" he said.

Hades didn't answer.

"Those are people who believe in you. They think you're going to return to save them. To save everyone." He rumbled with gravelly laughter. "They have such hope. It will be so *delightful* to squash."

Hades glared at him. *I look forward to the look on your face when we emerge from your lord triumphant,* he thought.

Typhon heard nothing of these thoughts. Still chortling, he turned back around and urged the horses up the road.

Fifteen minutes later, the wagon lurched to a stop at the top of the processional road. "Passage within," said Typhon.

The guard at the gate came up to the cart, eyes wandering over imaginary piles of fruit. "We weren't expecting you," he said grudgingly. "And this fruit looks moldy."

Tom pulled the illusion from the cart. The guard recoiled in shock, his eyes meeting Hades'. He stumbled back, stuttering out apologies as he waved them through. "I had no idea — humblest regrets —"

Typhon leaned out of the driver's side and smiled. "Oh, you *will* regret questioning me," he said, and flicked the reins. The horses pulled forward. Hades struggled to sit up. His head was pounding from lack of water and food. As the gate closed behind him he saw the beginnings of a gaping crowd. Now everyone would know.

The outer courtyard of the palace was a sea of polished black stone from wall to wall. Guards and workers buzzed about, but all fell silent as the prison cart rattled toward the inner gate. Tom and Typhon sat proudly upon it, and even Echidna had stopped her note-taking and started to look a little nervous. The guards at the inner gate pulled open the doors and stood aside without having to be asked. Hades watched as a sea of stricken faces passed him by — people who worked for Kronos, but perhaps not by choice, he thought. People who had perhaps held out hope that the tyrant could be defeated.

"Brothers," he whispered. He couldn't bring his voice to full power. He met each of their eyes, willing them to understand. Whatever happened now, happened to them together.

They passed through the second courtyard and drove up to a set of wide black stairs. Here the carriage stopped, and Typhon and Tom dismounted. Echidna leapt lightly to the ground. She turned and, taking an elaborate key, inserted it into the lock. Magic whispered around the lock and it slid open.

"I trust you can take it from here," she said. "I've been away from the lab for far too long, someone's bound to have destroyed an experiment in the process." She wrinkled her nose.

"You don't wish to share in the glory?" Tom sounded surprised.

"I told you I'd be making my own report." Her smile was thin and cold.

Typhon pulled the gods out one by one, hauling them by their ropes and reminding Hades that he'd barely been able to move in the cramped wagon. His shoulders screamed as Typhon grabbed his arm and tossed him to the ground. The magical harpoon hadn't bled, so Echidna had left it in him to 'see what happens'. The strength spell still sucked at his power, a way to keep him down during the long journey.

Tom watched Typhon manhandle them all to standing. "I am sorry about this," he told them as he linked their ropes together. "Your brother was my friend, even if he was a spy. I wish you'd seen sense."

Zeus spat at him, though the gesture was largely symbolic as he had no water to spare. Poseidon curled his lip. Hades ignored him, looking straight ahead. Tom's excuses meant nothing. He lacked the courage and the faith to do what must be done.

Tom took the end of the rope and began to walk, pulling his prisoners behind him. They left the burning heat of the black courtyard and passed into halls as dark as the tomb, lit only by the occasional flickering torch. Their footsteps echoed against the bare walls.

Tom drew up in front of two obsidian doors, carved with scythes that swept through a field of grain — or was it people? The door was flanked by two statues in pale marble, a man and a woman, each with an expression of deep terror. A tiny raised tear was halfway down the man's face. The statues were so grotesque that even the guards at the door wanted nothing to do with them, stepping carefully around them with distaste as they made way for Tom and Typhon and the prisoners.

"This is it," muttered Zeus.

"Silence!" Typhon barked, and shoved him. Tom pulled on their rope and pushed open the door, ushering them inside.

The throne room looked little different from the hall: tall walls, all black, a floor polished until it shone like an onyx mirror, candlelight that bounced around the room and gave the illusion of a spring of fire on all sides. Unlike the corridors, the throne room was filled with more ghastly statues like those that had once lined the road from Novaris up to the palace. The statues on the main road had been the most terrifying, the last glimpse into the lives of people that had died in pain and terror. The statues here were almost elegant, beautiful. The nearest woman to Hades had faced her death with grace, standing tall and staring ahead, unwilling to show her fear. He could see it in the back of her eyes, though, dimmed but present.

"Incredible, isn't she?" rumbled a deep voice from the front of the throne room.

The voice was like its own kind of magic, pulling Hades' attention unwillingly from the heroine next to him. His eyes were drawn toward the front of the room. The black throne glittered strangely, flame and shadow dancing along its hard lines. A hooded figure sat on the throne, cloaked in darkness save the long, pale, bony fingers, which protruded from the wide sleeves of his robe and tapped on the arm of his throne. Hades felt the piercing gaze of Kronos pinning him to the spot.

The hooded figure laughed, a rasping and sinister sound that twisted in Hades' gut and made his legs tremble. He wanted to fall to the floor, to cover his ears, to pray for it all to be over. He forced his shoulders back and his head high. He would not be cowed by this man — this god — whatever he was. He was no more than Hades' own brother, after all. "I keep my most special kills here, in the throne room with me. She makes for a good reminder: defiance means nothing in the end. Dignity means nothing. Everyone bows to me, whether in life or death."

He lifted one skeletal finger and beckoned. Tom dropped the rope and hurried forward, then knelt and touched his head to the floor. "My faithful one," Kronos said. Hades thought he saw Tom wince.

"Always," Tom said, voice quivering.

"You have brought me that which I seek, and you will be mightily rewarded," Kronos promised. "To think that a mere insignificant ant could ensnare my flesh and blood! Though I suppose I should not be surprised. For you too are insignificant ants in my presence. The dirt you walk is not fit to be beneath my feet. The power you wield is less than the power I hold in one finger." He lifted a finger as if to demonstrate.

The ropes around Hades tightened, and he found himself being dragged forward. He tried to dig his heels into the ground, but the floor was slick as ice. He was swept toward Kronos as if on a tide, with Poseidon and Zeus dragged behind him.

He was pulled up short at the edge of the throne, face to face with the dark hood. Even up close, it was utterly black within. The hood tilted, as though Kronos were observing him. "You seek to be a leader of men," intoned Kronos.

"I seek nothing. I merely follow my destiny," Hades replied. Getting the words out was a struggle, as though the air in front of his face were thick, trying to drown him. His voice sounded thin and reedy, a boy's voice in the presence of a mighty god.

Kronos chuckled blackly, sending shivers over Hades' skin. "Ah, yes. *Destiny*. The destiny our dear mother imparted unto you. The destiny that you would one day be mightier than I. But if you were to be raised to defeat me, how is it that she made you weak?"

He let go of the spell that had dragged Hades, and in that moment Hades found that all his strength had gone as well. He collapsed at the foot of the throne. Kronos laughed again. "She feared me because she could not control me. And so she sought to create new life, life that she could order about or work like one of her puppets. She thought that together you could defeat me.

Instead, your fate will be as dire as the fate that befell your beloved brother. Worse, perhaps."

Hades had smashed his lip against his teeth on the steps of the dais. He lifted his head now and spoke through a bloodied mouth. "We will defeat you," he said. "We're stronger together, stronger even than you."

His bravado did nothing but amuse Kronos. "Are you, now? You think you can take me?"

"Of course we can." Zeus managed to sound arrogant and cocksure even in the presence of an almighty god, Hades marveled. His voice didn't even tremble. "Look at you. You don't even have the courage to face us."

Tom gasped from his place right behind and to the side of Hades. But Kronos laughed again. "Wish to see my face, do you?" he said. "Wish to see me as I really am?"

He stood suddenly. A chill wind swept through the throne room, and the torches around the walls guttered and went out.

"Allow me to grant your wish," said Kronos' voice in the darkness.

The light flared again, making Hades wince. This time, though, the fire around the hall was not the flickering red-orange of normal flame, but a cold, high blue-white. The hooded figure raised his hands to his face, and the hood fell away.

The face beyond was nearly unrecognizable, warped by the use and misuse of magic. His skin was pale as a corpse, sagging against his sunken face and clinging to his skull. It looked like it might fall off but for the thick beard that curled over his jaw, lined with silver and glowing in the strange firelight. His nose was withered, wide nostrils evoking the image of a skull, and the sockets of his eyes were deep pits, as though the skin there sank into nothing. From deep within burned two bright lights, his crimson pupils. Hades's mouth went dry. His arms trembled, and for a moment he thought he'd be robbed of the power to even lift himself halfway off the floor.

Kronos stood. He was tall, taller than Hades, taller than even Atlas had been. Taller than his high-backed throne. He raised his arms and gave a guttural cry that froze the brothers' hearts. He was taller than anyone Hades had ever seen before, taller than any man had ever grown —

No. That wasn't right. He was *growing* right now. The wind snaked through the room again, brushing across Hades' ankles and shoulders, and he watched with awe as his brother, the tyrant, the god, expanded his body. His shoulders grew wider, his legs taller. The robe extended and glittered with dots of cold light like stars. His hands brushed against the walls of the throne room, sending torches tumbling to the floor. His head scraped the ceiling and he stooped, circling his arms down like the bars of a great prison around the brothers, kneeling to fit his entire body within the vast space.

Hades now truly *felt* like an ant. An insignificant creature, unable to comprehend the power and abilities of the being before him. Chill dread settled in his stomach. Behind him, Typhon and Tom had thrown themselves on the ground in awe.

"What is it I should fear, brother?" Kronos spoke softly, but his voice shook the ground and reverberated in Hades' ears. Hades clapped his hands over his head. His whole body convulsed as Kronos laughed. "Should I truly be so scared of you? You, a thing I could crush under the weight of my thumb?"

He drummed his fingers on the floor as if to demonstrate. His thumb was indeed as large as the brothers themselves. At the slam of his fingers on the stone the entire room trembled. Statues toppled, losing their arms or legs or heads as they smashed on the throne room floor.

The thumb looked…weak, though. Stripped of muscle, tendons and knuckles pushing against skin. Hades forced himself to look up. The horrific face of Kronos grinned down at him like a god of death, revealing sharp teeth like swords, but the flesh was, if anything, paler now, stretched even thinner. This little display had cost him. As much as he tried to prove otherwise, there were limits to his power.

For a moment the two brothers locked eyes: maroon to crimson. Kronos regarded him a moment, exhaling an icy breath that nearly knocked him over and sent cold needles of fear into his heart. Hades rallied what strength he had and pushed himself to his feet. Their moment was coming, the moment of truth. The deciding moment for all of Olympus.

The silence seemed to stretch forever. In it, Hades' mind flashed with memories. He could smell the crisp scent of rain, feel the glow of the fireflies as he had the night his parents had received Atlas and Poseidon in their care. He felt the way his heart had stopped, stricken, the moment he'd first laid eyes on Persephone. His fingers tingled with the memory of her hand in his, and his mouth flushed and buzzed as he thought of the first time he'd kissed her. He felt again the swell of meaning and happiness as Diana lay Achilles in his arms for the first time. All the moments of a life, and a life well lived even if it hadn't been as long as he'd have liked.

He took another breath, and time spiraled away from him, toward the future. He saw his boy grow, win his first fight in the training yard, bring home his first self-shot wild boar, have his first kiss, stand under the sacred tree with his last love. Hold his own first child.

He had to do this. He pushed his shoulders back, and raised his chin. He was a warrior, and he would not go cowering to his death.

Then Kronos laughed, and the moment broke. His hand swept toward them.

Kronos' thumb did not bear down on Hades as he had suggested. Instead he scooped the brothers into his palm. His skin was dry; it stank of death and was cold as snow. Hades' hands flew out, gripping his brothers' in solidarity. Poseidon's mouth was open, he was probably screaming — but Hades could hear nothing over the rumbling laughter coming from Kronos' mouth.

The hand bore them up, and up, and behind the swordlike teeth Kronos' maw gaped black and desolate. He tipped his head back, opening his jaws wide, then wider still, wider than any man should be able to.

He dropped them within.

Hades squeezed his eyes shut. Any moment now those teeth would come down on him, grinding his legs or arms or head, severing him like a serving of meat at a party. He bounced off something slimy and thick — the tongue, maybe? — and then he was free falling, with nothing to hold on to but his brothers, feeling the air around him grow colder and colder. He imagined his breath would puff in the air, if he had the courage to open his eyes and look at it. But he didn't open his eyes, not until they had hit the ground, or what passed for it: a soft, spongy surface that absorbed their fall as though they'd merely jumped from a high rock, and not fallen from towering heights.

They were alive. They were already shivering, and they'd been eaten, but they were still alive. Hades opened his eyes.

The world around him was cold and dark, black as the interior of Kronos' palace and without lamps to light it. Hades grit his teeth and summoned a ball of fire to illuminate the space.

He saw nothing but black. Next to him Poseidon sat up, rubbing his head. He looked up. Hades raised the lamp but the walls of their prison stretched past his light, up and up toward oblivion.

"So." Zeus lay on his back. His eyes were wide with shock, but his voice was as normal as though he were commenting on the weather. "Here we are."

CHAPTER SEVEN: THE POWER OF UNITY

"We have no time to lose. He wants our power, and he'll start draining it at once," Hades said.

Poseidon grinned. "So let's give it to him."

"This is what, the stomach?" Zeus prodded at the spongy floor. His lip curled. "I'm not sure I'd have signed up for this if I'd known it was going to be so disgusting."

"You don't have to tell this part in the tales afterward," Poseidon reminded him. "Come on, hero. The sooner we get out of here, the sooner we're breathing real air again."

Zeus put a hand to his nose. "Don't remind me," he choked.

They hadn't known precisely what might lie within Kronos' mighty being, but icy cold was something Hades could work with. He was tired, he was weakened from lack of food and drink, but resolve was a better energizer than rest or sustenance. He would succeed, for he would not see this world pass down to his child.

He reached up to his shoulder, where Echidna's crossbow bolt still sat. He snapped off the shaft and yanked it free. The pain of the shaft passing through muscle made him scream through gritted teeth, but a moment later the wound cooled. Poseidon's hands were on his shoulder and covered in water. He worked quickly to clean out the wound and heal it. Hades nodded in relief. With his other hand he grabbed Tom Ambrose's spell, the one that sapped his strength, and pulled. The spell writhed and hissed. Zeus sent a shock of electricity through it and it dissipated in a spray of foul magic.

Hades felt a sudden opening, like the unlocking of a door he hadn't realized was closed. The spell had cut off his connection to Olympus — not weakening his power, but separating him from it. With a roar of joy he summoned the power of the planet. *Let's not be parted again.*

The last time he'd caused an eruption, it had been from loss and rage and pain. He'd watched his beloved take the blow that was meant for the tyrant, giving up her life for his cause. He brought forth this eruption for her, too, but not out of a sense of anger. It was a sense of justice, of this battle turning a full circle, of his weakness becoming his strength. *For you,* he thought, allowing himself one last selfish thought of Persephone before he turned all his concentration on the task at hand.

This ground was odd ground for a volcanic eruption, but it was still connected to the planet, and so Hades could still use it. The black ice walls around them bubbled and began to stream, making rivulets of water that soon turned to torrents. Poseidon joined him, shoulder to shoulder, guiding the water to flow around them.

The walls began to rumble. Hades grinned at his brothers. It seemed Kronos was having a spot of indigestion. He truly should have done more to subdue them before allowing them access to his body. His hubris would be his downfall. Poseidon pushed at the air with his hands and the water followed his orders, pressing against the walls of their prison — Kronos' stomach. At the same time, they began to rise on a spit of dirt.

Hades' forehead was burning. The ground under their feet rumbled and he slipped, and was only saved when Zeus grabbed his elbow. Zeus hissed at his brother's touch; the air around them was starting to steam, the water bubbling. Hades was running too hot. But he had to continue. They had to rise higher, and higher still. They couldn't be sure they wouldn't be caught up in the explosion, not until they saw the light of day.

The world tilted and the brothers scrambled to orient themselves. Kronos must be doing something on the outside — shrinking? Or would he be clutching his stomach?

"Stop," came Zeus's voice close to his ear. "Take a break."

But they couldn't take a break. An icy blast reinforced the walls of their prison. Kronos was taking their power and using it to reinforce their captivity. They had to break out now, before Kronos understood the true extent of their abilities, or they would never succeed. He shook his head, even though his vision swam with spots and strange whorls, and his hands began to glow.

"Now?" Poseidon said through gritted teeth.

"Not yet." Hades looked up. They weren't close enough to the gullet — all he saw was black, spiraling upward and outward, into infinity. He scraped the edges of his power and poured them into their rising tongue of land. He could feel himself faltering but he dug deeper yet, summoning what power was left in his body.

His ears were ringing, and the world was going fuzzy before his eyes. "He's going too far," he heard Zeus shout, but the voice was so far away. Zeus must be talking about someone else, something else. Everything was starting to feel like a dream. He just had to keep going, keep going…

"Then we can't wait any longer. Do it!" Poseidon shouted.

The world flashed blindingly bright. Hades' concentration broke. Poseidon slipped his arm around his brother as he started to topple from their tiny, high shelf of land.

Lightning branched out over the ice and cracked on the water with a *boom* that rang in Hades' ears. The world jolted again. "More!" shouted Poseidon.

Zeus' face twisted in furious concentration. He raised his arms, and white power shimmered along the length of his body. Lightning solidified into a crackling spear of white twice the length of his body. He hurled it down, into the middle of the melted sea. It blasted outward. Electricity crawled up the sides of the ice prison around them.

The space around them convulsed one final time, and the waters rose like a flood. Poseidon drew his arms up now, and water encased them in a sphere. Not a moment too soon, either, for they were rocketing through the air, up and up, flattened against the bottom of Poseidon's shield as they moved.

And then there was a light in the black, and the jumbled world of the throne room hurtled toward them with its fiery reflections over the floor and its marble statues, tossed this way and that in disarray. Tom and Typhon cowered in one corner, eyes wide as they watched the orb of water sail through the air.

The orb hit the floor. The impact was absorbed by the water, and Poseidon released his hold as they spun toward the door. Hades burned and sweated, delirious. He could think only of the cold water splashing around him as it lapped against the edges of the throne room like a sea. He barely noticed the second swell of water as Kronos continued to vomit, and he completely missed the great wavelike crash as the tyrant collapsed, prone and shaking, at the top of the dais. Hades barely heard the doors of the throne room bang open, hardly registering the splash of feet next to his head as boots thundered past.

A face hovered over him — *Persephone,* he thought wildly, but that was wrong, Persephone had pale hair and no wrinkles, she was young and vivacious — *Mother,* he realized as Raven drew him up by the shoulders.

"Did we do it?" he mumbled. "Did we win?"

Tears streamed down her face. She drew him into her chest, smiling. "My son, you did it."

CHAPTER EIGHT: JUST THE BEGINNING

The *power*. Zeus couldn't stop looking at his hands. They still glowed, even though he was safe to the touch. The sheer power he'd held, for one glorious moment. More potent than anything he'd ever wielded before. An incredulous laugh escaped him, something borne of relief and disbelief. The tyrant was done for. They'd destroyed him. Their destinies had been fulfilled.

While the brothers had prepared their trap Ethan had mustered what was left of the Cross of the Iron Phoenix, imploring them to return to the palace for one final assault. Anyone who'd realized they had one chance, and one only to destroy their tyrant, had joined forces. The Centaurs and the Minotaurs, led by Livia and Timotheus respectively, had broken down the doors, and the Outlaws had lent their expertise in the ways of spycraft and espionage to their army, allowing a large number of resistance members to infiltrate Novaris in advance of the day. Merlin and Harry Ambrose had joined them at the last minute, destroying parts of the keep walls while Kronos was distracted to allow the army to get through. Kronos would want to show off his new power, Merlin had advised them before the fight. In his cruelty, he would let the rebellion think they were winning, before rising greater and more terrible than ever before. He'd never made a backup plan. The idea of Kronos defeated was as unthinkable to him as the idea of swimming in the sky.

The god's pain had been palpable. The ground all around the keep had rumbled, the mortar had cracked at the sound of his screams. A great wind had torn most of the leaves from their trees. Kronos' guard had dropped their weapons at the sound, choosing to run or surrender once they realized their lord no longer held the power he'd once claimed. This, too, Merlin had foretold: "Most of them are working for the tyrant because they've no other means," he'd explained. "They don't want to die for this cause, and they don't particularly want to kill for it. Let us remember that if we are so lucky as to take prisoners."

Now Zeus stood in the throne room of a tyrant, covered in slime and strange water and gods knew what else, dizzy with victory. He looked around.

There was Poseidon, with his clothes plastered to his body and his hair slicked back from his head. He looked like he'd gone swimming, and his eyes were bright with exhilaration. As he spotted Zeus he waded through calf-deep water and embraced his brother. "We did it," he said, and took a deep breath. He hitched for a moment, hesitating. "We did it," he said, more quietly this time.

Zeus felt the emotion sweep over him in a wave, too. He understood his brother perfectly, and he squeezed Poseidon tight. Every breath they'd taken in their lives had been in service to this moment. Perhaps they hadn't known that, but it didn't make it less true. And now —

"Come on, you two!" It was Harper O'Donovan, the obnoxious head of the Outlaws and inexplicable best friend to Hades. "There's still so much work to be done."

Zeus and Poseidon broke apart. Zeus wished for the first time that Leda were here, to see him in the height of his victory and flush with power. He'd urged her to stay far from the fighting, of course, to keep Hercules and herself safe. They'd been so uncertain that this plan would work, after all. Now that it had, though, he sort of regretted his decision to send her away.

He looked for Hades. His brother sat on the floor, propped up by Raven and attended by Harry Ambrose. Hades put a still-glowing hand up to his head. He looked woozy. Zeus and Poseidon exchanged worried looks. Hades had pushed himself to the brink within Kronos. But when they splashed over to him, Harry stood. "He'll be alright," he said. "He needs rest. As I'm sure you do." His gaze moved beyond them and his mouth tightened. Zeus half turned and spotted Tom Ambrose and Typhon, both in the grip of Minotaurs. Tom's dark hair flopped over his head and glowing ropes bound his hands. He looked defeated. Typhon, on the other hand, roared and butted and kicked and spat, until the Minotaur that held his left arm grew tired of the fight and knocked him out cold. His body was heaved over a shoulder and trooped away, to some prison where he could await justice for his crimes.

"What will happen to him?" Zeus asked, nodding to Tom. The wizard was powerful — perhaps the second most powerful wizard on Olympus. *If you don't count us,* he thought smugly. There was no way Tom could be allowed to go free.

"He will have to be judged, same as all Kronos' men," said Harry. He sounded sad. "I don't expect he'll be let off lightly."

"On the bright side, he'll probably try to ingratiate himself with whoever's got power. He'll follow our lead now," Poseidon offered.

"Somehow I don't think that's enough," Harry murmured.

"Agreed," said Zeus as Harry went over to discuss securing

a perimeter with his father. "The little bastard should get a taste of what we got. Maybe we can construct a giant cold stomach for him to rot in for a little while."

"We might have a use for him," Poseidon cautioned him. "Let's not throw away resources."

Zeus snorted. The day he used Tom Ambrose as a resource would be a dark day indeed.

At the top of the dais, men and Centaurs and Minotaurs were inspecting Kronos' body. The tyrant lay face-down in the very fluid he'd expelled from his body. His robes were soaked. He was much smaller now — perhaps eight or nine feet in length, enough for two Minotaurs to carry him. And he looked like a stick, with his skull all but poking through his skin. "What a way to go," Zeus said, lip curling in a combination of disgust and pity. "Drowned in his own bodily fluids."

They drew closer. As they came near the body the nearest Outlaw stood up, saluting smartly. "He's still breathing," he said.

A cold fist formed in Zeus' gut. "You're joking." But even as the Outlaw shook his head, Zeus knew the truth. He could see the minuscule rise and fall of the robe against Kronos' prone body. Well then. "Stand aside," he said in the most powerful voice he could muster. He called the power to him, and in his hand the lightning bolt took shape: a deadly double-edged sword.

"We should get Hades." Poseidon sounded nervous.

"Why? The mission was to kill Kronos, and we're going to kill Kronos. We don't need Hades' approval for that." The sword flashed up, and before anyone else had time to object, Zeus swung it down at the intersection of Kronos' head and his body.

There was a crack, and the smell of hot stone filled the air. A blast of power knocked Zeus off his feet and sent the lightning sword flying. Poseidon flung an orb of water after it and caught it mid air, letting the lightning web over the water.

Zeus pushed a flop of soaking hair out of his face. His backside ached, but he wasn't about to rub it in front of all these people. And before him Kronos still lay on the dais, breathing, head and neck still very much attached.

He heard the splash of feet. "You won't be able to kill him, I'm afraid," came Merlin's voice.

Zeus looked up at the old man, uncomprehending. "What?"

"Kronos is too powerful to be killed." Merlin held his robes above the water as he made his way toward the dais.

"Too powerful to be killed?" When Zeus' entire purpose in life had been to kill him? "Then what, pray tell, was the point of all this?" He gestured wildly, voice rising in hysteria.

"Calm, now." Merlin himself was the picture of calm as he made his way up to the dais. "He can't be killed, but that doesn't mean he'll imminently rise again. Kronos has been defeated, and your hard work has reaped its rewards." He patted Zeus on the shoulder. "Don't worry, hero. All will be well."

###

Not everyone was convinced that all would be well. As the rebellion swept through Novaris and news of Kronos' defeat traveled like lightning, Merlin and Harry dismantled the traps and incantations around Tom Ambrose's manor home close to the palace and brought the heads of the rebellion in to take up residence. Hades refused to rest until he'd heard the full account of the battle from his father's eyes, and understood that Kronos was vanquished but not extinguished.

"He must be kept powerless." Hades sagged against the headboard of Tom's bed, a massive overstuffed thing with a purple coverlet embroidered in astrological symbols. His eyes were sunken, his face sallow. He took a sip of the broth that Raven brought for him.

"Of course. That's the point of this exercise." Merlin sounded irritated.

Hades tried to focus. The old wizard kept swimming in and out of his vision. He was utterly drained — physically, emotionally, almost spiritually. He was almost too tired to sleep. When he reached for the power of Olympus, the power of the mountain and of flame, it was nearly painful to the touch. Merlin gave him a sharp look as he tried to make his fingers glow. "Enough of that," he said sharply. "Rest. What sort of fool would you look if you died of overexertion *after* the battle?"

"You're stalling," Hades accused. Merlin's gaze dropped guiltily. "You don't know how to contain him, do you?"

"We're working on it," Merlin said, tilting his chin in a way that made him look lofty and noble. He didn't like not knowing things, especially magical things. "For now, we're confident that the damage done to his body is not easily repaired. He is in a coma, of sorts, and looks as though he will remain there for some time."

"Some time?" Hades echoed. That was hardly a scientific

measurement.

"Long enough for us to figure out what to really do with him." Harry Ambrose poked his head around the door. "Father, he thinks he's found something."

"Who?" said Hades as Merlin rose.

The wizard looked guilty again. "Focus on getting better," he said.

Hades tried to summon a fireball, but Merlin smacked his hand. "What did I tell you?"

"It's what you won't tell me that's weighing on my mind," Hades grumbled.

"You will have to tell him eventually." Harry Ambrose looked around the room, wrinkling his nose. Tom Ambrose was the sort of man who'd been obsessed with status, and he'd decorated his manor with anything that might proclaim he had it. His bed was a high four-poster, covered in the softest silk sheets Hades had ever laid on. There were three or four pillows just for decoration, velvet with little golden tassels. Paintings covered every inch of wall. Hades recognized the wardrobe as the work of one of the most renowned Sherwood woodworkers, and the desk next to it was no less fine, ornately carved with scenes of foxes and deer and unicorns. It was a far cry from the simplicity in which he'd been raised.

"Only one man lies at the intersection of great magical power and an intimate knowledge of Kronos' true abilities," Merlin said grudgingly.

Hades tried to follow his words, but the pounding in his temples was threatening to block out everything else. "Which means what?" he said.

Harry sighed at his father. "It means my brother might have the key to keeping Kronos captured. He's been helping us in exchange for amnesty."

What? Hades tried to sit forward; he failed and slumped against the headboard again. "You can't do that. He'll betray us in an instant."

"To whom?" Merlin waved a liver-spotted hand. "His old master lies prone, and a hostile army has taken over his palace. He has no choice but to work with us."

"Tom is a coward," Harry said quietly. "It meant he never dared stray from his loyalty to Kronos, but it also means he'll do whatever it takes to stay on our good side now. We've shown that Kronos can be beaten, and that makes *you* the most powerful person on Olympus. Tom won't double cross you; he'll try to suck up to you." Harry considered, then pushed his glasses up his nose and shuddered. "Which is almost worse."

"Who did you consult about this?" Fury was giving him more energy, and he struggled to slide his feet out of bed. If the wizards wouldn't cooperate with him, he'd deal with this problem himself. "Who gave you permission to pardon one of Olympus' greatest traitors? The man who killed my brother, and tried to kill us?"

"I did," said Ethan, pushing past Harry and coming into the room. He stopped, shook his head at Hades, and came around to the side of the bed. He was standing straighter, Hades thought as his father carefully slid his legs back under the covers and pushed him against the headboard. Ethan handed him the cup of broth and raised his eyebrows expectantly. *Drink.* Hades had swallowed half the cup before he even realized what he was doing.

Ethan waited until he'd drunk all the broth, then refilled his cup from a teapot that sat on the side table. "You need rest, son."

Hades couldn't rest. He tried to turn his fury on his father instead, but the feeling was dulled by fatigue. Maybe he could sleep for two or three days first — *then* he could wake up angry and ready to deal with this mess. "How could you do this? It hasn't even been a day. And he —" He'd been given chance after chance to help them, to do the right thing. He'd chosen wrong every time. Hades changed tack. "Did you talk to Zeus and Poseidon about this? Are they on board?"

"They are not the leaders of the Cross of the Iron Phoenix. We are." Ethan ran his hand along his beard and sighed, looking at a point somewhere over Hades' head. He was thinking deeply. "We have spoken to you often of sacrifice, my son. You sacrificed having a happy and carefree life in exchange for serving this cause. You sacrificed raising your own son to assure yourself of this victory. You even sacrificed your love in the battle." He paused here, swallowing, and Hades saw tears swimming in his eyes. For the first time he wondered if Ethan felt...guilty for all he'd put his sons through. Yet why should he? It was their destiny, and he'd been given a role to play. A role he'd played to perfection.

"There is another kind of sacrifice, a hard kind, but the kind that comes after victory. It is the sacrifice of justice."

"Justice?" Hades echoed. "Everything we've fought for?" His hands clenched around the coverlet, nails digging into the thick brocade.

"Yes. Not everyone faces justice, or at least the kind of justice we'd like them to face. Some brutes, like Typhon, used their power to torture the innocent. Without a master to protect him, he will surely pay for his crimes. But some, like Tom, have knowledge that cannot be replaced. Knowledge that is, regrettably, invaluable. And knowledge that we need to access. So we make deals with people like Tom, and let them keep their fine houses and the lives they had, more or less, before the rebellion. We keep them on a tight leash, of course — and Tom will always know that it is our mercy that spared him. He will strive to ingratiate himself with us always, out of the same fear he had for Kronos — that once he has run out our mercy, he will be punished."

"I…" Hades let out a sigh. "I don't see how that makes us better than Kronos."

"We'll never kill him, for a start." Ethan chuckled. Then his expression sobered. "The revolution was hard work. But what comes next might be even harder. Many people did distasteful things under Kronos' watch, and most did not want to. There will have to be some measure of forgiveness, if Olympus is to move into a time of peace and prosperity." He paused. "You're not drinking your broth."

Hades obediently tipped the cup to his lips again. He was half afraid that Ethan would fill the cup a third time, but when he was finished his father merely took it from him and set it on the side table next to the pot. "Sleep now," he said. "The coming days will be difficult."

Hades didn't think he could sleep. But he let his father push him gently down into the bed, and before he'd had a moment to contemplate all Ethan had said, the darkness overtook him.

###

He woke some time in the middle of the night with a clear head and enough energy to get out of bed. He rummaged in Tom's wardrobe, discarding silk robes decorated with demons and devils, fancy shirts with collars of frippery, velvet coats and cravats. At last he found something that looked simple — a cotton shirt and comfortable trousers, something that looked as though Tom had worn it for one of his many ruses in the Novaris market. Then he padded out into the house to take a look around.

All was quiet. The house was dark, and Hades summoned a light to hover at his shoulder. His power tugged at him a little, resisting — it was still exhausted, he surmised. Well, as long as he didn't have to conduct any complicated spells or displays of power, he ought to be able to power a simple light while he looked around.

The walls here were crowded with paintings, too. Portraits, cityscapes, fanciful imaginings of demons and magical creatures. At the front of the main hall was a portrait of the man himself, at least as tall as Hades, set opposite the front door. Hades stopped to regard it, looking at the regal and arrogant expression on Tom's face. His hands flashed hot, and he imagined hurling his light at the painting, letting it catch on the canvas, watching the flames lick at Tom's cold, traitorous eyes. But another look at those eyes stayed his hand.

The artist, whoever he was, had been a master of his craft. Folded within that arrogant expression Hades thought he could see a hint of fear in the set of Tom's shoulders, in the curl of his fingers. Tom had lived his entire life in fear, and that was a hard way to live. Even now, if they offered him amnesty in exchange for binding Kronos, he would continue to live in fear, unable to comprehend that the Cross would keep its word.

Tom was punishing himself.

Something about it still irked him as wrong. But he knew it was the best justice he was likely to get where Tom Ambrose was concerned. He lowered the light, and continued down the hall.

The manor was a maze of rooms and corridors, and Hades walked them at random. He passed rooms that were locked and rooms that stood wide open, rooms with summoning circles on the floor. At least two libraries — he passed five rooms that were filled with books, but couldn't tell if he was walking by the same room from a different angle. After fifteen minutes or so of walking, Hades realized he was moving with purpose, heading deeper and deeper toward the heart of the house.

He passed formal dining rooms, tea rooms, book binding rooms, studies. He passed more locked doors that he knew without trying not to open. Finally the doors stopped appearing, and the corridor was one long stretch of hall with one door at the end.

He went up to the door. It opened at his touch. He knew, somehow, what he would find within.

The room was small and cold. A long counter ran across one end, strewn with papers and ink. Shelves above held powders and spices and magical items waiting to be used. In the middle of the room was a stone table, and on the table lay Kronos.

He was the smallest Hades had ever seen him: shorter than Hades himself, with thin shoulders and spindly legs. He looked less like a warrior and more like a corpse, yet Hades could see the gentle rise and fall of his chest. Thick bands of glowing blue magic ran over his chest, his waist, his pelvis and his calves. His eyes were closed. His robe had been removed and he wore a simple linen shift to give him what little dignity he deserved.

Hades didn't know how long he stood for. He stared at this god, this man, this brother. Odd that he felt some kinship with the tyrant even now. Perhaps it was a feeling of obligation; he'd spent so long caring for three brothers that a fourth was almost natural.

Yet Kronos had been anything but natural. A kinslayer, a power-hungry tyrant, who drew evil to him and reflected it back tenfold. Hades was glad, suddenly, that Kronos couldn't die. Now he wouldn't share in the kinslayer title.

But if he wasn't here to try and kill Kronos, then why was he here?

A gentle glow began to fill the room. It reminded Hades of starlight on leaves, of moonlight in the sacred groves. It reminded him of waking up to more brothers. He turned as Gaia entered the room.

Her dark skin contrasted with the glow of the leafy dress she wore. White flowers bloomed on it, giving off their own glow. Her green eyes were luminous. A shining tear fell from her eye as she turned to Hades. "I hope you understand that I grieve for my son," she said.

Hades nodded.

"I lost him long ago, in truth. But even after I put this plan in motion, twenty-eight long years ago, I held out hope that he might become gentler. See the error of his ways. Understand that love was a more powerful motivator than fear."

For a while they were silent. Gaia had brought the sounds of the forest with her, and Hades listened to the rustle of the wind. If he closed his eyes, he could almost fool himself that it was the echo of Persephone's voice.

"I don't know what to do now," he confessed.

"Your work is far from over," Gaia warned.

"Oh, I know that." He laughed. "I think it's gotten more complicated, actually." His stomach growled, and he winced. "And maybe it's hard to think on an empty stomach." Broth wasn't exactly filling.

Gaia laughed, a bright tinkling sound that made little pink flowers bloom all down the front of her dress. "Come, my boy. We will sit together until the sun comes up, and we will meet with your brothers. I have much news, and much guidance to give you."

###

They sat in the kitchen, eating day-old bread. At first they sat in silence. Hades appreciated that Gaia didn't ask him if he was all right. He sat and contemplated his bread, listening to the wind and turning over a singular question in his mind.

At long last he asked: "What happened to her?"

Gaia set her bread down. "After she died?" she said gently.

"Yes." He had to know. Had Persephone's vibrant soul merely…vanished?

Gaia pressed her hands together. "My son, Olympus has no afterlife, no Underworld. That intangible part of us that we call the soul stays, perhaps, for a while. Or leaves."

"And we never know what our own loved ones have chosen to do," Hades said hoarsely.

"Such is the nature of death," Gaia told him. "Those who cling to this world may stay for a time, but in the end all are gone."

And so those who died were cursed to sit in a world that had not been made for them, living out the echo of their lives while those who'd loved them tried to hear their voices on the wind. Hades found himself tapping on the table in agitation. Something about this arrangement did not feel right. Something could be improved.

There was a noise at the threshold, and Raven came in. She cast them both a befuddled look. But all she said was, "Are you sure you should be up?"

"I'm fine, Mom —" he stopped and tried not to look at Gaia. "I'm fine. And I'm old enough to take care of myself, by the way."

She leaned over to plant a kiss on his brow. "Old enough and capable enough are two different things." Then she got to work, humming, on making fresh loaves.

Gaia was watching Hades, a question in her eyes. He didn't resume their prior topic of conversation. It felt too personal, somehow. Besides, he was starting to get an idea. A way to properly care for the souls of the dead. Did he not have some kind of obligation to it, after all, now that he'd led a rebellion that had cost many lives?

Zeus arrived next. He looked rumpled in his shirt, and hadn't put on any trousers, which set the two kitchen girls who were still working here into fits of giggles. He grinned at them and swaggered over to the table. "Good to see you up," he told Hades.

"Good to be up." Hades rolled his shoulders. "Ready to get to work?"

"No." Zeus laughed and took a roll. "Saving the world made me hungry. We can talk about breakfast."

And so they did. They crowded around the kitchen table as they would have done at home. Raven found some cold smoked meat and cheese, and before the sun was fully over the horizon Ethan and Poseidon had joined them. They greeted Gaia with hugs — an awkward one, in Poseidon's case — and crowded in. Soon Zeus and Poseidon had them laughing with good-natured jokes about who would defeat who in the training ring now, and mirth bounced off the walls, warming Hades better than any fire could. Things would be all right, he thought.

When breakfast had finished and they'd washed their plates, Ethan cleared his throat. "It looks like our commander is back on his feet," he said. Zeus and Poseidon whooped, and Hades felt his cheeks turn hot. He grinned. "So we're ready to talk strategy. I've sent for Merlin to meet us in the blue study."

"Will there be tea?" Zeus snagged one final roll.

Ethan stared at him. "You just ate."

"So?" he said through a full mouth.

Ethan shook his head and ushered the children — and Gaia

— out.

The blue study was so named for its color. Blue couches embroidered with fantastic birds Hades had never seen before sat on a floor of rich brown wood, covered in blue rugs. The wallpaper was striped blue and white, but he could hardly see it for the paintings lining the walls, all featuring blue prominently. Merlin and Harry already sat on a couch, hands folded in their laps. Slouched across from them was Tom.

Hades stopped, drew a deep breath. Tom caught his eye and flicked his dark hair out of his face. "Enjoying the master suite?" he said, and his voice held a tinge of anger. "I designed it myself, for the ultimate comfort. Which is quite your due, of course."

"I will say that I was *never* consulted on whether I wanted the master suite," said Zeus, taking the chair next to Tom. He shot him a dark look, and Tom flinched away.

"Enough. Hades needed, and still needs, time to recover. But he's here now, and I understand you and your family have a solution to our tyrant problem." Ethan spoke as gently and professionally as he would to any member of the Cross. How did he do it?

Hades tried to clear his thoughts. Tom was their ally now. No way around that.

"There is a spell that has never been done before," Tom said.

"Because it can't be done," muttered Harry.

"Because it has always lacked power. Power that we three wizards have, if we work together." His lip curled up slightly, but he cleared his throat. "The Chronostasis Eternus."

He lifted his chin as though expecting gasps of 'It can't be done!' from the rest of them.

Zeus picked at his teeth. "Chronowhatsis whatsis?"

"Chronostasis Eternus," Merlin said. He steepled his fingers and gave Zeus a look of such reprimand that the young one straightened and folded his hands in his lap, looking abashed. "Chrono, for time. Stasis, stop. Eternus: forever. Time stops forever for your brother. He lies there, so that even when he wakes from his coma he is trapped for the rest of eternity."

Hades looked at Zeus and Poseidon. Zeus' eyes were alight. Poseidon's, troubled. "I think I'd rather die, if it were up to me," he said.

"Death is, unfortunately, not an option," Merlin said. "Kronos is a god, and gods cannot die."

"But you're saying this can be done?" Zeus said.

"I'm not saying that," Harry put in quickly.

Merlin waved a hand at his second son. "Tom believes it can be done, and so do I. I'm willing to stake my reputation as the world's greatest wizard on it. It is, however, a fiddly spell…"

"And easily broken," Tom put in. He swallowed. "If one of Kronos'…loyal subjects were to interrupt the field we erected around him, the spell would falter. They would, in short, bring time back to him by their passage."

"So not only do we have to perform a spell that has never been done before, but we have to put it in a place that no one will ever go?" Hades said.

"I vote for the Brown Swamp. It's horrible," Zeus said.

"Would the dragons of Etna guard it?" Poseidon asked. "Or we could put it at the bottom of the sea. Or in a volcano." He nodded to Hades.

"What he needs is a different space to accompany his different time," Gaia broke in. She sat calmly, hands resting on her lap. The flowers on her dress were a pale blue to match the room. Her gentle smile had not wavered since Hades had seen her that morning.

All eyes turned to her. "What do you mean by that?" Ethan asked.

Gaia looked at Hades. "I am the mother of creation," she said simply. "I will create. A prison that sits outside of time for Kronos, a place that no one can touch him. A place that mortals cannot venture."

All was silent in the wake of her proposal. Her green eyes bore into Hades, as though trying to tell him something.

Tom's mouth hung open. "You can do that?"

Harry rolled his eyes. "Tom doesn't believe *anyone's* got more magic than him."

"That's not true," Tom snapped. "But maybe if you understood the metaphysical properties of space creation, you'd realize that it's impossible for any mortal man to do what she's suggesting."

"Well, she's not a mortal man," Harry said.

"That is enough,"Merlin commanded, and his sons fell silent. Hades tried not to smile. In some respects all families were the same, even the ones with brothers on opposite sides of a rebellion. "We must attempt the spell in the place where he is to rest. So this other world shall be prepared, and then we will perform the spell. And *then* it shall be separated from the mortal realm, so that no one may venture to it again."

"He'll need a guard," Hades said absentmindedly. Then he blinked, thinking. The others were looking at him. "Just in case. If the spell fails, or our enemies *do* find some way to get to him…" Or if Tom Ambrose put in some sort of loophole that would allow Kronos to return to his full faculties. Hades wouldn't put it past him.

Tom glared at him. "She said no one could go into the prison and live. Who's going to guard him?"

Zeus sent him a little zap of lightning, and he yelped. "Mind your betters," Zeus said.

"Men will die," Hades said slowly, thinking. He looked at Gaia, the mother of creation, and his mother. "But not everyone in this room is a man. Would a god survive this?"

The gentle smile on Gaia's mouth deepened. "I believe they would."

"Then it has to be one of us." Hades looked around, swallowing, realizing suddenly what that meant. "It has to be me."

Zeus was too flighty. He'd get bored, go wandering, and defeat the whole point. Poseidon also lacked the patience, and might be lured away from his vigil if there were some sort of crisis. But Hades had learned to look before he leapt, to consider his options. He knew that guarding Kronos would always be the most important task in his life.

"That's ridiculous," Zeus said. "The whole point of finding somewhere no one can go is so that he'll never be disturbed. If he's never disturbed, he doesn't need to be guarded."

"We can't risk anything going wrong." Hades turned to Gaia. "Will I be able to return to Olympus?"

Gaia considered him for a few long moments. "You will," she said at last. "But you will not be able to bring anything with you from Olympus to this other world."

Something cold settled in his stomach. *My son.* If he took on this duty, he would never see Achilles again. His would be a lonely existence on the edge of nothing, with no one to keep him company —

Or would it? His mind began to churn with all Gaia had said that morning. "What if we made a place? A place where the souls of Olympus could rest? Where the good people who live good lives can go and just…be? As long as they wouldn't interfere with the imprisonment, of course," he hastened to add.

"They would also exist outside the confines of time. So it should be safe from them. But…I would like to understand your full vision, my boy," Gaia said. "Tell me what this realm would look like."

Hades was silent as he thought about it. When the silence dragged on too long, talk turned to other things — ensuring that the farmers got their crops in, buying enough goods to distribute to everyone to keep the cities of Olympus from falling prey to famine and replacing infrastructure to ensure that the land would stay stable. Ethan drew up a list of envoys that he wanted to send to every city, people who might convince the powerful there to accompany them in their new vision. His sons were at the top of the list, but Gaia shook her head. "I think they will have more than enough to occupy their time," she said.

Hades listened with half an ear, but his thoughts moved like lightning from place to place. A world of souls. A place for the dead. The chance to meet, perhaps, someone he had lost long before her time.

CHAPTER: NINE: THE UNDERWORLD

They met at the front of Tom Ambrose's house five days later: Hades, Poseidon, Zeus, Ethan, Merlin, Harry and Tom. The wizards had brought Kronos with them, the god lying flat on the stone slab, which floated next to him like a cloud. In one hand Harry clutched a sheaf of notes. He stood between Tom and the body; Tom, for his part, avoided looking at his old master.

"If you're sure it'll work," Ethan said, clapping him on the shoulder.

"Not at all," said Merlin cheerfully. Hades exchanged a glance with his brothers.

The green and golden glow that signaled the arrival of Gaia emanated from the top of the staircase. A moment later she was there, descending, smiling that beatific smile and surveying the people grouped before her. "You are ready," she said.

"Ready," said Hades.

"Ready," said Zeus and Poseidon in tandem.

"Ready." Merlin patted the stone slab.

"Ready," murmured Tom and Harry.

Ethan nodded.

"Then we shall go." Gaia lifted her arms, and Hades felt a tugging somewhere behind his chest. The ground moved beneath them in a blur; it was as though they were a few inches above it and far, far up at the same time. Cities flashed beneath their feet, then fields, then trees. Then cities again. Not five seconds later they hit the ground with a lurch that sent Hades stumbling. Poseidon reached out to steady their father and Merlin sprawled against his slab. Tom sat heavily in the dirt in surprise, then grimaced and rubbed his backside. Hades stifled a smirk and turned away.

They stood at the green and scrubby base of a mountain — the mountain Hades still saw every time he closed his eyes. It rose sharply into the azure sky, craggy and populated by goats. The River of Life sparkled as it wound lazily out of one side. The air smelled of olive trees and hibiscus flowers.

Mount Etna.

"This is a place of much magic," Gaia said. "It is the place where you were born, Hades, and it is the place where your power is greatest. Here we will do what you have proposed. Are you prepared?"

Hades' mouth was dry. Perhaps it was poetic, that where he'd lost his love was where he might find her again. "I'm—I'm missing something," he realized.

He met Gaia's verdant green eyes with his maroon ones. The great Mother laughed in understanding. "Naturally," she said, and swirled her hand.

It was strange to feel the spell from the other side, as though Gaia were reaching across the world to find her quarry. Hades focused on the feeling of the magic, the jolt of recognition when she found what he was looking for. She pulled back, and Hades watched him come at high speeds, zooming over the ground and deposited in front of them so abruptly that he chased his tail three times, then toppled.

Cerberus.

"Ugh!" Tom recoiled and reached for his wand.

Merlin swatted his hand. "Do you think you're the only villain reformed?"

"I know, I know," Tom groused, rubbing at the back of his hand. "But it takes some getting used to." Cerberus growled.

Hades knelt and spread his arms. "Here, friend," he said, and Cerberus loped obediently to him. The dog butted his future head against Hades' hand, while his present head stayed trained on Tom. "Don't worry about him," Hades laughed. The past head whined, and he scratched its silver ears. Then he looked past the dog to Gaia. "Now we are ready," he said.

Gaia closed her eyes. The ground beneath them trembled. Then a crack rent the air, startling the goats on the mountainside and sending up a cloud of dust that tickled the inside of Hades' nose and sent Cerberus scuttling behind his master. Gaia pushed gently at the air and the crack in the ground widened, deepened, and hollowed out into a circular tunnel, with a staircase that led straight down. "The gateway to the other world: the Underworld. It will reveal itself only to my sons, Ethan and Merlin," she declared.

She turned to the wizards first. "Are you certain that you wish to go within now? I will try to protect you, but cannot guarantee that you will survive."

Merlin patted the stone slab. "I am a man of my word. I will do this. And so what if I die? No one's meant to live forever, and I have had a good run." He smiled briefly. "Of course, I will gladly take whatever protection you give me."

Harry lifted hs chin. "I'm not going to change my mind."

"Can I?" said Tom, running a hand through his dark hair.

"No," said Harry and Merlin at once.

Tom sighed. "Well, we're already doing one impossible thing today. What's one more?"

Gaia turned to Ethan next. "I make the same statement to you," she said.

"And I make the same reply," Ethan said heavily. "I have a wife and two other boys I wish to live for, but I will see this through."

"You have always had unyielding faith in your son." Gaia smiled at him. "Your guidance and support have saved the world, and Hades will no doubt seek your advice for years to come. You should know the way to reach him, should the need arise."

She breathed deep, and it was as though the world breathed in with her. The wind ceased rustling and weaving over the plain, the water calmed, the birds stopped their singing. Without another word she turned and led them down.

As Hades crossed the threshold of this new realm — *his* new realm, he corrected silently — he felt a tingle, and the air around them glittered. They were passing through an invisible veil, something that would keep out wandering animals and travelers. The moment they were all on the stairs, the opening knit up behind them and the world was dark.

It took a moment for Hades' eyes to adjust, but they did, thanks to a faint glow coming from the stairs. It was enough to see his feet as he walked. Their steps pattered like drumbeats on the stone as the six of them went down, and down, and down yet more. The further they walked from the surface, the more Hades was gripped by a sense of calm. The air around them smelled of dirt and stone, but was far from cold. It was almost like a blanket, wrapping around him in a reassuring way. At first he thought this Underworld was silent, but then he heard the soft murmur of a waterfall somewhere far out of sight. The sound increased gently until at last they were at the bottom of the stone stairs, facing a great blank hall.

Gaia turned to them as they finished descending the stairs. "Hades asked for three vast halls," she said into the silence. "The first should be the prison of Kronos, into which nothing, soul or physical being, should go. His eternal prison will be within this hall, and it is here that Merlin and his sons will cast not only the Chronostasis Eternus, but spells of protection and warning as well, should anyone breach the hall and go seeking the tyrant."

She gently pushed at the air again, and Hades had the vast sense of moving backwards. Nothing else changed, but a moment later a grand door of black stone appeared on the far wall. "Wizards, go to your work," she commanded. "It would be unwise for you to tarry here longer than you must."

The old man bowed. Then he nudged his sons. They followed suit. Then they disappeared through the black door.

Gaia turned next to Hades. "You will be the lord of this realm, the keeper of this castle. It will be your home, and the home of countless other souls. It is up to you, my boy, to decide what it should look like."

Hades had a picture in his mind, a home as tranquil as the forest, as joyful as the community in which he'd grown up. He bit his lip and wrinkled his brow. His magic was not made for this sort of creation. But Gaia took his hand, and he felt something as cool as water flow through him. "Make a picture in your mind," she advised. "See this place as you want it to be."

Hades closed his eyes, and began to build his perfect home. He concentrated on the gentle trickle of water from the waterfalls, and added to it the soft percussion of the wind, rustling through the trees. He thought of the fireflies that buzzed around the trees of Sherwood and the gentle glow that first emanated at nightfall. He thought of the way the forest teemed with life: crickets and grasshoppers, deer and boar and rabbits and foxes, squirrels and mice, butterflies and bees. And the people who lived among them, grateful every day for the bounties the forest provided.

Next to him, Poseidon gasped. Sounds like whispers added to the leaves and the water. Hades opened his eyes.

Trees had sprung up in shades of gray, from bright and shining silver to dark, almost gunmetal in color. Their leaves rattled against each other, shining in a gentle and cold light reminiscent of moonlight. Their branches curled gently in spiraling patterns no real trees could boast, creating swooping and elegant shadows on the ground. The ground itself was paved with a gentle mist that felt like walking on the finest of carpets.

Hades looked up. There was no ceiling above them, but a darkness that stretched forever like the night sky. In that darkness there were no stars, but the tiny pinpricks of light that he saw danced about, spinning with each other or going their own way, growing larger as they drifted down towards the ground. As they got closer, they grew to nearly the size of his hand. As the nearest orb touched the mist it resolved into the lanky, translucent, silver body of a hare that dashed off, threading through the trees. A moment later another orb became a young fawn who cantered after it.

More orbs were falling now, drifting softly to the ground like snow. Among the animals, people began to resolve, looking at their hands and clothes in wonder, gazing at the trees.

Hades concentrated and a tall, glowing building rose in a series of spires around them. It sparkled like crystal, and beyond its clear walls they could see the trees of the forest. "Here is where the souls will come when they first arrive in the Underworld," he decided. "They can rest, understand their new existence, and perhaps make friends with whom they can explore the forest beyond."

"A hall where the dead will find peace," Gaia said. "Those who led good lives and sought nothing but prosperity for themselves and their neighbors. This hall is the Halls of Eternal Peace, and the people here will look to you for whatever they need."

Zeus, Poseidon and Ethan were wide-eyed as they looked around. "It feels like I could stay here forever." Ethan sounded a little mournful.

"Your time will come," Hades laughed. He turned to Gaia. "What about the other thing?"

She squeezed the hand that was encased in his. "You must dream it, and it will be."

Hades closed his eyes again and took a deep breath. He imagined a magnificent structure, a tower of obsidian in contrast to the crystal, that sparkled like stardust in the gentle light of the Underworld. The doors of the tower were decorated with a broken sword. In time the sanctum would fill, but for now he shaped two statues, the first two that visitors would see when they entered the tower itself.

He opened his eyes, and saw it shimmering above the tops of the trees in the distance. "Come," he said. He wanted his family to see it before they left.

Gaia transported them to the front of the tower, and Hades let go of her hand to address his family. "My world would not be complete without the memory of how it came to be, and all that we sacrificed for it," he said. His voice trembled a little. "This is the Sanctum of Fallen Heroes. Anyone may enter, and remember those people we loved who sacrificed themselves to give us a free world."

He cast a thought, and the doors behind him opened. Silver light emanated from within.

The inside of the sanctum was hollow, with a ramp running the length of the wall and slowly sloping up to the top. Alcoves dotted the walls at regular intervals, alcoves that waited for their commemorative statues. In the center of the sanctum stood Atlas, nearly seven feet tall, holding the world on his shoulder as his bronze statue had done in Labyrinth City. He looked as if it were easy, smiling broadly down at his brothers. It was so like him, down to the dimple on his chin, that Ethan let out a strangled sob and embraced the statue at the waist.

"I do not know where his soul has departed to," murmured Hades, putting a hand on his father's shoulder. "But wherever it is, I hope he finds his way back to us. And until he does, we will properly remember him."

They turned, and Hades gestured to the first alcove in the sanctum. There stood Diana, proud and regal, with one hand on her hip. She, too, looked lifelike enough that Poseidon ran a wondering finger down her cheek. "Do you think she'll come here?" he asked.

"If she does, you'll be the first to know," Hades assured him.

"What of Persephone?" Ethan asked. The next alcove was bare, as were all of them, all the way up to the top of the tower.

"All our heroes will be here in time," Hades replied. "It is simply…fatiguing. My talents are better put to use, for the moment, with making sure that the details are perfect in the halls of Eternal Peace." He didn't feel like telling his family the real reason he hadn't included Persephone — that he thought, deep at night and alone with his thoughts, that he could hear her voice, feel her presence. That he hoped beyond hope that she was still out there somewhere, waiting to come home to him.

Gaia tilted her head suddenly. "It is done," she said, and waved her hand. The ground spun beneath them, and a moment later they had moved again. They stood before a wall of black fog, a roiling and pulsing mass. The air here was colder and settled uneasily in Hades' gut. Magic, he realized, some sort of spell to turn back any souls who wandered this way. He looked back over the swirling mist. The trees were thinner here, and the Sanctum and his own palace were mere dots in the distance. A soul would have to wander far indeed, to get here.

He brushed at the fog with his hand, summoning a gentle wind. The fog momentarily cleared to show the black doors of Kronos' prison. They were shut tight.

Merlin, Tom and Harry emerged from the fog. Their faces were pale, even by the gray light of the Underworld, and Merlin's hands shook. He leaned heavily on Harry's arm. As they drew near he said, "The prison has been constructed, the Chronostasis Eternus has been cast. Kronos will sleep until he is interrupted."

"Which he must never be," Hades added.

He turned to his faithful companion. Cerberus' gray coat gleamed in the light, and all three heads looked up at Hades hopefully. Currently the dog came up to his waist, his tail thumping against Hades' side.

"You see the past, the present and the future," Hades said. "You know who has been loyal to Kronos and who will try to free him. You know every soul that comes into my realm. Will you take up the mantle of guardian, ensuring that the world is safe from him forever?"

Cerberus' red eyes glowed. All six pairs focused on Hades. The dog yipped once, tossing his head as if to say, *Yes.* He knew his master's will, and he ceded to it. Then he whined and bent until his head was on the ground, a gesture of submission. His tail tucked between his legs.

Hades crouched. He thought he might know what Cerberus meant. "You will never be chained again," he promised. "I trust you to know your business. You may wander free, and I will come here often to be with you. And you may come and seek me out, if you know that there is a threat."

Cerberus nodded again, then yelped and took off over the field, perhaps in pursuit of some ethereal rabbit.

Ethan cocked his head as he watched the dog run. "Fitting, I suppose," he said at last. "Once, he guarded his master. Now he guards his master in an entirely different way."

"Indeed." Hades smiled.

"Are you prepared to be the guardian of all souls?" Gaia asked him seriously.

Hades swallowed. He was unsure, on the one hand — on the other, he had never been destined to lead a quiet life, even after the defeat of Kronos. And who else would take care of those who had perished at his hand? "As prepared as I will ever be," he replied.

"I think there is one more thing you need," Gaia said.

She waved her hand, and they moved again, back to the heart of the forest. They were in a clearing Hades did not remember creating. In the middle of the clearing sat a manor. It sat between four trees — indeed the trees were the corners of the manor itself, stretching toward the sky with smooth black bark and stark white leaves. Two little towers, carved like trees, framed a large door. The polished surface reflected the glow of the mist upon which they walked, and when Hades opened the door the walls glowed with the same inner light. He stared at the wide foyer in some shock. His entire house at Sherwood could fit in here. And now he was supposed to live here alone?

Not alone, he reminded himself. *Hopefully.*

He led his family from room to room. Large windows let in the light, and the mist on the floor provided more. Carvings and reliefs covered every inch of wall, stories of heroes and legends both long past and yet to come. A library held a vast assortment of scrolls and books, some real and some incorporeal, books that held the told and untold secrets of the universe.

Gaia led Hades through the library and opened a door at the back. It led out to a little pond of crystal clear water lined with black stones. Three white fish swam in it, eying the newcomers curiously. A black bench sat at the edge of the pond. It was perfect for a moment of contemplation.

"You will need knowledge in your new duties," Gaia said. "You will need to take action, and sometimes you will need to meet with your subjects. Sometimes, however, you will need to be alone, to contemplate death and life after death. Remember to take your solitude seriously — as seriously as your other work," she said. She came closer and put a hand to his cheek. "You must be tranquil, or else the Underworld cannot be tranquil."

He nodded. "I understand."

That tranquility filled him as he looked around. Here he had a place that was his and his alone, a place where he would never have to hide himself or his destiny. Perhaps he could truly be *Hades* here. Perhaps he could find out who Hades *was,* now that his grand destiny had been fulfilled.

No. He could not do that until he had one more person by his side.

There was no time to dwell on that. His birth mother clapped her hands and turned to the group.

"We have been here long enough. Wise, I think, to depart before our mortal friends' souls anchor here forever." Gaia lifted her arms, and the world spun about them. They rose above the manor, past the falling orbs of souls, rose until the forest looked like a carpet beneath them and the Sanctum of Fallen Heroes and

the Hall of Eternal Peace were tiny twinkling stars. Hades smelled bitter sulfur, then ash and dust, then the myriad complex stinks of life. In a rush of heat they were back on solid ground.

CHAPTER TEN: ATLANTIS

The sudden warmth of the world caught Poseidon off guard, but he welcomed it a moment later. Calm the Underworld had been, but it hadn't quite been for him. Let Hades walk in a world of black and silver and gray. Poseidon would take the vibrant blues and greens. Yet he envied his brother, even though he was happy for him. Hades had found his place.

"I have favored my eldest son with a realm of his own," Gaia proclaimed. "Yet my eldest is not the only one who has sacrificed. My second eldest has also given his life to the cause, has loved and lost. Your brother, your cherished Diana — both have been taken from you."

Poseidon thought suddenly of the perfect likenesses of Atlas and Diana, silent and still in the Sanctum of Fallen Heros, and swallowed the lump in his throat.

"No gift could ever fill the emptiness of their loss. Yet you remain selfless and committed to others. Now it is time to think of the things you need. What may I do for you? What needs may be addressed?"

Poseidon blinked. He'd never really thought of *needing* things. Not until he'd seen Diana, and needed that love and intimacy that a family could provide. And they needed no other prison, now that Kronos was confined to the Underworld…

Gaia seemed to understand his hesitation and confusion. "Think of what *you* wish for," she said gently. "What you need for yourself, not what you think others need."

"I need…peace," he realized. "Sanctuary." That was what

he'd been jealous of with his brother. Not the Underworld, but a realm that fit Hades so perfectly, a realm that gave him plenty of responsibilities to take care of, but also plenty of opportunities to be himself. "I did lose much." A twin, a love, an entire life. "I don't want to lose my memories of them, though. Can I have a place to remember Diana, a place that honors my brother, without having to go to the Sanctum of Fallen Heroes every time I wish to see them?"

"Your wish shall be granted." Gaia lifted her hands.

"Somewhere close to the water," he blurted, then blushed. Surely whatever his birth mother offered should be enough...

Gaia smiled again. "Anything you want," she said.

A moment later Ethan, Merlin, Zeus, Hades and Poseidon stood on the edge of a riverbank. The land around them was steep and mountainous, verdant with moss and bushes. The river burbled as it wound past them into a cave. The air smelled of fresh water and moss.

Gaia gestured to the river. "Here is the entrance to your realm, your sanctuary. What will you call it?"

Poseidon felt a prickling in his whole body. "Atlantis," he breathed, the name coming to him as if from a far-off memory.

Something knocked against the shore — a boat made of smooth dark wood and elegantly carved to look like a leaf that had been lost to the current. Poseidon helped his father and Merlin in, then steadied the boat while Hades and Zeus clambered after. Gaia took her place at the prow, and Poseidon climbed in last, taking a seat at the stern of the little boat. He picked up the oars and dipped them into the water, rowing them toward the mouth of the cave. At the same instant Gaia raised a finger, and a gentle breeze nudged them. They slipped into the cave and Poseidon watched as the light became dimmer, little sparkling slivers on the current. Then even that light disappeared, and for a few long minutes they saw nothing, hearing only the rush of water against the river bank. From the front of the boat Gaia made a thrumming noise, deep in her throat, and Poseidon knew she was concentrating. Making something.

Light appeared faintly above them: a glowing moss on the ceiling of the cave that wound like a river of its own, showing off the white of Merlin's hair, the slope of Zeus's proud shoulder. Poseidon continued to row. Gaia stood proud, unmoving.

He felt the pull of something deep ahead of them. A vastness of water, far greater than this little river. Almost without thinking he pulled water over them, creating a shield to trap their air and protect them.

The boat tilted down suddenly. Poseidon gasped, moving his oars to push them off the rocks as they started to careen down the river. Zeus shouted and the others clung to the side of the boat. They bounced off a boulder and smacked heavily in the water, spinning toward the side of the cave. Poseidon caught the side with one oar and pushed with all his might, until they had turned back into the current and began to drift smoothly again.

Ahead, light filtered through another opening in the tunnel. Seized by a sudden instinct, Poseidon directed them toward the light.

They came out from beneath the stone cave and found

themselves on a river at the bottom of the ocean.

The sea had been pushed out to create a vast palace. Poseidon dropped his protective bubble of air, for Gaia had made one of her own that expanded over the ocean bed to create a place where humans breathe as if they walked on Olympus above. A palace twisted before him like intricately entwined coral against a perfect turquoise backdrop of sea. Beyond the bubble he saw the flash of colorful fish, the sweep of dolphins and even sharks as they investigated this new part of their home. A flash of longing seized him, to go swim with the denizens of the deep.

The little boat bumped against a pale marble dock and they alighted. Poseidon tied the boat to a shining steel ring, then joined his mother to lead the procession toward the palace. It sprawled over the seabed, winding across little flats of land in between shallow pools that teemed with tiny crabs and other life. Around them, the ocean moved and rolled, its gentle roar soothing.

The front doors were of pure white stone, edged with bright pink coral. Gaia opened them onto a vast hall lined with tile made from crushed coral of every shade. Poseidon stopped dead. Next to him, Hades and Zeus drew in sharp breaths.

"Oh, my son," murmured Ethan, and Poseidon couldn't tell whether he was close to smiling or crying.

At the front of the hall stood Atlas. Another statue, but this one had nothing of the world, no hint of the sacrifice or pain Atlas had gone through at the hands of the tyrant. Poseidon didn't want to remember him that way. He wanted to remember the laughing brother, the brother who was always game for a joke, always ready to move, to fight. Atlas had always been full of life and action, and it was this way Poseidon wanted to remember him, always.

The statue had been plucked from his memory and made real. He remembered the morning well. It had been close to Maia's birth, and they'd crowded around his tiny apartment kitchen. Poseidon had told some joke — he couldn't even remember it — but Atlas, tired from days of hard manual labor and nights trying to keep Ivy comfortable, had howled with mirth. No matter that the joke hadn't been that funny. The fact that he laughed so hard made it all the funnier, and they'd ended the evening with tears rolling down their cheeks.

Thinking about it brought tears of a different sort to Poseidon's eyes now. That time shouldn't have been simpler, yet somehow it was.

He felt a cool hand in his, and looked down. Gaia pressed his fingers. "Come," she said.

She took him to a throne room, which felt both odd and right at once ("For this is your realm, and you must tend to its needs as a ruler," she said), then to a few rooms of state, a banquet hall, then out and over a little bridge that connected them to the next part of the palace. They skirted several buildings that Poseidon determined to examine later before finally crossing a bridge that led them to a little mossy island surrounded by water that teemed with fish no larger than his pinky finger. A small octagonal structure sat here, one of glass and stone. Gaia motioned for him to open the unassuming wood door.

Inside the structure was Diana. It was a shrine.

This was no memory, though. It was her. Her body, turned to

stone by the evil chimera Medusa. She knelt in a shallow pool of warm water. Her eyes were open wide. Poseidon knelt, too.

She looked so calm. Most of Medusa's victims had been wracked with terror in their final moments, but Diana had left this world the way she had always walked in it: utterly serene. Light bathed her face. It was almost a shock to find her skin cold to the touch.

Her eyes glinted as though a speck of life remained in them. The corners of her mouth were turned up in the start of a smile. She looked…peaceful. Around her legs yellow and pink sea flowers twined.

Poseidon blinked. He didn't realize he was crying until a tear hit the water and the flowers swirled about him. "I thought…" he murmured. He thought she'd died alone and afraid, abandoned by him on the battlefield. In truth, she'd faced her destiny with her eternal grace. Now, fittingly, she would be remembered for that. He bowed his head. "Thank you, mother," he whispered.

###

There was much to explore in Atlantis. The palace sprawled so that it was almost more like a city than a single palace, with dozens of guest houses, chambers and courtyards sprawled over the little islands at the bottom of the sea. Light refracted by the ocean above them played over columns of coral and pearl. The palace was designed for many visitors, and Poseidon looked forward to welcoming them all. Yet he found his gaze constantly pulled away, toward the sea. Bright colors flashed as fish played and scattered before the snouts of sharks.

"Do you think your brothers might explore the palace on their own for a while?" Gaia was looking at him sidelong. "Perhaps you and I could go for a swim."

"Point me in the direction of the dining room and I'm happy," Zeus said. He patted his belly. "Watching you make two new kingdoms is hungry work."

Hades rolled his eyes. "We'll be fine," he said. "And I'll keep Zeus out of trouble. If anyone can do it, a god and a master wizard can."

Gaia led Poseidon to the edge of the palace, to where another dock extended past the air bubble and into the water. She breathed deep, closing her eyes, then stepped through the bubble, smiling.

And then she transformed.

Her brown hands grew delicate pale webbing, fingers lengthening. Her green gown shimmered and knit down her body, covering her legs. Her bare feet widened into powerful flippers. Poseidon stared.

His birth mother gestured with her hand. *Come.* Heart pounding, Poseidon stepped out of the air and into the water.

He had no need to breathe. That was his first thought, and he put his hand up to his neck in wonder, finding three shallow slashes under each ear. Gills. He felt a burst of energy and looked down in time to see his legs merge together, the tan skin of his body turning a vibrant blue as scales shimmered into existence over his torso. His tail had a powerful fin, like a small whale's. He twitched it once and shot through the water, disturbing a cloud of silver fish that scattered in panic. He laughed. The sound bubbled out into the sea.

His mother swam easily to join him. *Shall we explore this new world?* she asked.

"Yes," Poseidon tried to say, but the noise was nothing in his mouth. *Yes.*

She dipped her pointed chin and turned, leading him away from his palace and into the depths.

The ocean was a marvel. Poseidon had always loved the water, but never had he had so much of it at his disposal before. As they swam into the darkness of the open sea they were joined by little bioluminescent fish that radiated blue-green light as bright as lanterns, skimming over the black sea bed. They were joined by another school, this one red and purple, and soon a whole rainbow had gathered around Poseidon. The fish were curious, nibbling at his arms and beard until he laughed, darting away at the strange sound that emanated from his mouth. *Apologies,* he thought to the fish, and he didn't know whether they heard him or not, but they returned to examine his ears and nose.

He turned to his mother. *What else lives down here?* he asked.

Many things, she replied, and swam deeper. Poseidon followed. They entered a sudden cold spot and the little fish scattered. A moment later a long snout, glittering and glowing purple and blue, emerged from the dark. Ridges like teeth adorned its head, and two long antennas waved in the water. The head of the sea serpent was at least as large as Poseidon's, but its body was long and lithe, whipping through the water propelled only by its tail and guided by a thin fin that feathered down its

150

back. Its scales rippled like bark, and in its eyes Poseidon saw a depth of intelligence and wisdom that could only come from long decades.

The serpent nodded to him, as a ruler would nod to another ruler. Poseidon nodded back. *You will need advisors, as all good kings do,* Gaia said. *Do not be afraid to draw on the wisdom of the Deep.*

They swam on. They saw a pod of Krakens, many-armed sea creatures larger than the largest animal Poseidon had ever witnessed on land. Their tentacles were spread out over the ground, gently caressing the algae, checking each strand for signs of decay, picking little creatures and bits of food from the ocean floor. They were gardening, he realized, carefully tending a crop. They waved to him and Gaia as they swam past.

Beyond the Krakens lay clams so large his whole family could have fit inside. Pearls lay scattered around their shells like rubble. The clams were tended by tiny creatures, things that looked much like Poseidon looked now — human from the waist up, with gills instead of noses, but resembling a variety of fish and crustaceans from the waist down. They were perhaps half as long as Poseidon himself. Their eyes were wide, glowing slightly from their years far beneath the ocean's surface. They blinked rapidly as Poseidon swam by, stroking their clams idly with one hand.

They saw sea nymphs, darting in and out of coral palaces in their games of hide and seek. They saw giant turtles, carrying entire small islands on their backs as they made their unhurried way through the ocean. There were warriors here, and wise men, treasures of civilization that had learned to live in relative harmony.

You are not their king, not precisely, Gaia said as they swam.

I do not think I could be their king, Poseidon confessed. The things he was seeing could make even Zeus humble.

This world is united, connected, Gaia told him. *Kronos cared nothing for the sea; he thought it full of creatures unworthy of his attention. It was fortunate for them, but you know the truth: the sea is full of beautiful, bountiful life. It is life that must be preserved. Where possible, you must work together with your brothers on Olympus and on solid ground. You must ensure that the sea is heard. All the creatures here deserve a voice. That is what you are.*

Not a king, or a ruler. A voice for the people. Poseidon spun around in the water.

He liked that. He'd never been much interested in ruling anyway.

Some of his thoughts must have slipped out, for Gaia laughed. *I am not sure the two things are so distinct — not when ruling is done well, anyway. But it is good that you see and accept responsibility for your new role.*

Poseidon stopped. *Perseus,* he said. *Can he come here? Shall he inherit this position? This title?*

Gaia held out her hand and let a swarm of minnows cluster around her palm. *Perseus' destiny is his own,* she replied. *Even I cannot see the future as it will be, only as it may be. But there is no reason the two of you should not be united again.*

His little one. He'd teach Perseus the value of being a good listener. And maybe Perseus wouldn't have to be parted from Maia and Ivy. The palace had room for many guests.

Many family members, he silently corrected himself. He had a feeling Atlas would want it that way. He'd hate for Ivy to wander the world alone, for Maia to be cut off from her uncles.

We must return. Gaia began to swim back in the direction they'd come. *My energy and resources are not endless, and there is yet one more realm to create.*

CHAPTER ELEVEN: A REALM BUILT FOR TITANS

Zeus couldn't help it: all this water made him nervous. He was the master of storms, after all, and the mix of lightning and water was deadly.

Even though the ocean was held at bay, he could almost feel it pushing down on him. He had to remember that he could breathe. He wandered the island buildings of Atlantis, glaring at a tiny crab when it pinched his toe. "Watch it," he said. "I could eat you in one mouthful." How he must look to it: as immense as Kronos had been to him and his brothers. The thought made him shudder, and he swiftly walked on.

He spotted Poseidon and Gaia swimming at the edge of the bubble. His brother's long legs had transformed into an undulating tail. The muscles beneath his blue-green scales shifted as he swam easily through the water, laughing. The sight was at once jarring and beautiful. Zeus wasn't sure how he felt about it. He felt joy in his brother's joy, kinship at his laughter. Yet it was a joy he could not truly share, for it was the joy of the sea, and something ugly and unhappy stabbed his heart at the thought of it. He turned from Poseidon, too.

He should be getting back to the main hall anyway. If Poseidon was returning, then surely they would be planning what to do next — and as his two brothers had gotten a realm of their own, surely Zeus was owed something as well. An anticipatory smile curved his lips as he made his way over the rocky islands and through gorgeous halls carved with sea murals and studded with pearls.

The main hall was nearly empty when he arrived. Only Hades sat there, so still that Zeus wasn't sure his brother even noticed him. Hades' chin was propped on his fist, his eyes fixed on the laughing statue of Atlas. He looked like he'd been sitting there for hours.

Zeus sat next to him. Their brother looked almost alive, as though his booming voice should ring out over the hall any moment. He found he disliked it. It was as though he kept expecting his brother to be there, and he wasn't.

"I hope that some part of him shares in our victories," Hades murmured. "That wherever his soul is now, he can rejoice.

"Do you think he will come to you?" Zeus asked.

Hades raised his brows and sighed. "I don't know. Before, when normal souls died, Gaia says they wandered the world until they faded away. But what happens to people like us? Because we're not really people, are we? We're not even wizards."

No, Zeus thought. They were something so much more.

The door opened and Ethan and Merlin came in, deep in conversation, followed by Gaia and Poseidon. "The long term maintenance of a spell of such magnitude would prove impossible for all but the most powerful wizards. And even if I were to put it together, it would require constant vigilance, day and night, to continuously engage the feedback loop. Remember, there's no such thing as perpetual motion."

The old man always gave him such a headache. "What are you going on about?" Zeus said.

Ethan shot him a reproachful look. *Mind your manners*, it said. "We're discussing the possibility of an underwater base. As far as I understand it, Merlin's telling me it's impossible for anyone who's not my son." He glanced at Poseidon proudly.

"Gaia did all the work," Poseidon said, though he turned pink at the edges of his ears. His legs were back, clad in the same trousers and sandals he'd worn when they first arrived.

"But your power will keep Atlantis safe and secure for any who wish to seek refuge here," Gaia told him. "Tend it well."

She approached Hades and Zeus. "Come." She was smiling. "We have one more location to visit."

A buzzing started up in Zeus' belly. This was it. It had to be. He stood, and Hades did the same. Gaia raised her hands and the ground beneath them shifted again. Water swirled around them, turning to gold and brown dust as they emerged from the water and made their way over land. Zeus grew dizzy with their speed, and when they landed again he staggered into Hades. His brother's strong but lanky arms gripped him and helped him steady himself, and he nodded his thanks.

They stood upon a vast stretch of green and golden grass, dotted with flowers and grazing goats. The plain was fairly flat, but when Zeus turned he gasped. Before him stood a mountain, taller even than Mount Etna, sloping into the sky. It was so tall that fluffy white clouds obscured its peak. He felt his hands clench. As the master of the storm — as, perhaps, the most powerful of his brothers — this would be a fitting home indeed.

A marble arch gleamed in the sunlight, sparkling with flecks of gold, veined in red and blue. Above the arch a golden sign had been etched with the words: MOUNT OLYMPIA, HOME OF THE TITANS.

Zeus stared. A clear white path wound up the mountain — a path meant for contemplation and purpose. His feet itched to walk it. But he had to wait until Gaia gave the word.

"Well?" She looked at him. "What do you think?"

He opened his mouth, but for once he struggled to find something to say. *It's beautiful* didn't really do the mountain justice. It fairly glowed in the sun, with brilliant moss and white and black stones scattered across its surface. A waterfall burbled down one side of it and the bushes were filled with trilling birds. Small trees dotted the mountain, the perfect place to sit and think, or lie with a loved one. He thought of Leda with a sudden pang.

"Excuse me, Gaia," said Hades. He cleared his throat. "I mean —" He frowned. Zeus almost laughed. In all these years, his brother could still be awkward. "Gaia? M-mom?"

Gaia tilted her head, smiling. "It makes you uncomfortable to think of me as your mother."

"Yes," Hades admitted.

Zeus had met Gaia twice in his life, and he doubted Hades had seen more of her. Her influence had pervaded their upbringing, their destiny, their very life — but she'd always been far away, distant as the enemy.

"I have always been Gaia to you, although I regretted it," she said. "I gave up the right to be called 'Mom' long ago. That belongs to Raven now."

She cast her eyes down, and Zeus thought he saw the shimmer of tears in them. Hades, though, sounded relieved when he continued. "Titans." He pointed at the gate. "Who are they, exactly? And why are we at their residence?"

Their residence? Zeus felt a clench of disappointment in his gut.

A moment later that clench turned into an electric energy. Gaia's smile became indulgent. "Dear children, the Titans are the three of you. Kronos styled himself a god, and the people need to be shed of his memory. When you go out among them, 'Titan' is the title by which they will come to know you. They will know that they can rely upon you to care for and govern Olympus, to ensure the harmonious functioning of this world and all its living creatures. That was Kronos' original purpose, the purpose from which he strayed in his constant, fearful quest for power. It is the purpose I now entrust to you."

She turned. Thunder rumbled over the mountain. The trees bent their bows in a sudden breeze, and the waterfall began to splash merrily. Next to it the ground broke open and a second waterfall, this one glowing with magma, began to flow. Zeus felt a shifting at his feet, a tugging as though he were being drawn somewhere, to fix something.

"Every element of Olympus is interconnected and relies on a balanced synergy," Gaia said. "If there is any imbalance, the planet will communicate this to you. All you must do is be attentive."

A life of lounging around Olympus, punctuated by brief adventures into the world beyond? "That doesn't sound so difficult," Zeus said.

"Oh, your duties will be fitting for the hardworking manner in which you were raised," Gaia told him, a mischievous glint in her eye. Like she was trying not to laugh at him. "The sun must rise and set each day, as must the moon. Take care that they are not thrown out of balance. Storms must fall in the right place, to enrich the soil and let the cattle and goats and sheep graze without flooding the land. Life must flow in its circle, as it is meant to do. And once life has ended, the good people and creatures of Olympus will let their bodies return to the soil of Olympus, and their souls venture into the Underworld."

Zeus swallowed. Suddenly this *did* seem like a lot of work. And he was powerful, yes, but…everything he'd done up to now sounded like a party trick compared to what Gaia wanted him to do next.

"It was a mistake to ask Kronos to rule Olympus alone," Gaia said. "I see that now. The three of you will work together as gentle gods, in harmony regarding the development of the world. This is the place to convene. There will be quarters for Poseidon and Hades during your visits, so that you may all be comfortable in your home while you ponder the fate of Olympus." She turned now to Merlin and Ethan, and her smile was tinged with sadness. "This is a sacred mountain, much like the Underworld. It is not a place for mortals. I will protect you for now, but this is the last visit you will make to this revered place."

Merlin clapped his wizened hands together. "Imagine climbing the mount of the gods," he said, and smiled. He looked almost like a child in his excitement.

Ethan nodded, gripping his staff, and Zeus could see his father's anticipation too. Well, the boys had gotten their sense of adventure from somewhere.

Gaia spread her hand, inviting, and they began to climb.

It was an easy walk. The path was steady beneath their feet, almost as if it had a mind of its own and wished for them not to fall. Zeus smelled ripe olives and pomegranates, and his stomach rumbled.

"I have a question." Poseidon sounded troubled.

"Please, ask," Gaia said.

"You've tasked us with making sure the world goes round…and, well, did Kronos really do all that? I'm not sure I could manage to tend more than the sea you gave me," Poseidon confessed. "There is a limit to our power, is there not?"

"A wise question, my son," Gaia said. "There is a limit to your power. But the limit will grow or shrink, depending on the people of Olympus. You see, the more belief a mortal being has in you and in your power to shape their fate, the more power you will possess. Kronos sought to ensure his power through fear, though I begged him many times to take a gentler approach. And had he done so, his powers would have been ten times as great as they were. Inducing fear is not the only way to make people believe in you, or pray to your power. It is not even the best way. Love and admiration are immensely more potent. If you treat your subjects with love and respect, they will return it, and your powers will grow beyond your wildest dreams."

Zeus tilted his face up toward the warmth of the sun. Power beyond his wildest dreams? Well, he could dream of quite a bit.

He didn't mind the idea of people showing him deference, either.

They wound up and up the mountain. The air grew crisper

and cooler as they went. Zeus' feet were getting pleasantly sore when he saw the first signs of building: high white marble walls, gleaming in the sun, piercing the blue sky like lightning bolts. It wrapped around the summit of the mountain, fitting seamlessly with the stone at its base.

At the front of the building stood a pair of spectacular golden doors, etched with scenes. As Zeus came closer he recognized Gaia, fleeing with a bundle in her arms, then an image of the four brothers in their Sherwood home. Scenes of hunting, Hades' first defeat of Typhon, the gods bursting forth from Kronos in his great defeat. Zeus felt a swell of something as he looked at the door, something that was not quite pride. It was — astonishment, perhaps. That he had managed to do all these things. That someone had found them worthy enough to carve on a door.

The doors opened onto an equally grand foyer, strung with tapestries depicting the flora and fauna of Mount Olympus itself. It was adorned with white tile, and plinths lined the sides of the room, carrying vases full of flowers. The grand hall had four different doors: one was adorned with the bident staff Hades had begun to carry; one held a crackling lightning bolt, and one a winding sea dragon. The fourth door was curiously blank.

Before Zeus could ask what it was, Gaia opened the blank door and went through it. They followed her down a long, opulent corridor. Murals had been painted over the marble, depicting battles and divine revelations from ages past. Their footsteps echoed in the hall, and none of them spoke, as if somehow afraid to disturb this space.

At the end of the corridor stood another door, also blank.

Gaia opened it onto a large round room with a triangular obsidian table in the middle. Zeus wandered over to the table, running his fingers over the golden lightning bolt on one corner. The walls of the room were painted with the various cities, fields and forests of Olympus, with a large window in the middle of one wall where they could look out over the mountainside. Above them, the ceiling was painted a blue so dark it was nearly black, dotted with twinkling lights. The stars of Olympus, Zeus realized. It gave the room a sort of cosmic glow.

"Here is a place where you may ponder together on the needs of the world," Gaia told them. "You are all equals, and so sit equally at the table. I know that, working in tandem, you will make Olympus prosper. And when you have spent long hours at your work, you may retire to your own quarters, entirely suitable for you. Zeus."

Zeus startled at his name. He'd been staring at the stars and only half paying attention.

"Would you like to see your rooms?" Gaia asked.

His rooms. His own palace. "Yes," he whispered.

Gaia left the others in the council chamber and led him back down the hall. "Your suite is the largest, of course," she told him as she walked, her feet somehow soundless on the floor while Zeus' boots echoed in the narrow corridor. "As this will be your permanent house, and your brothers will only need a few amenities here. Just as, I am sure, you will have a guest house at their lodgings."

Zeus couldn't really fathom why he would want to go far under the crust of Olympus to Hades, or feel the weight of the ocean again with Poseidon, but he nodded. Surely his brothers would be here all the time, discussing the important business of ruling the world.

They emerged into the foyer and Gaia crossed to the door with the lightning bolt. Another corridor, as ornate as the one linking the foyer with the Chamber, stretched before them. This one held scenes of the storm: swirling clouds, slashing rain, cutting lightning. A figure rode the lightning in one depiction, and Zeus felt a thrill of anticipation. Was that figure meant to be him? Could he do something like that?

The suite at the other end of the hall certainly suggested it.

Like the Chamber, Zeus' suite had no ceiling. Instead clouds swirled high above, the deep blue of impending storm. Instead of painted walls he had windows all around, with a sweeping view of the mountain as it sloped down to the plain. From this high he could see the curve of the world. He looked down upon birds that circled for prey. There was a wide white bed, a counter with a bowl of fruit and a loaf of bread, and a desk. A separate room led to a toilet, and another to a pool of bubbling warm water, an eternal bath. In the distance, thunder rumbled. Zeus felt the shimmer of power under his skin.

He sat on the corner of the bed as a sudden thought occurred to him. "Leda," he said. "You said that mortals…"

Gaia bent her head. "I am sorry, my son," she replied. "Leda is also mortal, as is Hercules. They have their own home now, and you may go to them whenever you wish."

Whenever he wished. But they couldn't come here. His life as a Titan was something they would be forever removed from.

Something twisted in his chest. So this was what Gaia and Ethan meant when they'd said there were still sacrifices to be made. In the end, all four brothers would be separated from their partners.

You can visit, whispered a part of his mind. But Zeus knew it wasn't the same.

Gaia's cool hand fell on his shoulder, dark against his pale skin. "Come, my boy," she said gently. "I can feel my power drawing thin. We must say goodbye to your father, and leave you to your work."

His feet and heart felt heavier as he followed her back down the hall. So many years he'd spent in refuge with his father or his wife. Now he truly was parting from them — he couldn't even bring them to visit. At the same time, the churning anticipation in his belly couldn't be denied, either: there was work to be done, and Zeus was eager to do it. Eager to use his power as a force for good. To see how far he could push it.

Back in the foyer, the five of them faced each other one last time. Ethan gripped his staff and let the tears fall freely from his eyes. "My sons," he rasped. "You have exceeded my wildest hopes for you. I hope you will grace Sherwood with your presence, and remember your old man."

He embraced each of them in turn, pressing their shoulders. When he hugged Zeus he murmured, "Don't let yourself be too alone up here."

"Of course not," Zeus promised.

Merlin came next, opting to shake hands. "Might your first prayer from a supplicant be from me?" he said. "I would beg that you visit Novaris, to begin sorting out the mess Kronos has made of it. People are fighting over scraps of power. But we can make it beautiful yet."

Gaia looked from brother to brother. "My sons," she said at last, and she sounded wondering. "Shepherd this great power you have inherited. Take care of it. Always use it for good." Her eyes lingered on Zeus for a moment, searching. Then she smiled, and the flowers on her dress broke open in bloom. Then they turned and exited the grand entry hall through the golden doors, walking carefully on the white path down the mountain.

The brothers watched them until they had disappeared beneath the white clouds.

CHAPTER TWELVE: FROM CHAOS TO ORDER

The sun shone, the wind whistled through the crags of the mountain, and the three brothers stood alone.

Poseidon clapped his hands. "I suppose we'd better get down to it."

"Of course, of course. Brothers, shall we return to the Chamber?" Hades proposed.

They were both looking at Zeus. "Right," he said, trying to keep the strange energy that threatened to fill him at bay. He wanted to walk, to explore, to see what it was to be a god. He didn't want to start his first day in power with administration.

But his brothers were probably right. They usually were. He followed them back to the council chamber.

The triangular table was etched with a circle he hadn't noticed before. Within the circle sat a map of Olympus.

"I'm not even sure where to start," Poseidon remarked.

"That's the challenge, isn't it?" Hades agreed. "But remember what Dad used to do."

"When he was running the world?" Zeus asked sarcastically.

Hades flicked a hand at him. "He delegated Cross duties to people who had a better understanding of the situations they were in. There were leaders in every city and different leaders for different beings. We need something like that: appointed spokespersons or leaders that can determine what kinds of problems need the attention of the Titans, and how to bring it to our attention."

"Agreed," Poseidon said immediately.

Delegation sounded like a grand solution to their problems. "Agreed," Zeus said easily. "What's next?" Maybe this administration stuff wouldn't be so bad.

"Space," Hades said.

Zeus looked up, first, into the cosmos that drifted peacefully above their heads. "What do you mean?"

"I mean physical space. Labyrinth city is packed, the poor quarters of Novaris are nearly overrun, and Centennial City won't even rent out full houses anymore. If we increase the actual landmass of Olympus, we can make sure that people have the space they need. We need places for the Centaurs to run, for the Dragons and Griffins to hunt, for the Minotaurs to enjoy their solitude. We only expect the population to grow."

"Agreed," said Poseidon again.

This made Zeus furrow his brow. It was a noble sentiment, yes. His brother was full of those. But... "How exactly do you propose we create entire new continents?" he said.

"I think it's a simple enough matter, really. How strong of a storm can you summon?" Hades asked.

Zeus grinned. "Is that a challenge?"

Hades leaned forward, grinning back. "Yes."

Zeus stood. All right, administrative work really *was* turning out to be fun. He breathed deep, and he called to the winds and the rain and the clouds, to the electricity in the air. A low keening began around them as the wind whipped up the mountain.

Hades stood too, then, and closed his eyes. Zeus felt the summoning of power about him. Hades' eyes snapped open, glowing red-orange. "Now," he said in a voice that roared like magma.

The room around them shifted — or perhaps it was they who were shifting, moving away from Olympus to the edge of the known world. The green-gray sea stretched out beyond them, tossed and darkened by Zeus' storm. From above Zeus recognized Mount Etna, the place of his brother's birth, the place of disastrous battles. The mountain was rumbling now. Dragons and Griffins streamed from her cone as jets of ash spewed into the air and were swirled about by the wind.

Lava came next, erupting from the mountain and flowing as thick as a river. It was all moving down one side, Zeus noticed, the side nearest the storm-tossed sea. The sea itself drew back, gathering in a mighty wave that crashed over the lava, creating a cloud of steam and cooling it to Olympus. "Zeus," Hades called, and Zeus knew what he wanted. Harnessing the power of the storm, he directed the winds gently — *that way*, he thought, pushing them toward the sea. They roared joyously as they followed his direction, slamming into the coast and carrying the new volcanic formations away from land. He guided the winds, pulled the storm, sent the volcanic ash and dirt away from the towns on Etna's opposite side, so that the people there would not be suffocated, their animals smothered. He worked until his arms ached and there was a tiny spit of land far out into the sea, until the red sun was low on the horizon, glaring through a screen of ash and smoke. Yet their land was so pitifully tiny, hardly fit for a few families to settle. They needed more. Their work was far from done.

Etna spewed into the night and beyond. The seas raged and

churned. The winds howled. And yet there was more to do, always more. Zeus kept at it as the sun rose. Fatigue threatened him, but as the day grew bright he felt a sudden surge of power that surprised him.

"Look," said Poseidon, pointing down. Zeus followed his finger. Beneath them stood a crowd of people, watching with open mouths and wide eyes.

Adoration. Respect. Prayers. *Yes.* If this was what being a god was like, no wonder Kronos hadn't wanted to give up his power. The people would ensure that Zeus could do anything. And so he made the storm fiercer yet, angrier, churning with angry clouds and spitting lightning that struck the little islands in a spectacular show.

After a while he lost track of time. There was only the flow of the storm, the swell of the waves, the unending flow of lava. And bit by bit the islands grew larger, solidified, became something vast and great and dark. The sun set, and the moon fought to be seen through the clouds. The sun rose again, and the day began anew.

Then Hades touched his arm. "I think we've done it," he said.

The island wasn't an island anymore. It was a vast landmass, still cooling and bare of life, though birds and Dragons winged over it in curiosity.

Part of Zeus wanted to keep the storm spinning forever. The other part of him wondered when he'd last slept.

"We have been at this for six days," Hades told him. Zeus felt his jaw go slack. "Maybe we should take a well-deserved day to rest."

Next to him Poseidon looked pale and drained. His eyes, though, were feverish with an excitement Zeus recognized. "Are you sure? We could always make it a little bigger —"

"Dear brother," Hades laughed. "Of course I'm not sure. But who knows what has sprung up in our absence. Let's rest, and find out what Olympus needs next."

A moment later, they stood in the Chamber of the Trinity again. Zeus felt the last of his strength leave him as they snapped the connection with the people of the plains, the vigil-holders. He sagged against the table.

Poseidon clutched his head. "I think I have to go lie down," he muttered.

"Good plan."

Zeus wasn't sure how he got into his bed. He didn't remember the trip back to the foyer, or into his room. He didn't try to explain to his brothers where they should go, either. They were clever enough to figure it out. He collapsed on his mattress and had enough time to think that it was as soft as a cloud before closing his eyes, and knowing no more.

###

He opened his eyes to the gentle sounds of thunder, to brief flashes of lightning in the cloud ceiling above him. It calmed him. The rumble soothed his heart while the lightning suggested the sort of gentle storm that lulled him to sleep as a child. But he wasn't tired anymore.

Zeus ran a hand over his face, feeling the soft stubble of a six-day beard. And by the gods — well, he supposed he couldn't say that anymore — by *whatever,* he was hungry. He sat up and looked over at the table.

The bread and fruit on it looked as fresh as it had the day he'd arrived. He launched himself out of bed, grabbing the loaf and tearing off an end before shoving it into his mouth. The bread was light and full of seeds. As he chewed he realized how parched he was. He grabbed a cup and, finding nothing to drink, summoned a little cloud to rain into it. Then he drank deeply and gratefully. Wine would have been better, but this was nice enough.

He ate the entire loaf, then broke open a pomegranate and enjoyed some of its seeds. Once he was full and his fingers stained fuschia, he went into the little room with the warm pool and slid in, letting the water come up to his chin. He leaned back and contemplated the sky-ceiling above for a while.

He didn't shift until he heard movement from the other side of the door. It cracked open. "So that's what you're doing," Poseidon said.

"Haven't you ever heard of knocking?" Zeus asked, leaning back and closing his eyes again.

"I did knock. On your front door. We're ready to reconvene."

"That's nice," Zeus commented. The silence became thick with disapproval. He opened one eye and rolled it at Poseidon. "I'm kidding. I'm coming."

He'd only been half kidding, but since Poseidon wasn't about to relax and have a bath himself, he saw no other choice but to get up and dry himself off with a length of cloth, then wrap a robe around his figure. He summoned a small wind to dry his hair as they walked.

Hades already sat in the Chamber of the Trinity, contemplating the stars. He still looked exhausted, with deep circles under his eyes, but he smiled brightly as his brothers came in and stood up to greet them. "I could feel it in the night," he said. "Could you?"

"Feel what?" Zeus asked. He'd been dead to the world.

"The belief. The power. People saw what we did and they believe in us now. As more than revolutionaries or replacements. This is perfect. The perfect opportunity to focus on the people themselves."

Zeus was still wondering why he'd had to get out of the bath. "I take it you have a suggestion?" he said, trying not to sound grumpy.

"Now's the time to appoint leaders," Hades said, maroon eyes shining. "People will naturally begin asking for our help, our favor. The sooner we put a system in place for that, the easier it will be."

"We can't possibly help everyone who asks for every little thing." Zeus could already see it: long queues around the base of Mount Olympia as people came to lay their petty grievances at his feet. "I can't be tossing judgments like lightning bolts."

Poseidon snorted. "I don't know, it might keep you humble." He flashed a smile. "But...Zeus is right." He snorted as Zeus mimed falling over in disbelief.

Hades paid neither of them any mind. "I propose we focus on the needs of the planet herself. Community leaders can resolve disputes between neighbors. We must ensure that the rivers flow and the sun and moon rise and set."

He lay his hands on the triangular table which. The map, Zeus noticed, now included their newly-made landmass. "My duties encompass the Underworld. I will tend to the souls that come to my halls and guard Kronos. I will also be here to take care of making new landmasses and controlling the volcanoes."

"I will safeguard the seas and rivers," Poseidon said. "The leaders of the sea peoples can always come to Atlantis, and I will have a greater understanding of the world around me."

Zeus thought of the water, pressing down, and suppressed a shudder. "Fine by me. Which leaves me…" He looked at the map and felt a swelling sense of duty. Of importance. Of power. "The land of the living."

"Your storms will be integral to watering crops and grazing lands," Hades said. "Your control of the sun and the moon will keep Olympus in its rhythm, and you will hear the prayers of those on land in need of help. I trust you can bring the most relevant of those prayers to us, where we can decide what to do with them. That way, should there be any failure in communication with the leaders of Olympus, the people will not be in peril."

For a single, striking moment, Zeus felt the weight of this responsibility as heavy as the sea that had so unnerved him in Atlantis. Then he straightened his shoulders. This was the task of a lifetime, a task no one else could fulfill. It was a destiny that even his brothers did not share, not really. "Let's turn to the next order of business, then," he said, in as mature a voice as he could muster. "Who are these great leaders of Olympus?"

That debate took less time than they'd thought: the obvious candidates were the leaders who'd formed the backbone of the Cross of the Iron Phoenix. It was determined that they would approach Ethan, Livia, Merlin and Timotheus. Livia and Timotheus would represent not only the Centaurs and Minotaurs, but the Dragons, Griffins and other magical beings that were mostly found on Mount Etna. Poseidon would establish his underwater kingdom and consult with the creatures there about who were their natural leaders. Ethan, wise as he was, could listen to the complaints of men and determine which ones were relevant. And Merlin could shepherd Olympus into a new age, an age that combined magic and technology and celebrated cooperation between peoples. For too long, Kronos had tried to keep everyone separate. That would change now.

They talked long into the night. Food appeared when they needed it, but Zeus never felt the need for sleep. Perhaps it was related to his sudden increase in power, but even in the middle of the night he felt invigorated, ready for adventure. He itched to explore the new continent, to set foot where he'd never been before.

"The problem is, how are we going to convince people to work together?" he said, taking an apple from a bowl and biting into its crisp flesh. "They've been taught to stick to themselves."

"We'll have to spread the word that great innovation happens when we work together." Hades drank deep from a cup of wine. The carafe had appeared on the table some time around twilight, and it was some of the finest vintage Zeus had ever tasted. "If we must walk among the people ourselves, so be it —"

"No," Poseidon warned. "You've got a job, now. You've got a kingdom to run."

"Our brother of the sea is right." Zeus wagged a finger. It wasn't often he got to feel on the right side of an argument, especially when Hades was the one on the other side. "We must use the leaders of Olympus to bring us news of any struggle or catastrophe, but we should also use them to spread our own messages to the people. And this is the first one: work together, to rebuild what has been destroyed. To make it better."

"Agreed." Poseidon raised his glass in a toast.

"Agreed." Hades smiled wryly, raising his own glass. Zeus completed the triad and they drank.

The sun was a low fire on the horizon. Zeus couldn't consciously remember calling it back to rise. It felt as though the night preceding it had been too short, and the day too long. His brothers were silent; Poseidon stared deep into his wine glass, and Hades was looking out the wide window of the Chamber, a faraway look in his eyes. Zeus recognized that look. His brother was daydreaming.

"We all have a lot to think about. And we all have much work to begin. Why don't we adjourn this meeting, and schedule another for another time?" Zeus suggested. "Let's see how the first phase of the plan works and what we need to do next."

"Good idea." Poseidon stroked his beard. "Shall we use the usual? Signal rocks?"

"Maybe something a little more...detailed," Hades suggested. He closed his eyes, thinking. Then he laid his hand flat over the corner of the table on which the little golden bident was carved. A moment later, a little rectangular tower of black stone rose from the table, the golden bident still crisp on top. Zeus looked down. His own symbol had raised from the table as well, as had Poseidon's.

"When one of us wishes to meet, all we must do is put a hand on our symbol, and think of the time. The others will feel the pull of the summons, and be able to see the next date. For example —"

He placed his hand on his tower. A moment later golden script scrawled down the side. Zeus inhaled sharply as his own tower grew hot under his hands and he felt a hooking sensation, like an itch at the back of his mind. He watched the date appear on his tower. "Next week?"

"Just a check in." Hades smiled.

"Brilliant," Poseidon decided. Zeus nodded. It *was* brilliant. He wished he'd thought of it himself.

"Well, then. If that concludes the first meeting of the Titans of Olympus, I shall bid my brothers good day." Hades stood. Zeus thought he caught a particular hunger in his eye. Perhaps it was the same hunger Zeus had, the need to explore this world they were remaking. Perhaps, though, it was something else.

He didn't get a chance to ask. "Until next time, brothers," said Hades briskly, and took his leave.

CHAPTER THIRTEEN: A PROMISE KEPT

How many days had he been away from the Underworld? How many souls had found their way to its depths? Hades' belly twisted nervously. He felt like a boy again. He had duties, naturally. And he needed to attend to them. But he couldn't help the hope that somehow, she was there…that she'd found her way to him again in her soul's wandering.

He couldn't transport himself while he was in the palace on Mount Olympia, but as soon as he'd gone through the front door he took himself to Etna and the mouth of the Underworld. His transportation wasn't as elegant as Gaia's, and it left him with a lurching seasickness that took a minute to subside. By the time his world stopped spinning the ground had unfolded before him into the long staircase that descended to the dark.

He reminded himself to take the stairs carefully, trying to reflect on the meeting and all that had happened there. He'd changed the face of the world above. He ought to be exhilarated by that. But in truth, all he could think of was the vast world below, unfolding as he descended.

As he reached the bottom the stair resolved into the top of the Hall of Peace. Plain steps gave way to smooth stairs and a banister ornamented with delicate carvings of the heroes of Olympus. As souls fell gently to the stairs they resolved into silvery people who drew themselves up, looked wonderingly at their hands, then began to survey the world around them. Their expressions ranged from serene to incredulous. This time Hades descended the stairs with them, entering the mingling crowd below.

He forced himself to pause at the bottom of the stairs, to greet the people here and welcome them to the Underworld. Some of them looked at him with confusion; others with awe. Some had already found people they knew; they embraced joyfully and tears fell from their faces like starlight. None of them were Persephone.

Hades found his way to the front of the Hall, where double doors allowed ready souls to exit and explore the Underworld. He stepped out into the leafy forest and looked up at the eternal twilight above him: the darkening abyss that wasn't really a sky, filled with stars that weren't really stars. He cast his mind out toward Tartarus. Cerberus was chasing a rabbit. He hadn't expected any trouble yet, but it was good to confirm that all was well with their prisoner.

He stuck his hands in his pockets and set off down a path of mist. Around him the trees and bushes rustled as the souls of animals played and chased and flew. Birds trilled curiously at him from nearby branches, and a squirrel paused in its gathering of silvery nuts to observe him.

The walk to his own private home was long, and it gave his mind time to settle. It was hard to be anything but calm in the Underworld, and by the time he saw the magnificent front door of his manor he'd almost convinced himself to accept things as they were. Persephone wasn't here. He'd suspected, from the beginning, that it was a risk: with nowhere for her soul to go after death, perhaps it had simply...

That thought was too painful to follow to its conclusion, but the first step — that she had not come to the Underworld (not yet, he prayed, not yet) — was one he tried to take as he opened his front door.

He removed his coat and hung it on a nearby hook. He would lose himself in work. There was always more work, wasn't there? He had volunteered to contact the leaders of Olympus, since Zeus had so much to do himself, and the past nine or ten days' effort was beginning to catch up to him. He entered his private chambers and froze.

A figure stood, silhouetted by the large window in his front room, looking out into the peaceful wood beyond. He viscerally recognized the fall of her raven hair, the set of her slim shoulders, the curve of her nose as she turned towards the sound of the opening door.

"You made it feel like home," Persephone said, simply.

Hades found he could say nothing at all. He strode forward and swept her into his arms, letting his tears fall freely. He could taste hers, too, as he kissed her.

###

He woke the next morning feeling more well rested and content than he remembered being in a long time. Persephone's head lay on his shoulder. For a moment he thought she was still sleeping, but then she tilted her head up to him for a morning kiss.

He still couldn't believe it was her. But he'd spent the night assuring himself that every freckle on her body was exactly where he'd left it. Remembering her in her living form, washing away the last horrible sight he'd had of her. *This* was why he'd taken charge of the Underworld. Not for Kronos or all the other souls. For her. Perhaps it was a selfish move, but right now it was hard to care.

"Did I wake you?" he asked when he broke their kiss.

"I don't sleep anymore," Persephone said. Her fingers ran lightly over his shoulder. They felt as real as they'd been the day he'd taken her hand in marriage. He still couldn't fathom it. But there was a gray pallor to her skin, a sort of paleness that could drift into translucence if he wasn't paying enough attention. "I can sort of drift, like I'm meditating. But I'm always aware."

"Do you still eat?" Hades said. He was suddenly famished.

"I don't have to." She smiled. "But I enjoy it."

He summoned a spread of fruit and olives and bread and butter, and as they feasted he recounted the events following their devastating defeat at Mount Etna. Persephone's mouth fell open at his story. "So everything we fought for…"

"We won. As much as we lost on the way, we won." He pressed her hand.

But if she was to be Queen of the Underworld, she needed to know the whole truth. After breakfast he took her to Tartarus and showed her the prisoner that lay there. Her body turned entirely translucent as they went inside, as if in fear, but she kept her head high and her face impassive.

She liked Cerberus, to his great relief. She wrapped her arms around the dog's middle neck and held it tight. "You poor thing," she murmured, and it whined pathetically, whipping its tail against her side and licking her face.

"How brave he must be," she remarked as Cerberus took off after a stick Hades threw. "To turn his back on the master that created him."

"That master was cruel," Hades replied, watching Cerberus come loping out of the mist, three heads fighting over who got to give the stick back.

"But look at all the things he created that never turned against him. Typhon, Medusa…" Persephone shuddered, moved by an inner chill. "I think it is a brave creature indeed that turns to kindness when it has only known hate." She knelt, and Cerberus ran past Hades to bask in her attention. "And a very good boy. A *very good boy*…"

When Hades finally pried his dog and his wife apart they walked again. This time, Persephone told her side of the story. How the pain had faded and she'd watched, as if from a distance, as Mount Etna began to erupt. "I called for you then," she said, sounding a little mournful. "I don't think you heard me."

Hades' own recollection was hazy, and when he tried to scratch the surface the memories were a raw lash against his heart. Even with Persephone beside him again, he couldn't bring himself to recall that day. "I don't think I heard anything," he replied quietly. *Anything but the sound of my own heart, breaking.*

"It took me a little while to truly understand that I was dead," she continued, slipping her hand into his and admiring the trees as they walked. "I think it was only my constant focus on you, *just* you, that kept my soul from drifting apart. I learned after a while that I had to concentrate constantly to be near you, and that small pieces of my mind kept wanting to…wander off. I watched it happen to others, too — they had nothing to tether them here, and they became like pollen on the wind. I resolved that it wouldn't happen to me, that I would try until one day, you heard me."

Hades thought of the way the wind had sometimes caressed his ear, sounded like her voice. "I think I did hear you," he murmured, turning to bury his nose in her hair. It didn't matter if she was a spirit, it felt real and true. It smelled of pomegranate flowers and clean soap. And holding on to him seemed to be keeping her more solid, anchored. One more reason to never let her go.

"I felt the pull when you created the Underworld, too," Persephone said. "I was afraid, at first. I was looking in on Achilles and I didn't know where you were. I thought I was finally reaching the end. And I suppose I was — I didn't know what the end was then." She laughed. Her laugh still sounded like clear crystal bells. "Then I came down here and saw all the others getting their bodies back, able to wander...but I drifted. It was like I'd forgotten what my body had been. I couldn't become whole until I found my way to your manor, your chambers."

A lump rose in Hades' throat. "I thought I'd lost you forever," he said huskily, stopping under the cover of the trees. He didn't need the people of his realm to see him break down.

Persephone cupped his head in her hands. Her fingers were cool and soothing like the mist of the underworld, and her eyes were bright pools, shining with silver tears. "I never stopped fighting to be with you, in life and in death," she said gently, and kissed him. It was a kiss he could fall into forever, a kiss he could live in. They never had to be parted again.

At last, all was as it should be. His Queen would share his life and realm. And he wanted to show her everything. Warm energy filled him, and he gently broke the kiss. "Come with me."

He took her to the Hall of Fallen Heroes. She was silent as she walked among the statues, wiping away shining tears as she looked upon Atlas and Diana. "We have lost so much," she mused. "I pray that it's worth it. The three of you always had the best intentions."

Hades nudged her with his hip. Here in the Hall of Fallen heroes she was even less substantial, and his body went right through hers. "What's that supposed to mean?" he said.

Persephone smiled, but her eyes were serious. "Of the four of you, you and Atlas were the most ambitious about leadership. You were preparing to take your father's place, and Atlas...I think Atlas wanted to be where the action was. But Poseidon was most at home training the new recruits or sitting around the campfire, swapping stories. And Zeus has always been..." She weighed her words. "Impulsive," she decided.

Hades had to laugh at his wife's tact. "You're right." He leaned in to kiss her, forgetting her insubstantial state. "But I think that Poseidon's qualities will make him a good leader. He likes to spend time among the people. He could always tell us what the rebellion needed from the perspective of the men. Zeus...he is impulsive." Hades found his brow wrinkling. "But that means I trust him to act with speed should any problems arise."

"But you said he also will control the rhythm of the sun and the moon," Persephone pointed out. "That's far from an impulsive job."

She was right. She was always right. It was such a relief to be back with his wife, who was always right. "He was always the least mature of us, and not only because he was the youngest. But he deserves a chance, doesn't he?" said Hades.

"He might also benefit from some help, to ensure that he isn't overwhelmed by all he must do alone. After all, you told me Poseidon had moved Ivy into Atlantis. She will be a valuable advisor to him. And now you have me. Who does Zeus have, if Leda can't join him at the top of Mount Olympus?"

Again, she was right. Hades would have to think on it. But he also thought, privately, that Zeus should have the chance to prove him and Persephone wrong, too. What if these tasks were what his brother needed to reach his potential?

###

Hades did not know how long they explored the Underworld together. He just knew that he had to show his beloved every corner, to seek her approval on every leaf and every path and every wall. Persephone was generous with her praise, stopping to pluck flowers for her hair or stroke the muzzle of a bold deer that knew it had nothing to fear from them. Persephone had most substance when she was in Hades' manor: she was as solid as he was, able to hold things and kiss him and dance the way they used to. Toward the edges of his realm she was most like a spirit, most difficult to hold on to. But Hades didn't mind spending most of his time here, with her. If he never left the manor house again he'd be content, as long as she were in here with him.

Later that day, after they'd returned and spent a leisurely afternoon on the couch in one of the many sitting rooms, with Persephone's head in his lap, she sighed wistfully. "I would be perfectly happy if I could know if our son is all right."

She twisted to look up at him. But Hades had frozen, a cold shock flushing out from his belly. Achilles, his beloved boy. *Was he all right?*

"I..." He bowed his head. "I've failed you," he said.

"What do you mean?" She sat up, eyes filled with concern. "He can't be...well, he'd be here with us if he were." She put a hand to her chest.

"I'm sure he's alive. But after I sent him away...well, we didn't want to bring the children back too quickly, in case some of Kronos' allies and underlings thought to get revenge on us through them. And then we were building an entire continent, and discussing the fate of the world..."

"It's a lot of work," Persephone agreed gently.

"But is it worth giving up being a father?" he asked.

She didn't say anything. For a horrible moment he thought she'd say *no,* that he'd spend eternity with a wife who resented him.

"You had no choice," she said then, and he nearly wept from relief. "You were given a destiny. No one else could defeat Kronos. You and your brothers had to be the ones. But...promise me he's with a good family. You were raised by a good man who wasn't your father. If Achilles is given the love that you were, he'll be fine."

Hades swallowed. He wanted to assure Persephone that yes, Achilles was growing up happy and healthy, like any young boy should, in a way that would make his parents proud. But he couldn't make that promise. The last he'd seen of the boy, Ethan had taken him away. At Hades' request, of course, but all the same...

"I must go to him," he said, just as Persephone said, "You must go to him."

They stared at each other. Hades blinked. Persephone giggled. "I am glad we're thinking in the same way, my husband. But of course, you must go to him. Achilles must see what his father has become, and understand why he can't be with us."

"What if..." Hades swallowed. "What if he doesn't want to see me?"

Persephone leaned in, pressing her forehead to his. "It will be all right," she murmured, her words soothing him like a balm. "It will be all right."

Hades kissed her tenderly, relishing in the softness of her mouth, the way she yielded to him. "I'll return as soon as I can," he said. For now that he knew he must go, he could hardly think of anything else. The Underworld was working as it should; it could spare him for a few days. But he left his heart at home, smiling at him from the couch as he went to collect his coat and hat.

###

The trip to Sherwood was much simpler than in the days

before he'd been a full-fledged god. It was the work of a moment to transport himself to the edge of the forest, though he still had to stand with his hands on his knees for a moment, fighting to get his nausea under control.

This meeting could serve two purposes, he thought as he made his way into the forest. Ethan could apprise him of the sentiments of men, and he could inquire about his son.

But he stopped dead as he entered the forest. Sherwood looked new. Sherwood looked…repaired. Roads were smoothed over and people lived in their houses again. There were still signs of the all-but-abandoned forest, but the bones of houses were being reused to strengthen that of their neighbors, and leaky roofs were quickly being repaired.

It was almost as though Hades had gone forward in time.

He hurried along the path home, pulling his hat down to avoid being recognized. Dread pulled on him like a loose string slowly unraveling his wits.

The great house of his childhood was, miraculously, still standing. Its boughs dripped with leaves like hanging emeralds, branches twisting toward the sky, the glossy bark shining in the sun. Hades stared at it, feeling a mix of nostalgia and awe at the sprawling tree, when a voice said from next to him, "Took you long enough. Do you know how much work it was to take apart all those wards?"

The wards. They'd forgotten to dismantle them after the battle. "Sorry," Hades half laughed as he turned to embrace his mother. Then his laugh died on his lips. His mother's hair was completely silver now. The lines in her forehead were deep grooves, and there were ample wrinkles around her eyes and mouth."

Raven caught his look. "What's wrong?"

"Nothing." He swallowed. "I…I just didn't realize how much time had gone by." How one or two days in the realm of the dead could be years and years on Olympus.

"I'm sure you've been busy. As have we." Raven patted his hand and gestured. "Merlin said it was the most complicated magic he'd ever seen. No wizard could have made wards like that — or broken them," Raven added.

Which was probably why Tom Ambrose hadn't tried to attack them in their sleep. "I can't say I'm sorry we protected the old girl." Hades smiled up at the old home. It was too grand, and it had lived too long, to be felled by the petty squabbles of men and gods.

The yard around the house was flush with grass. A flock of chickens eyed him curiously as they dug around for worms and insects. The dirt pen that had sometimes been used for training was full of flower beds now. Raven hadn't wasted a minute of freedom.

"I suppose you're here to see your father," she said. "I'm not sure he'll thank you for all the extra work you've given him."

"You know he'd have done it whether I asked him to or not," Hades said.

"I know," Raven sighed. "Ethan is his own worst enemy sometimes."

Ethan was out late, meeting a group of mayors and important men from Centennial and Labyrinth City. He came home well after dark, face haggard and frowning, newly lined, and his limp was more pronounced. But at the sight of Hades his frown washed off his face and his eyes lit. "My son!"

They embraced, and Ethan moved to get them some tea. "Sit," Hades ordered. His father was even using his walking stick indoors now. "I know where the tea is."

"I'm glad you're here," Ethan called to him as he rooted about in the kitchen. "I was considering whether I should call for you myself. But I'm supposing you have your own reasons for showing up."

"Yes." Hades bit back a smile. "Dad, she's back."

He brought out the tea, and told Ethan all about Persephone's return. Ethan smiled broadly, and Hades even caught the glisten of a tear on his father's cheek as he spoke.

"Son." Ethan leaned over and gripped his hand. "Your mother and I always knew Persephone was like the other half of you. It was devastating to watch you suffer. We're so pleased she's back. And, of course, we look forward to seeing her again." He shot Hades a knowing look.

"In many years, please!" Hades laughed.

"I don't know. The Underworld seemed like a much more peaceful place than up here," Ethan groused. Then his face turned serious. "In the midst of all this joy, something is weighing on you, yes?"

Hades set his cup down. "It's my son."

"Achilles is thriving. Let me put your fears to rest," Ethan said immediately.

His father was telling the truth. But Hades had promised to

check personally. "Is it possible, at all, to see him? To assure him that we love him, and we didn't leave him by choice?"

Ethan tapped his fingers against the teacup for a little while, thinking. "Terri and Gene are hardworking and proud people. I knew they would take their role as guardians seriously, and you risk offending them if you think they don't. But they wanted their boy to have a grandfather figure, so they come over once a week for dinner. If you stay for two days, you'll get to meet them…provided they agree, of course."

"Of course." Hades tried to conceal the wash of relief that flooded him.

"In the meantime, you can help rebuild Sherwood," Ethan told him. "Strong hands are valuable here."

And so the next two days were filled with hauling boards, hammering nails, clambering up trees and thatching roofs. Hades was a worker in high demand: he never needed to rest, replenished as he was by the energy of belief and love that still suffused Olympus at his victory over Kronos. For his part, he was almost grateful for the simple work, concentrating on tying bundles of thatch and setting the doors on their hinges.

The men around him worked from sunup to sundown. Toward the end of the day their feet dragged and their minds dulled, and he sent more than one down from the roof, too afraid the man would fall and find his way to the Underworld sooner than he ought. Though everyone went home when the day was done, they returned the next morning still exhausted.

After finishing one roof by lamplight, Hades came down and headed home, rubbing the ache from his hands and whistling softly as he approached the front door. But when he remarked upon it to his mother, he caught the strained look she shot his father. "The people of Sherwood have always worked from sunup to sundown," she said carefully. "But sunup is quite long these days. Except for the days where it's short."

Hades glanced at Ethan. "What's that supposed to mean?"

Ethan sighed and rubbed at one eye. "Might I suggest that you take the long way back to Etna, when you go home? See how the people of Olympus are faring for yourself. I take my duties to you quite seriously, but there's nothing like hearing the truth unfiltered, from the mouths of the common people."

Odd, thought Hades, and filed it away for later.

The afternoon he was to meet his son, Hades couldn't concentrate. He hammered his thumb when fixing a roofing tile, dropped his lunch in the dirt, and every time Raven asked him a question she had to repeat herself. Finally she gave him a light shove. "Go home and wash up," she said. "Even Titans sweat."

Hades scrubbed himself in the bath until his skin felt raw. As he combed his hair a strange stillness took hold of him. What if his son didn't want to see him at all? What if Terri and Gene were forcing him to come? Perhaps Hades should never have disturbed their peace. If Ethan said the boy was doing well, then the boy was doing well. Hades shouldn't confuse him by showing up, pretending to be another parent.

Then he thought of Persephone. The way her eyes had filled with longing as she talked of their son. The sorrow in her heart that she could not be reunited with him until he had lived a long and fulfilled life on Olympus, nurtured by other people. Hades had to meet with Achilles for her — for both of them.

Ethan knocked gently before opening his bedroom door. "They're here," he said.

Ethan led Hades not to their living room, but to the small office he'd used during his work with The Cross of the Iron Phoenix. Now he had an office in Sherwood's city hall, but the little room here was still stacked with books and papers. There was just enough space for a man and woman to stand on the fine wooden floor.

They both had olive skin and dark, curly hair. The man had a crooked nose and silver streaks in his trim beard, and kind blue eyes that filled with reverence as he bowed his head to Hades. Hades felt an accompanying swell of energy. The woman was as tall as her husband, with a strong frame obviously used to the hard labor of the forest. Her bow, a fine yew specimen, leaned against Ethan's desk. She bowed as well, her dark eyes full of emotion. Hades thought he saw reverence therein, but also worry.

Perhaps she thought he was here to take his son away again. While part of him mourned that he wouldn't, he sought to alleviate her fears as he ushered them both to rise. "My father tells me that your care for my son is exemplary," he began.

"We're doing our best," Gene said, eyes still averted.

"Your best is very good indeed. Will you tell me a little of his lessons?" Hades asked.

Gene swallowed. Raven had thoughtfully placed a tray of tea on the desk, and Hades poured a cup for each of them. As Gene took a cup his shoulders sagged a little and he even spared a smile. "He's a remarkable child with any weapon we put in his hand,"

Gene said. "He trains every morning for three or four hours. He's already bested his first teacher. Harper O'Donovan's been helping us, but he thinks that Achilles will have learned all he can teach in a few years or so."

Hades raised his eyebrows. "Impressive indeed," he murmured. Not one of his brothers had been able to reliably defeat Harper, even Atlas.

"We know that he is destined to be a leader of men, so in the afternoon he has quieter lessons," Terri added. "We help the neighbors with gardening and building so that he may learn what society — real society — is built on. We study history and language, and once a week we come here where Ethan teaches him of politics."

"And how does he do in these quieter lessons?" Hades asked.

"He is a kind boy," Terri said. "Sometimes impulsive, but his impulses are always toward generosity. And he's clever. Sometimes it's hard to keep up!" She laughed. "The neighbors love him. He's always at someone's house building something in exchange for cake or listening to the neighbors tell stories of the war. He loves to—" She stopped, and cleared her throat. "He loves to hear about his father."

Hades looked down at his tea and blinked until the tears were gone. "Most impressive," he said when he'd mastered himself. He looked up again. "I'm touched by the love that is obviously in your hearts," Hades said, for Terri and Gene were brimming with pride. "Thank you both, for your remarkable care."

Terri and Gene exchanged a surprised glance. "We are the ones who should be thanking you," Gene said. "For the honor of raising the boy."

"And for all the work you do to ensure the well-being of Olympus," Terri added.

They spoke for a few more minutes. Hades told them a little about his work in the Underworld, the vast silver world that awaited them, a respite from work and a space to relax. Death was so often an occasion for sorrow, but the Underworld should be a place of joy. He wasn't sure whether he imagined it or not, but he thought he saw the weight on Gene' brow lighten as he described it. They spoke a bit more of life up here, as well: Achilles had been hard at work building a dam for one of the Sherwood streams and repairing roofs after a flood. Another odd thing, Hades reflected, thinking back on Ethan's request. Flooding shouldn't be something that happened in Sherwood. Poseidon and Zeus should see to that.

When conversation petered out, Hades cleared his throat and asked the question he'd longed to ask since first entering the room. "May I...speak with him?"

"Of course," said Terri immediately, and Hades felt his body sag with relief.

Gene opened the study door. "Achilles," he called.

There was a pause, then the light patter of feet. Then a gangly silhouette stood in the doorway.

Achilles was astonishingly tall. Hades felt another swell of sorrow at the years that had slipped away without his notice. The boy shared his mother's raven-black hair and delicate nose, her pointed chin. But his eyes were all his father's, maroon and wide and somber. He was lanky like both his parents, but Hades could see the muscles of his arms under his tunic, a testament to his constant physical work. His face was bright with intelligence and curiosity.

Hades began to tremble. So much time lost, that the tiny infant he'd held in his arms had grown into such a boy. He dropped to his knees and felt hot tears slide down his face, flaking to ash as they cooled on his cheeks. Terri and Gene quietly slipped past him and out of the office, shutting the door behind him. He held out his arms.

Achilles came toward him slowly, confused. "Do you know who I am?" Hades asked, suddenly afraid.

"You're my father," Achilles replied. "The god of the Underworld."

"Yes," said Hades, joy washing through him. "I am."

Achilles stepped into the circle of his arms and Hades carefully embraced his son. The boy was obviously uncertain, confused. But slowly his arms came up and around Hades' back, drawing him close.

They stayed like that for many long moments. At last Hades broke away. "I'm told you're doing very well," he said softly.

"Mother and Father — I mean, Terri and Gene..." Achilles' face grew red.

"Please, they are your mother and your father," said Hades, recalling what Gaia had said to him. The words set his heart aglow with fresh pain, but he knew it was the right thing to say. "They are raising you, and they deserve the honor of those names."

"They say that I am going to be a great leader." Achilles

looked down and scratched at the floorboards with one toe. "That it's my destiny."

"And you're uncertain about that?" Hades smiled. Well he could remember such conversations with his own father. He hadn't learned of his specific destiny until he'd unlocked his powers, but Ethan had always spoken to him as though he'd had a grand purpose. It hadn't always been easy to believe.

"I suppose it is." Achilles sounded far from certain.

"Being one of the people is an important part of being a great leader." Hades put his hands on the boy's shoulders. "For now, I'm told you excel in all your lessons. Concentrate on them, and let everything else come. I will be with you in spirit, and I'll come to visit you as well. And you can always ask to see me, if you're not so certain about these lessons of yours." He smiled. "Would that be agreeable to you?"

Achilles nodded. "How often can you come?" he asked in a small voice.

Hades blinked back more tears. "I cannot be with you every day, but I will visit often. And —" he reached into his pocket. "I have something for you. A token from me...and your mother."

He drew out a necklace of shining obsidian beads. A small medallion hung in the middle, stamped with a golden bident spear. "Your mother is in the halls of the Underworld now," he said as he fastened the necklace about Achilles' neck. "She cannot come up to the land of the living, but she loves you beyond measure. And she and I will always be with you."

They stayed in the study until dinner, then went out to sit at the table with both their adoptive parents. Achilles, so somber in the study, became more relaxed and curious around the adults he knew well, helping to set the table and asking questions about everything in the stew Raven had been simmering all day. It filled Hades with a mix of pride and sorrow. His boy was growing well, but Hades would never truly know him as a son.

They ate, and chatted, and Achilles showed off some of his hand fighting forms in the middle of the room until Gene shook his head and declared it time to go home to bed.

Hades stood as well. "I will begin my walk home as well," he announced.

"It's dark," Raven protested.

"I wish to get to the boundaries of Sherwood by dawn," Hades explained. "Then, in the morning, I can begin visiting new places, as you recommended." He nodded to Ethan.

He knelt in front of Achilles again. The boy's hand went to his throat, touching the necklace. "We will be with you always," he reminded Achilles gently. "Be a good boy and listen to your parents." He was proud of himself for not stuttering at the word *parents.*

They put on their coats in silence. Then he shook Gene's hand and hugged Terri. He embraced Achilles one final time, and held back his tears until the family was at the end of the yard. Then he let them flow.

It was a time he had so longed for, the time to raise a child of his own. And now it was lost to him forever. He would miss so many moments that made fatherhood real — the long hours playing together, teaching Achilles the most valuable things in life, discussing problems and deep philosophical questions as his son asked them with a child's simplicity and wisdom. He would never have that.

But he still had his son. He might miss moments, but he must still be the best father he could. He could never forget that.

He couldn't bear to go back upstairs and say goodbye to his own father. He put on his coat and hat, and set out into the dark.

CHAPTER FOURTEEN: THE OLYMPIANS

Hades traveled through the night, stopping briefly to rest where Sherwood Forest gave way to plains and farmland. It was more to settle his mind than his body; since receiving power through prayers and belief, he was never empty of energy. After watching the birds build nests and the bees investigate spring flowers for a while, he got up and started walking again. He thought ruefully of what Persephone would say when he returned; he would be gone a lot longer than he'd promised. He'd have to make it up to her. But surely she understood that the duties of Olympus sometimes changed his best-laid plans. He watched a rain cloud drift across the sky without releasing itself on the field. He took off his hat and let the sun warm the back of his neck. Sun was one thing he missed about the Underworld.

As he walked the plain grew drier. The river that flowed from Sherwood toward Novaris grew lower and lower on its banks until it was reduced to a muddy trickle. The grass was dry and crunched underfoot, and the air smelled of dust. *The rain cloud that had drifted by earlier certainly could have been used here*, he thought.

He came upon a farm at the outskirts of the Market Place, a small merchant city where one could buy anything that existed on Olympus. Three thin sheep; he fished some apples out of his pack and was nearly stampeded by eager animals. The sheep let him pat their ears as they munched, then nosed at his pack for more.

As he retrieved more apples for them he saw a farmer in a long tunic come striding toward him. The farmer was frowning, but before Hades could apologize he called out, "Looking to buy? They make good wool, and acceptable meat. Though I'd stew it a good while, they're none of 'em lambs anymore."

"Why would you sell your flock?" Hades asked.

"I used to sell the wool." The farmer grimaced and picked at a tooth with his littlest finger, glaring up at the sun. "Had a beautiful flock. But we don't grow enough to feed 'em. Can't afford to buy grain, either. The crop's been failing over half the continent and prices are high. We've only got enough for the household, really."

That's not how it's supposed to be. "Mind if I take a look?" Hades asked.

The farmer's gaze swept up and down. "You don't look much like a man of the land, if you don't mind me saying. But if you want, I won't stop you. Especially if you take some of those sheep off my hands."

Hades walked the farm. It was dry, and the crops the farmer had managed to grow were withered and stunted. Not how it was supposed to be at all. The ground here had always been fertile, so what were Poseidon and Zeus doing? He sent the farmer back into the farmhouse to retrieve something, and while the man was gone he knelt in the soil. Planting his hands firmly, he sent a little shiver through the land.

The soil here should be richer now. He couldn't do much for this year's harvest, but next year's, hopefully, would be better.

The man came back, and Hades paid for the sheep with silver. The farmer stared. "What kind of fancy man are you?" he asked at last.

Hades patted him on the shoulder. "The kind who'll see what he can do for you and your family," he said. "By the way, did you...talk to anyone about this?"

"It's all anyone talks about," the farmer replied bitterly. "The sun stays high in the sky for hours, like it's noon for days straight. Drives us mad when we can't sleep. Then it goes down, and stays down, or it barely comes up before it's setting again." He shook his head. "When the Tyrant was around, taxes were high and you couldn't breathe the wrong word, but you could at least rely on the sun to come up."

Hades paled, and thanked the man, moving on. To be compared *unfavorably* with Kronos...he understood why Ethan had sent him out to walk.

By the time he entered the Market Place he was almost out of apples. People at the market eyed the sheep without much interest; Hades would have gladly sold them for less than he'd paid for them, but the creatures were rather sorry-looking and no one had the resources to pity-buy livestock.

The Market Place had always been bustling, if small. In the richer quarters, long avenues ran along storefronts and charming half-timber buildings where merchants could live and store their stock in the same building from which they sold it. Those who couldn't afford a building could rent a stall in one of the many long brick halls, and those who preferred the outdoors and didn't mind chancing the weather could set up in the winding alleys of the souk. Everything was divided by type of good: the livestock and butchery were in one neighborhood, while cloth goods and furniture took up another. Dry foods and household items sat in another quarter, and fruits and vegetables yet another.

Hades first wandered among the livestock, but when no one volunteered to buy his sheep he moved on. He spoke to the merchants as a curious and chatty buyer, and found that they all had the same problem: the market was virtually empty an hour after opening.

"Sometimes the sun only comes out for a couple of hours a day," said one merchant as he measured out nuts for Hades to eat on the road. "Nobody wants to do their shopping in the dark. So they rush to buy in the morning, and then they leave. It's a mess. I can't shift stock fast enough."

"And don't forget the robberies," said the woman next to him, who was trying to sell limes.

"Robberies?" Hades asked.

"Everyone's getting robbed, seems like. I have to keep my money on my person, all the time. If I'm here in the dark, someone could well be breaking into my rooms to see what I've got." He shrugged. "It's hard to blame them."

"*I* can blame them just fine," said the lime seller, her face as sour as her wares.

"Nobody's got money. Grain's so expensive we can't make bread. Though my nut flour's selling a treat." He held some up toward Hades.

"No, thank you," Hades replied. "It's terrible that people can't eat."

"Yes, well, some people also like to be hoodlums," grumbled the lime seller. "It's not all stealing to survive. And these long nights only help with that."

"I see. Thank you for telling me this," Hades said seriously.

"I'd like to be wherever you're from, that you don't know it," the nut seller replied.

"Soon enough." Hades gave him a bland smile, and gave a walnut to each of the sheep.

He kept walking. Everywhere he went it was the same. He elected to transport himself magically to Labyrinth City, checking in on Timotheus and the Minotaurs. Timotheus gave him grim news: the Minotaurs were doing worse than ever, unable to find work as there wasn't enough daylight to pay them proper wages. Merlin, sequestered in Centennial City, had the same reports. "We're working on some devices that can do certain household tasks," he said, gesturing around his workshop, which was strewn with both parts and students tinkering. "Washing your dishes for you, or your clothes, that sort of thing. If a device can do it, it won't matter whether it's day or night. But people have been complaining a lot, yes." He frowned. "I included this in my last report."

Which Hades had never received. He followed up this visit with a visit to Etna, where he spoke to Livia and the Centaurs. The constant fluctuations of daylight were affecting them, too — it was nearly impossible to hunt when daylight — walking animals never came out of their burrows. The Centaurs saw better in the light, and were struggling to feed themselves, much less cure the meat and pelts they sold to others.

Hades thought about leaving the sheep on the slopes of Etna, but when he caught a Dragon looking at them hungrily, he lost his nerve.

Instead, he transported them all to the slopes of Olympus. He was getting better at this magic; his head only slightly swam. The sheep bleated and glared at him, shaking their fuzzy heads.

He pulled off their rope harnesses and patted them on the heads. "Be free," he said. "I will know you when you reach the end of your lives, and you can be doted on by Persephone and get all the Underworld fruit you can eat."

Then he set off, up the smooth path to the top of the mountain.

He let himself in and headed first to the Chamber. Pressing his hand to his symbol, he let it flare. Golden words inscribed on the side of the little tower with the time and date of the requested meeting: *NOW*. Then he went off in search of his brother.

He found Zeus in his chambers. The room was dark, and he spotted the shape of his brother beneath the gray sheets on his bed. "Zeus," he said, voice hard.

A bit of lightning sparked over Zeus' head. He grunted.

"Zeus, get up. Meeting. Now."

Zeus grunted again and rolled over. "Hades?" He summoned a ball of lightning to act as a lamp as he peered at his brother. "What are you doing here? It's the middle of the night."

"It's not supposed to be." He heard the soft slap of footsteps in the foyer. Poseidon was here. "Come on. We have to talk."

###

Hades tried to be practical and factual about the situation. He spoke of the fast-traveling sun, the long nights that grew deeply cold, summoning frost that killed what crops survived the droughts. He spoke of the complaints of the merchants about crime and low sales, of the struggle the Centaurs and Minotaurs had in feeding themselves. "Merlin says he corresponded about this." He looked from Zeus to Poseidon.

"I correspond with my brethren of the sea," Poseidon reminded him. "I've received no note from Merlin."

"Me either," Zeus said, but his eyes shifted from side to side.

"Zeus," Hades warned.

"I...Maybe I forgot to check my mail sometimes. I've got a lot to do and it appears in a little drawer on my desk..."

Hades took a deep breath. Now was not the time to fight. They needed solutions. "Why don't you go get it, and we'll take a look together?" he suggested.

Zeus was turning red, his eyes flashing with anger and embarrassment. Hades kept himself calm until the door to the Chamber had clicked shut behind the one brother, then he turned to the other. "What's going on? I thought you two were working together."

"We are." Poseidon leaned back, spreading his arms. "We agreed that I would make the water and he would send the storms out around Olympus. I've been making exactly as much as I've been asked to make." He frowned and chewed on his lower lip. "Which means that if some areas aren't getting enough water, others are getting..."

"Too much," Hades finished for him.

The door opened behind them and Zeus staggered in under a mountain of messages.

He dropped them on the table. "I thought we were going to get updates only," he complained.

Hades started flicking through letters. "They are updates only," he realized. He could sort them into four different hands — Ethan, Merlin, Timotheus and Livia.

The letters told a dire story, of hard situations getting harder, of frustrated people asking for help.

"They could've come up and asked," grumbled Zeus as Poseidon read the fifth update from Labyrinth City aloud.

"No, they can't." Hades tried to keep his voice even. "No mortal can ascend Olympus."

"I know that," Zeus snapped, far too quick. "I just…forgot it for a second. Look, you can't give me the hardest job of the three and then dance back to your perfect Underworld palace and your perfect Underworld wife. You have all this support, and what have I got? A mountain and a pile of work to do, that never stops."

"You said you were ready for this role." Hades met his brother's eye and refused to look away. "Gaia told us how fragile the ecosystem is, and how it needs constant care. You said you could do it."

"Well, I didn't know what all of 'it' was, did I?" Zeus shoved his chair back and stood. Lightning appeared in both fists.

"Hey!" Poseidon stood, too. "Calm down." He folded his arms and glared at Zeus.

Zeus didn't sit, but he did extinguish the lightning. He glared at Hades.

"You're right. None of us knew how hard this would be. We all took on difficult tasks, and I don't think yours is the least difficult. But that's not what's important. What's important is, we made a promise to this world. We have to fulfill it. We can't have people wishing for the good old days of Kronos, can we?" Hades asked.

Zeus opened his mouth as if to answer, then worked it soundlessly for a few moments. Then he shut it. He took another deep breath. "No," he agreed. "We can't." He shook his head. "But both of you have others to help you remember what day it is, what has to be done. I'm by myself here. But I'm going to start by calling up the sun. And then —" He sniffed his armpit and made a face. "I'm going to take a bath. And then maybe…we can talk about how to fix this?"

His electric blue eyes were so earnest that Hades felt his anger melt away, just as when they were boys and Zeus had gotten himself into some sort of trouble with a Sherwood girl. "Go take a bath," he agreed. "You'll feel a lot better."

Zeus left them alone with a pile of messages and even more misgivings.

"He is the youngest of us," Poseidon said into the silence that followed. He ran a hand along his chin, down through his beard. "I noticed the days felt out of alignment, but I thought it was a matter of adjusting to life under the sea. I should have been paying better attention."

"As should I." Hades put his head in his hands. "I should have checked in on the both of you."

"That's not your job anymore, brother." Poseidon sounded amused. "Don't neglect your own kingdom through micromanaging ours."

It wouldn't solve the real problem, anyway. Zeus needed to be around other people. Hades could see it now — his little brother was lonely and depressed. He, too, was separated from his wife and son, but he had no one to help him with the demands of the day. Where Poseidon could receive human visitors, take comfort in the playing of his son and seek advice from Ivy, Zeus could only follow his own advice.

And, if Hades was being honest, Zeus' impulses had rarely led him to good places. He benefited from positive guidance, as did they all.

"I think even *we* need help," Hades decided. "I think this calls for a higher power than us."

"You mean —" Poseidon looked at him questioningly.

"Gaia." Hades put his hand on his summoning block. He'd never tried to send for his mother before. He wasn't sure this would work. But he closed his eyes anyway, and sent the request out into Olympus. *Gaia. We need you. Come.*

Then he opened his eyes, and they waited as the cosmos swirled above them. They waited as the first pink fingers of dawn touched down on the snow-clad mountain top around them. The pink washed away to gold as the sun rose over the edge of the world.

Sunlight was halfway down the mountain when Hades caught her scent: roses and moss, dirt and decay. All of life and death encapsulated in one woman. The Chamber door opened and she came in.

"My sons," she said, looking from one to the other with her rich eyes. "You call, and I come. How may I serve the masters of

Olympus?"

Hades and Poseidon exchanged looks. Poseidon dipped his head, urging Hades to speak, and Hades thought for a moment. "It is we who wish to serve," he said carefully. He noticed the way Gaia's eyes rested on the messages strewn about the table. "We are dedicated to ensuring that Olympus thrives. Yet we did not entirely understand the demands of the work when we set out to do it. The Keeping of the Underworld and the safeguarding of Kronos take up much of my time, and I don't dare spend too long away. Poseidon must take care of a kingdom of his own, and half of the one above the water. And Zeus…" Hades stopped, thinking.

"Is alone with the rest of it," Poseidon finished. Hades nodded to him.

"We want to surpass the legacy of Kronos," Hades said. "We don't want people to regret the way they supported us."

"And so what is it that you ask of me?" Gaia tilted her head. "Do you think I perhaps squirreled away a few more brothers?"

Hades laughed. Poseidon snorted. Even Gaia smiled at that. But then Poseidon's expression became thoughtful. "Well, what if you could help…make more of us?" he said.

"My childbearing days are long over," Gaia replied, causing Poseidon to blush. "No, my sons, there are no others like you. But perhaps I can do something to create others who can come and go from the mountain, who can do Zeus' bidding and focus on those tasks that would take up too much of his time." She tapped her finger to her lips. "I think I have the thing. Come. Let us call for your brother."

###

There was a gentle glow in Zeus' chamber. That was new: he didn't remember recalling the sun so soon after dawn. But the glow was different from sunlight — not harsh and directed from above, but suffusing everything around him in a green-gold wash.

His heart leapt. He recognized this glow.

He slid out of his bath and pulled on a shirt. Padding out of his room, he made his way down the elaborately carved hall, running his hands along the stormy motifs as he walked.

He knew she would be in the foyer before he even opened the door. Something about Gaia's presence called to him. Perhaps that of child to mother. He did not expect to see all the others.

His mother stood resplendent in an ivy green dress dotted with tiny blue flowers. Her blazing green eyes settled on him and a smile curved her lips. She held out her arms.

"Gaia!" He bowed, then hurried forward to embrace her. His mind swirled with confusion. Only the Titans could climb Mount Olympia — and Gaia, of course. And indeed his brothers stood off to the side. But there were several more figures milling about. "What…?" He straightened and tried to look as though he hadn't rolled out of bed a minute ago. "Who are these…people? To what do I owe the honor of your visit?"

"I have come to render assistance," Gaia said serenely. "It has come to my attention that the pressures of ruling the world are high, and it was unfair of me to lay such work at your door."

Come to my attention. Zeus' eyes flicked to Hades. Was he imagining things, or did his brother look slightly guilty?

"There is no shame in delegating your work," Gaia said. "And thus, I have created seven gods whose purpose is to assist you. Helios and Selene."

Two gods stepped forward. They looked like any other man and woman, except Zeus detected a faint glow about them. The man was tan-skinned, golden-haired, with amber eyes and a generous mouth above a strong chin. He had a runner's physique, lithe and strong, and the glow surrounding him was a gentle gold, like the hour before sunset. "This is Helios. He will shepherd the sun across the sky," Gaia said.

Gaia gestured to the woman next. She was much paler, with skin the color of porcelain and hair so pale it was nearly white. Her eyes were a light gray, her mouth thin and bloodless. "This is Selene, and she will do for the moon what her brother does for the sun."

Gaia presented the rest of the gods one by one. A young, curly-haired fellow with light red eyes was Eos, of the dawn. A tall, curvy woman with a proud face and a rich smile was Hera, goddess of marriage and fertility. Zeus felt a jolt somewhere in the vicinity of his stomach as he looked at her, but it was soured by his growing anger. He waited patiently as Gaia introduced a harvest goddess as golden as wheat, Demeter, and a god with dark skin and a blacksmith's apron, Hephaestus. Finally she bade a young god step forward, and introduced Hermes as a messenger and guard for Olympus. "To ensure that people feel safe, that the sun rises and the crops grow," she finished. "They are here to serve the planet, and to do your bidding."

Anger writhed in his gut. His mouth was dry. "So." He

swallowed. "You don't trust me to do anything that you asked of me. Why is that?"

"You are still the bringer of storms, which in turn bring life —" Gaia began.

"I told you I would handle it," Zeus snapped, this time to Hades. "You gave me what, a day?"

"Zeus, we were asking so much of you, and all we want is for you to succeed," Hades began.

"So you took all chances of success away from me and gave them to someone else." Lightning zapped from his hands and scorched the foyer floor in front of him. "This is so like you. You couldn't bear the idea that I'd get credit for doing something more impressive than you, so you made out like I couldn't do it at all."

"That's not what we were thinking," Poseidon began.

"You can stay out of this," Zeus barked, and his brother recoiled as though he'd been slapped. "All you've ever done is be duped by the golden child, the brother who can do everything, who's *smartest* and *wisest* and *best* and knows how to do everyone's job for them —"

"You were hurting people," Hades cut in. His voice was quiet, but firm, and years of listening to it shut Zeus up as effectively as if he'd shouted. "You didn't mean to, and you weren't doing anything directly to cause it. But that's just it, brother. You weren't doing anything. The people of Olympus needed more than the occasional storm. They needed concrete planning, which was never your strong suit."

"And it is yours," Zeus replied bitterly. "Like everything

212

else."

Hades took a deep breath, and Zeus thought he saw a flash of red-orange beneath his skin, like magma trying to break free. "I'm not perfect," he began.

"Tell that to the rest of Olympus." Zeus was snarling now, but he didn't care. His brother was the best brother, always. No matter how hard he worked, he would never get any credit. People offered it to Hades instead, and he was happy to take it. "Everyone thinks you're the only one who can save the world, so why don't you do it?"

Hades threw his arms in the air. His composure finally cracked. "I did do it," he yelled, smoke pouring from his mouth. The new gods took a step back in tandem, looking between themselves in alarm. "I found a solution to your laziness and your inability to focus on your task, the most important task you've ever been given. You've always tried to make up for lack of planning with power, and it doesn't work. If you'd stopped to think, maybe you'd keep the sun rising on time every day. If you'd stopped to think, we might have won the battle on Mount Etna instead of losing half our men. If you'd stopped to think, my *wife might be alive* —"

Poseidon put a hand on his brother's shoulder. There was a hiss of water meeting magma, and ash flaked off Hades' arm to the floor. Hades stopped, took a deep breath. He closed his maroon eyes. Zeus stared at him, agape. A bitter feeling, somewhere between triumph and resentment, churned in his belly. *He never forgave me.* It had all been a front. Was that why Hades was undermining him now? To make him pay?

Well, two could bring up the past. He forced his voice to soften. "All decisions have consequences, and that was a terrible consequence. It is true that I prefer to act, and sometimes acting means that things happen too swiftly to stop. But is it better than always hesitating? Waiting and waiting for a right moment that never comes? After all, when *you* ordered us not to take action, did Atlas not try to fix things alone? Did your mistakes not kill anyone, brother?"

Poseidon's eyes grew wide. He stepped back like he expected the fight to get physical. And maybe it would be better if it did, Zeus thought. He could use a little outlet for his anger.

Hades let out a breath that sent a swirl of hot air around the room. "You're right," he replied softly, and Zeus almost scoffed. *That's a first.* "Had I resolved to make plans when Atlas first pushed for us to act, we might have defeated Kronos with the power of four. A lot of people who died might have lived. There's not a day that goes by where I don't wish for a different outcome. But I can't spend every day wallowing in what I did, and what I should have done. I have to move forward. I have to concentrate on what's best for Olympus. Maybe it's not glamorous. Maybe it doesn't make us feel like all-powerful heroes. But it will make life easier for the people down there." He gestured. "Both in their life and their death."

He stood for a moment, thinking. Zeus wanted to bite back, but he found he was out of things to say. He hadn't expected Hades to admit fault. He'd always assumed his brother thought he was as perfect as the rest of Olympus thought him.

It was infuriating that Hades could be both perfect and

humble about it.

Hades turned. "Welcome to the family," he told the seven new Gods, who were currently staring at the ground and probably wishing they were anywhere else. "Thank you for the duties you will perform. Your services *will* be necessary." And with that he strode out, leaving lightning crackling anew between Zeus' fingertips. The utter audacity —

He felt a cool hand on his shoulder and turned his head. Poseidon stood before him now. His blue eyes were as calm as the deep ocean. For a moment they stared at each other.

"I don't want to hear it," Zeus said shortly. For Poseidon was obviously still on Hades' side. Everyone always was.

"Tough." Poseidon's grip on Zeus' shoulder tightened, and beneath the calm Zeus caught a steely resolve. "I will be leaving, too, but before I go, you will hear me out." He took a deep breath. "The decision to defeat Kronos was a collective one. You share equal credit for his capture, just as we share equal responsibility for everyone who died in our moments of failure. But we all make individual choices, too, and we cannot escape the consequences. You can't blame Hades for failing in your responsibilities here. You could always have asked for help yourself, you know. But you never thought about that, did you? You never wanted to face accountability."

He turned, then, and strode through the cluster of new Gods, letting the grand doors of the palace slam shut behind him.

CHAPTER FIFTEEN: TEMPTATION

Hades could be interfering and insufferable, but the sad fact of the matter was that he was also often right, Zeus reflected much later. With the new gods, things became simpler almost immediately.

Gaia had created quarters for each of them, expanding the foyer to include seven new corridors to seven lush suites. At Selene and Helios' request, Zeus put an adjoining door between their suites, so that they could visit each other without having to come back out into the foyer and down another hall. Re-molding the palace to his will was surprisingly easy. He also created a separate chamber, one with a large rectangular table where he could meet with all seven of his gods to discuss the business of Olympus.

His mood improved almost immediately as well. He woke with the first light of the sun, bathed and dressed himself and took his breakfast in the Lesser Chamber, as he'd taken to calling it, in time to see Eos clamber back up the mountain from his duties. Zeus watched Helios at work for a while, then as the other gods trickled in he took reports on the state of Olympus. Demeter, the goddess of the harvest, told him where things were going well and where extra water was needed. Hermes reported a dramatic fall in crime once the day and night cycles were evened out, and was able to carry messages from the leaders of Olympus straight to Zeus' breakfast plate. Hera was often there to counsel him on the content of the messages. He found her liquid brown eyes and long lashes almost impossible to look away from whenever she read over correspondence from the world below. But he could sometimes tear his gaze away, if only to let it wander down to her lush red lips, so inviting whenever they smiled, the rich curves of her body beneath her toga. Her hips swayed as she walked, and she moved with a grace that nearly took his breath away. He hadn't realized how lonely he'd been before the gods had come to Olympus. Sometimes, when he was feeling in a mood, he supposed he ultimately had Hades to thank for that — but mostly his moods were few and far between. There was simply so much work to be done, and so much lively conversation to be had. Selene and Helios gossiped every day when they returned from their work, laughing about what they'd seen out in the world — the little conflicts and clevernesses of humans, the trysts and lies they got themselves embroiled in. Zeus enjoyed listening to them and at the same time felt a pang of longing, that he might wander the world and experience it the way normal men did. The way he once had.

But there was something appealing in being here, too. He was part of a family again, and this family gave him his due. No one chastised him or told him his plans were without merit. No one cautioned him to consider one more time, to think before he acted. The advice they gave him was always steered toward making his plans work, rather than convincing him that they would never succeed. They showed him the respect that Hades and Poseidon — and even Ethan and Raven — had denied him. They were a bit like siblings and a bit like children, especially young Hermes and Eos. But some obviously wanted to be something more. Zeus could hardly miss the way golden Demeter draped herself across the table when he came in, letting her toga dip low to show off the swell of her breast, smiling knowingly whenever Selene spoke of young lovers meeting, hushed, by the light of the moon.

But Zeus did not want Demeter. She was beautiful, and whenever she touched him his body responded with an ache that was only natural. But he recognized the sort of longing he had for her. He'd had it many times in his youth. It was the desire to be wanted, the desire to inspire that sort of want in other people. It was the need for a fling, and he was mature enough now to understand that what he *really* needed was…love. Respect. The foundation of a life with a partner.

You have a partner, whispered a treacherous part of his mind. But when he lay in his bed at night, tossing and turning and thinking of a soft body next to his, he knew that he could not return to Leda. She was mortal, and could not abide on Mount Olympia. And his duties kept him here. Surely it would be better for her to take another husband of her own, and it would be better for him to take another wife. Surely she would not begrudge him this.

He could write to her, of course. Release her from any perceived duties and urge her to love again. But the thought of it struck his heart like a lightning bolt and set thunder rumbling over the whole of Mount Olympia. He would kill any man who tried to wed her. Perhaps it did not make him so perfect as Hades, but what did Hades know? He'd found a way to stay with his one true love. He was playing house in the Underworld while Zeus did all the real work above.

###

One day he was woken unexpectedly when the door to his suite was flung open.

"Hades?" he said groggily, and not a little grumpy. "Those little boxes were your idea, you might as well use them."

"It's me," came Hera's rich voice, for once not promising or gentle, but brisk and no-nonsense. A shiver traveled down his spine. Leda had been no-nonsense like that. "There's been an incident."

Good thing he hadn't jokingly asked if she was going to bring him breakfast in bed. He sat up and reached for his shirt. "What's going on?" Guilt flared up, followed by confusion. He'd read all his messages. The crops were good, crime was low…

"There's trouble from within Poseidon's realm. A fight that triggered a tidal wave. Labyrinth City is entirely flooded."

He felt it a moment later: a surge of panicked power. Prayers, as people begged him to help, to save them and their homes. "But I'm not the god of the sea," he said.

"Whatever your brother is doing, it is taking all his attention," Hera said. "I've already tried to call him."

"That's a bit presumptive, isn't it?" Zeus said. He was only half-joking.

"There was no time to waste. I hope you trust me." Hera was pulling on one of his coats, fastening it over her waist. She looked magnificent.

She looked like someone he should trust implicitly. "What do I do?"

Hera wound her curly brown hair around her head and secured it in a loose knot at the base of her skull. "Only you know what you can do, my lord." She looked up at him through her lashes as she said it.

Maybe it was the imminent danger, or maybe it was the shock of having a woman in his rooms for the first time since the palace was built, but Zeus felt the power ripple through him and knew he could do anything. And he wanted to do it for her. He grabbed her hand. "Let's go," he said.

Her lips curved. "Are you certain?" she said. She looked like she wanted him to say *yes*.

"There will be lives to save, and you are the goddess of family," Zeus replied. "I need you."

Her eyes flashed, and her fingers squeezed his. Zeus clenched his other fist and a cloud enveloped them.

A moment later they were above Labyrinth City.

The vast walled metropolis was a devastating sight. Water had flooded most of the alleys and streets. In the inner part of the labyrinth the water came up to people's knees and they waded through it, trying to put their valuables and their small children above the waterline. But the closer to the edge of the city, the higher the water was. It came up to men's chests, then their chins, then above their heads. Many bodies floated unmoving, their souls already departed for the realm of Hades.

"There will have to be some kind of answer for this," Zeus said, stricken.

Hera clutched his arm tightly; not a situation to which he objected. "Later," she said soothingly, and he knew she was right.

"For now, let us focus on the most important things. How do we get the water out?"

The drainage systems must be overwhelmed. Zeus didn't dare think about Timotheus and the Minotaurs in the bowels of the city. Instead he summoned a little whirlwind and sent it down into the center of Labyrinth, where the statue of his brother stood tall and proud in the central square.

The whirlwind turned into a waterspout. Zeus concentrated on it until he was certain it would obey his every thought, then began to maneuver it carefully through the street. It wobbled, wanting to collapse, but he kept his grip tight. He would have control of this power.

Someone looked up, and he felt the bloom of power that came with a little extra wonder. The waterspout stabilized and picked up speed. Carefully, with his other hand, he began to craft a second one to follow the first.

It was tricky work. Labyrinth City was full of tiny dead-ends and threading alleys that connected two parts of the city. He also had to maneuver around bodies that might still be alive, around houses and belongings. And as his waterspouts took on more and more water, they grew taller, reaching for the sky. Hera put a hand to her mouth.

"They're getting too large," she whispered.

"Never." Hopefully. But Zeus felt the familiar spark of needing to show off. And today, at least, he was showing off for a good reason. He drew the water gently toward him, and took Hera's hand. She was the goddess of family matters, and through her he twirled the water as though it were thread on a spindle, turning it light and fluffy until it added to their cloud.

"Oh!" Hera gasped.

Sweat slid down Zeus' temple. The work was finicky and difficult, but he couldn't dare drop his concentration, even for a moment. He shepherded the waterspouts through the streets of Labyrinth while simultaneously drawing water up into his cloud, until it sagged with promise and lightning crackled beneath his feet, ready to be used.

At long last the waterspouts reached the edge of the city. He pushed them out to sea with a strong gust, leaving the city itself in ankle-deep water. Below, thousands of faces turned up to watch the cloud in astonishment as Zeus ushered it toward the slopes of Etna, where it broke in a crack of thunder that knocked both him and Hera off their feet.

She landed on top of him, and over the sound of the rain he heard her laugh, delighted and astonished and relieved. "You did it!"

He caught her wrist as she tried to push off his chest. She looked up at him. Her body was warm and soft against his, and a mere inch of crackling air sat between their mouths. Water droplets beaded in her hair and on her toga like diamonds. Her hand splayed and rested against his chest, toying with the edge of his shirt. Every time her fingers came in contact with his bare skin, more lightning arced down to the mountain below. "I never doubted you," she said.

Zeus leaned up and kissed her.

They stayed on that cloud until the downpour had turned into a light patter and the roar of thunder had subsided. Then they returned, soaked and with their clothes in disarray, to find the whole of Olympia waiting for them.

"The story has gone twice around Olympus already," Hermes said as applause broke out around the foyer. "Zeus has saved an entire city!" He bowed low, and presented a letter stamped with the golden seal of the Mintaurs. "With the greatest thanks from Lord Timotheus, a leader of Olympus," he added with a flourish.

"We saw the whole thing," said Hellos and Selene in tandem. They'd left their satellites momentarily unattended to come down to him.

"It was mighty indeed," rumbled Hephaestos. Eos nodded, pink cheeks flushed as they always were.

"You must be exhausted." Demeter came forward, an accented sway in her hips and a promise in her eyes. "There must be something we can do to help you relax."

Her coy smile left no room for interpretation. But Zeus didn't care one whit for it. He squeezed Hera's hand, and the golden goddess' smile became fixed as she noticed. "We're fine," he said.

And he led Hera past them all, through his hallway to his suite, and he didn't care that they all saw.

###

Life on Mount Olympia became magnificent.

Zeus made a door between his suite and Hera's, so that she could come and go as she pleased, without all of the other gods knowing — and so could he. Hera's suite was cozy, with a blazing fire and a large table at which she could entertain guests. She enjoyed baking bread and the smell of her suite reminded Zeus, with a pang, of his mother's house. He could relax around Hera; she knew of the challenges of being a powerful God yet never doubted he could rise to them. She listened when he spoke, she came to him when he held out his arms. He could take her for walks in the lush gardens that sat on the ruins of Kronos' palace, or to the best, most secluded spots of Olympus from which they could gaze upon the stars together. He made love to her in most of these places as well, covering them with a blanket of fog to protect them from the prying eyes of Selene and Helios, and any mortals that might come along. The other gods didn't mind their new relationship at all — Hephaestus often nudged him knowingly, and even Demeter only sulked for a day or two before she was back to normal.

He took to getting up later and later, enjoying the time he spent in his bed with his new love, letting Hermes bring him the news of Olympus and letting Demeter tell him when he needed to send a storm to water the crops.

And then came the announcement.

He'd spent a joyful night riding the lightning, whipping up a storm that would hit the new continent and continue out to sea. It was his favorite sort of storm, unhindered by the need to be gentle or think of people's homes and crops. It raged across the Black Forest, tearing leaves off the trees and howling at the edges of Sherwood. He'd thoroughly enjoyed the exercise. And then he'd come home, pulled off his sodden clothes and opened the door to Hera's suite.

To find her with Hephaestus.

They sat next to each other at the table. Hephaestus was leaning over her, hand on her belly. They looked up in surprise at the sound of the door. Zeus thought he saw a flicker of guilt cross Hephaestus' face.

Cold, jealous anger curdled in his stomach. "What is this?"

Hera was startled, but recovered with her usual grace. "My love, I have great news." She brushed Hephaestus aside and stood.

"Does your news have anything to do with him?" Zeus growled. Hera looked confused; Hephaestus shook his dark head with something approaching panic. "Then what are you doing here? Why are you here, with my woman —" he started forward.

Hera caught his arm. "Everyone is welcome in my rooms. They always have been. This you know. I am the homemaker, the mother, the advisor. And I was advising Hephaestus on some matters."

"Of engineering?" Zeus sneered. He couldn't bear to look at Hera. He wanted to believe her, but the way she'd looked, glowing as if with a secret. And Hephaestus...what need did he have of laying hands on Zeus' woman?

"It was a matter of a technology that will have a great effect on the population, my Lord," Hephaestus hastened to explain. "A new way of washing —"

"Do I look like I care?" Zeus snarled. "Get out. *Get out.*"

Hephaestus scrambled for the door. It slammed behind him.

Hera looked at him reprovingly. But before she could say anything he rounded on her. "How many times has he been to 'visit'? How often have you done this to me?"

Hera sighed. "Done what, my love?"

"Made a fool of me. Betrayed me. How many times have you invited Hephaestus into your bed? And what about the others? Helios? Hermes?"

Hera shook her head in exasperation. "Zeus —"

"Answer me," he screamed.

She reeled away like he'd struck her. He stood, mouth gaping at his own outburst. Her eyes grew wide and brimmed with tears. Zeus' heart hardened. He was wise to the way of women who cried to get themselves out of trouble.

"I'm pregnant," she said.

The world stopped.

Zeus couldn't breathe.

"Hephaestus did come to me for advice. And I wanted his advice in turn. I'm having twins, Zeus, and he may need to attend the childbirth as the God with the best understanding of medical intervention. And he wanted to see if he could feel the babies, so he put his hand on my stomach." She reached out. "That's all."

Zeus swayed. "You're…twins?"

Hera cracked a smile, though it looked small and scared. "Twins," she replied softly.

"I…that's…" *Wonderful.* He should say wonderful. He had the chance to be a father again, to raise his children right this time. But…shouldn't he have been the first person she told? Shouldn't she have reserved the joyous news for the father? "Are they mine?"

Hera's fists clenched, and the tears came back. This time they were accompanied by a righteous anger. "How can you ask me that?"

"That's not a denial," Zeus realized with a growing cold fury.

"Yes, they're yours. Happy now?" she spat. "Of course they're yours. I've only spent every minute of every waking day with you, I don't see why that shouldn't be enough to convince you."

"Well, Hephaestus was looking very comfortable with your body," Zeus snarled back.

Hera picked up a clay bread bowl and hurled it at his head. Zeus put up a hand. A lightning bolt shot from his palm. The bowl shattered, scattering ceramic shards over the floor. For a long moment they both stared at the remains of the bowl, breathing hard.

"You threw that at me," Zeus said plaintively.

"Get out," Hera told him. "Get out, and don't come back until you're ready to grovel for my forgiveness."

His anger surged anew. *He* should grovel to *her*? She was the one who'd thrown a bowl at his head. She was the one who'd been caught in a compromising position. And she refused to apologize for it, refused to see things the way he saw them.

"With pleasure," he replied. Soon enough she'd be the one groveling, begging him to forgive her and take her back. He stalked through the adjoining door and slammed it. Then, with a motion, he wiped the door from existence. If Hera wanted him so badly, she could traipse through the halls of Olympus and let her shame be known to all the gods. He stomped over to his bed and flopped down.

But as his anger subsided, he started to wonder if Hera was right and he was wrong. He hadn't given her even a moment to explain; he'd simply been...unable to contain himself. Why? Why hadn't he trusted Hera? Of course she was the most desirable of the goddesses, but she had always been faithful to him, hadn't she? She'd traveled with him, advised him, respected him.

But there were plenty of missions he'd taken on his own. Plenty of opportunities for infidelity. Zeus clenched his fist. Yes, he was right to be angry.

Then he smacked his hand to his forehead. Of course he had no right to be angry. Hera had always taken him at his word. Why shouldn't he do the same?

But the evidence. Maybe he should let himself get caught in a compromising position. Let Hera see how that felt. See if she understood then. He stood, half prepared to do something stupid.

Then it really hit him. Twins.

And of course they were his. He'd spent every night with Hera since the flooding of Labyrinth City. It only made sense that she was pregnant. Twins. Little ones who would sit on his lap for storytime and toddle around Olympus. He could teach them to wield lightning and summon storms. He could teach them everything he knew about being a leader. He could even take them to visit their uncles. Hades, he thought magnanimously, would enjoy the sight of children playing in his dreary Underworld.

And yet...fatherhood. He had responsibility enough being in charge of all Olympus. Now he was supposed to take on the responsibility of being a parent?

He'd done it before, he tried to remind himself.

And you'll have Hera, said the voice in his mind. *If she'll have you, of course.*

If. Zeus swallowed. He really would have to grovel to her. He'd never groveled before. It sounded horrible. But there was no other way.

He strode over to his wall and made a door with a wave of his hand. Then he opened it. "Look, I —"

He stopped.

This was not Hera's suite.

It was a bright mossy field, dotted with little wildflowers. A hot spring bubbled in one corner, and a thick bed of straw was overlaid with a number of silk sheets. A tree hung over the bed, ripe with fruit. The scent of apple blossoms and roses drifted on the air.

At the edge of the hot spring stood Demeter, one hand at her shoulder. She'd been in the process of taking off her toga for a bath.

It was at this point Zeus remembered he was completely naked.

Her eyes traveled languorously down his body. Zeus felt himself react, stand taller and straighter so that she could take him in. A slow smile spread across her face. "To what do I owe the pleasure?"

"I, uh." Sensibility returned for a moment. "Wrong room."

"Is it?" She smoothed her golden hand down her arm, and the shoulder of the toga came with it. Zeus followed the movement of that hand with a sudden hunger. "You can open doors to wherever you want. Are you really telling me you don't want this?"

Zeus' mouth was dry. "Hera's having twins," he blurted.

"Is she, now?" Demeter seemed unphased by the news. "That sounds like a big step in your relationship. Why don't you come in, and we'll talk about it?" She stepped free from her toga and turned so that he could admire her form for a moment before she slipped into the hot springs.

Zeus followed her body all the way down, and the restless energy that churned in him, somewhere between anger and shame and jealousy, found a new outlet.

"Actually." He stepped inside and let the door close behind him. "I don't really feel like talking."

CHAPTER SIXTEEN: TANGLED DESIRES

It was the beginning of the end, though little did Zeus know it. He woke in a tangle of silk in Demeter's suite, smelling of fresh hay and grain and lazy summer sun, and stumbled back to his own room to bathe her scent off him. He closed the door behind him and vanished it as shame cast its deep shadow over him. What had he done?

It was Hera's fault. She'd given him reason to doubt. She'd made him angry. If she'd just apologized, recognized that she'd hurt him — but her pride and stubbornness had gotten in the way. Zeus slid further under the water.

Down here in the silence it was easier to admit that he was the stubborn and prideful one. He should be the one begging for forgiveness. But it…wasn't that simple. He had a reputation to maintain, and leaders didn't gain respect by appearing weak.

He wanted, suddenly, the advice of his brothers. They would sigh, like they always had when he'd had girl trouble back in Sherwood, but they'd never failed to steer him on the right course before. Hades would probably be insufferable, and Poseidon amused. Zeus splashed at the water above him.

At length he got up and got dressed, and made his way into the Lesser Chamber. Demeter lounged in a dress that sagged over one shoulder, showing off an expanse of smooth gold skin that made his mouth water. Her smile was too knowing, too inviting. Zeus couldn't bring himself to look at her.

Fortunately Hermes was also in the room. "Tell me, messenger," Zeus said in a voice he hoped was imposing. "What do they say on Olympus?"

"They say that Poseidon has blessed the coast with an abundance of fish," Hermes replied, flopping into a chair and kicking his feet up on the table as he reached for a bunch of grapes. "Fish as tall as a man are being pulled from the sea. And they say that Hades has been walking above, turning the volcanic stone to ash and rich soil."

"And how is dear older brother?" Zeus took an apple, relishing the crisp *snap* as he bit into it.

"He is melancholy, they say. For everywhere he goes above, he must go without his most beloved wife. Bards have begun to compose music about it. Some of the tunes are very catchy." Hermes hummed a little in his clear voice. It *was* catchy. Zeus smiled without humor. To think that his brother, the most awkward suitor on the planet, was now considered the ideal lover of Olympus…

Well, it was ironic. That was all. Zeus didn't need to be known for that sort of nonsense.

The door to the lesser chamber opened, and Hera came in.

Zeus' heart did a complicated flop at the sight of her. She was so lovely, so proud. Her strong chin was held high and she moved with grace and assurance, sitting between Hermes and Demeter. Zeus flushed anew as Demeter winked at him.

Zeus waited for her to speak. He found himself aching for her to act as though everything were normal, and last night's argument had never happened.

Her steady gaze met his. Her mouth thinned. She wasn't going to say anything, he realized. She wanted him to grovel. In front of other Gods, no less.

Forget it. He stood. "Lots of work today," he said gruffly. "Riding the lightning and whatnot. I'll be back late."

He could feel the stares of the three gods on his back as he turned and left the table.

Eos was sitting on the mountaintop as he came out of the palace. The boy sunned himself and waved to Helios as he urged the sun up toward the horizon. Selene sat next to him, glowing contentedly after a long night's work.

"A good evening?" he asked. He still couldn't quite bury the sting that came from looking at her and her brother. They'd been brought into existence as a direct counterpoint to his own shortcomings. Hard to forget, really.

"The people of Olympus set out candles for the Lord of the Dead," Selene said, and smiled. "It was a little like looking at a vast sky below me, filled with twinkling stars."

Charming enough, Zeus thought. "Why do they do this?" he asked.

"It is known that the great Lord of the Underworld sometimes walks Olympus. People beg the favor of a visit from him. They hope it will bestow wisdom, long life and good crops."

Zeus couldn't resist. "What do they say about me?"

Selene cocked her head. "I do not know. When the storms howl in the deep night, the people and their thoughts are obscured to me."

Maybe I should go find out for myself. Zeus had plenty of storming to do.

But first — his brother.

He rode a cloud down Mount Olympia and let it rain itself out over Lumina, landing on the other side of the Greenwood Forest where the trees met the salt sea. There he called out for his brother, summoning an impressive waterspout that caused nearby fishermen to scramble. He tossed a few dizzy fish into their boats as compensation. He could almost hear the tales they would whisper tonight. *The God of the Sky provides.*

He felt something shift as his waterspout took on life of its own — the water, which he didn't control, battling with the air he did. The spout whirled over to land and deposited Poseidon on the rocky beach.

He wore a swimming loincloth and held a trident in his hand. His beard and hair dripped with water, and Zeus thought he saw the faint outline of scales on his brother's calves that quickly disappeared into the skin. "You could have come the usual way," Poseidon pointed out.

"The usual way isn't as fun." Zeus waved at the fishermen.

Poseidon shook his head. Then he wrapped Zeus in a strong hug that smelled of seaweed. "Better such a greeting than no greeting at all. It's good to see you. How long has it been?"

Zeus shrugged. "We've all been busy." No need to remember the day of his shame, the day when it became clear his brothers didn't think he could do his job. In a way, he ought to be grateful to them. They'd given him his companions. They'd given him his Hera. But they'd also caused Demeter's existence, so in a way they were the cause of his current problems, too.

"Then what brings you to the shore, where our kingdoms meet? Especially when you could request a meeting from

Olympus," Poseidon said.

"I need advice," Zeus confessed. "It's a...delicate matter."

"A delicate matter requiring some privacy?" Poseidon guessed. He sighed and shook his head, flinging little droplets of water that glittered in the sun like diamonds. "You always had a natural eye for trouble, brother. Come." And with a sweep of his hand he parted the waves, creating a tunnel that led down, down into the dark blue deep.

###

Zeus still found Poseidon's underwater palace unnerving. He tried to ignore the press of the water as he gave Ivy a perfunctory kiss on the cheek, ruffled Maia and Perseus' hair, and followed Poseidon into his personal chambers.

The chambers were like a sort of beach themselves, with a bed, a desk and a table for Poseidon in his human element, and a smooth floor of black stone that led into the sea. Whatever held the water out made it look like a large window — a large window that Poseidon could walk through at will. It made Zues slightly ill to look at, so he sat with his back to the vastness and helped himself to a seaweed salad on Poseidon's table.

Zeus summarized his relationship with Hera, then the fight and the revelation of the pregnancy. Then he confessed to his mistaken night with Demeter. Poseidon listened through all of this without speaking, though he shook his head. When Zeus was finished speaking, he sighed and examined his own forkful of salad before speaking. "You regret what you have done."

"Terribly," Zeus agreed.

"But instead of trying to make it right, you came here. To me."

"I needed...I needed to clear my head. To speak with someone who might understand how difficult it is to do all this." He waved his hand around the room. "To be responsible for an entire realm. To be so powerful that only *I* can bring the rain that will keep people from famine. It puts pressure on me, don't you see? And I need to relieve that pressure *somehow,* and if I'm worried my most beloved confidante will betray me..."

Poseidon sighed and tilted his head. "How worried are you? That she's betrayed you?"

Zeus stared at him. "It drove me into the arms of another woman, Poseidon, I'd say I'm pretty damned worried."

"You had a moment of frustration and uncertainty," Poseidon said in a gentle voice he must have learned since becoming a father. "But you said you took Hera into your confidence. You trusted her with your heart, your fears, your desires. Did you have reason to doubt her, before now?"

"None," Zeus asserted.

"Then perhaps...perhaps it is not her you doubt." Poseidon rubbed his beard. "I have a story for you. My boy Perseus is strong, like his father and his uncles. He can defeat almost anyone with nothing more than a stick. He is fast with a sword and a staff and a trident. Only Ivy and Maia can out-shoot him with a bow. And Perseus is clever. He can remember everything I say and I only have to say it once. Yet when it came to teaching him the administration of a house, he balked. He said that writing letters was boring, that half the staff hated him, that the mermaids bore a grudge. None of it was true, of course." Poseidon flicked a hand. "But he was afraid. He worried that he couldn't be good at these things. Maybe because they didn't come as naturally to him as fighting did. My valet chastised him once for knocking a vase off a plinth in the hall and now he thinks she'll never forgive him for any other slight."

"You know I love my nephew," said Zeus drily, "but what does this have to do with me?"

Poseidon smiled. "You are worried. Because some things are difficult for you, you are worried that it means that you'll never succeed at them. What if you can't take care of Hera, or the relationship goes poorly? But if you sabotage it from the start, then you don't have to face up to doing your best and still failing."

Zeus was struck with a sudden bitterness. *Doing your best and still failing.* That was what he'd been doing on Olympia before the advent of the gods, wasn't it? Failing, without his brothers to babysit him. "So what's the solution?" he asked, trying to push the unwelcome feelings aside.

"You must build your relationship on trust, respect and loyalty. Be honest with Hera. Communicate about the best way to move forward. Dedicate yourself to the well being of your new wife and her children." Poseidon swallowed and looked down. "You've been given a second chance at love. I envy you that. Don't mess it up."

They were silent for a few long moments. "I didn't realize you and Leda...is she all right?" Poseidon asked.

"Oh, she's fine." Zeus winced internally at the lie. After he was finished here he'd go look in on her, he resolved. He'd wanted to walk the land like his brother, hadn't he? He would make sure that she really *was* doing fine. Maybe leave her a note, telling her to find a new husband. "But we…it doesn't exactly work, does it, if we can't ever live together?"

"I can imagine it's difficult." Poseidon smiled at him. "You've grown, Zeus. I know this is hard, but I'm proud of you. And Hera sees something wonderful in you. Show her that what she sees is the real you, not this foolishness with another Goddess." He turned stern. "And don't do it again."

"Yes, brother," Zeus said meekly, though part of him chafed at being treated like a child. And right after Poseidon had praised him for his maturity.

"Anyway, I'm afraid I must go." Poseidon stood. "There's been a territorial dispute between the pearl harvesters and the serpents of the deep, and they refuse to see reason. I'll have to ride in on a sea dragon and put the fear of, well, *me* into them." He smiled and shook his head. "To think we'd end up where we are…"

Zeus gave his brother one last hug and allowed one of Poseidon's servants to escort him out of the palace, in an air corridor that led up to the River of Life. He didn't breathe properly until he stood on solid ground, surrounded by sky. Then he inhaled deeply, and flopped onto the Riverbank.

He had to come clean. He had to explain it all to Hera and beg her forgiveness. What else was there to do?

Let it drift like silt to the bottom of the sea, he thought as a dragonfly buzzed lazily overhead. He could pretend the infidelity had never happened. He could pretend that all was well. Of course, he should still beg Hera's forgiveness, but she didn't have to know the full extent of his remorse.

Be honest, Poseidon had exhorted him. But surely he was being honest, if he didn't tell her a direct lie…if she asked him if he'd had an affair with Demeter, he would have no choice but to admit it. But if she didn't…

And *affair* wasn't really the right word for it anyway. It had been an indiscretion. A momentary lapse in judgment, like Poseidon had said. Surely a God had to cheat at least twice for it to be an affair.

Zeus looked at the sky. It was past noon; he'd been in Atlantis longer than he realized. It was too late to pay a visit to Hades today, with all the work he had. Well, what would Hades have to say that his other brother wouldn't? Probably a few more platitudes about loyalty and love and trust, and how could Zeus do this, and all sorts of recriminations from someone who'd never been parted with his soul mate for more than a week. Who didn't understand how utterly lonely Zeus had been.

Zeus let the afternoon sun finish drying his skin, then sat up and shook his head. It was time to deliver some rain, as he'd sworn to do today. He summoned a cloud and rose into the air. Too late he remembered his promise to himself, that he would check in on Leda. *After the day's work is done,* he promised himself. *If there's time.*

He toiled long, until Selene rolled the moon into the sky. He couldn't arrive on Leda's doorstep at night, he decided: she might take that as an invitation. Or a dire insult. He should go back to his rooms, and the rooms of his beloved. He would handle one crisis at a time, and Hera's was the more urgent one.

Hera half stood when Zeus flung open the door. This time she was thankfully alone. Zeus fell to his knees in front of her. "Please," he said. "Forgive me."

Her mouth pursed, but her deep eyes glinted with a hint of mirth. "And why should I do that?"

"I was stupid," Zeus confessed. "I didn't know what to think, and I was so worried about our relationship, and then you said we were having children...and I did something horrible and stupid."

Do it, the back of his mind urged him. *Confess.* But once his lips were closed, he couldn't bring himself to open them again. He pressed his face into Hera's belly instead, willing himself to feel the sparks of life there. "Please, forgive me," he said again.

"You really were an ass," she told him, but one hand slid through his pale blond hair and rested on his scalp, sending shivers down his body. "But I suppose surprises of that nature can do things to a man."

Her hand moved down to cup his cheek, then his chin. She steered it away from her belly and tilted it up toward her face. "Do you trust me?"

"Of course. I was...I was overcome by stupidity," Zeus said again. On a sudden impulse he asked, "Do you trust me?"

"With my body and my heart." Hera pulled him toward her and let him press his mouth to hers. He relished the softness of her against him, the faint yeasty scent of rising bread, the way her hair tangled in his fingers as he brought his hand around the back of her neck. He broke away and pulled her up, back toward the bed. "Now let's have no more talk of petty arguments. Let's talk of our children, and how wonderful they will be."

###

They spent long hours lounging in Hera's bed. First Zeus apologized to her with his body, and then they murmured about baby names and how they would combine their suites when the children were born. Hera, exhausted by her pregnancy, spoke softer and softer until the only answers she had to Zeus' questions were the soft exhales of sleep. Zeus tucked her in and pulled on his clothes. He was famished. Famished and, he had to admit, somewhat dissatisfied. Not long ago they'd made love for hours. Now he found himself recalling how exhausting Hercules had been in the first few months of his life. How much worse would it be with *two*?

He made his way to the lesser chamber and summoned himself some bread and olives. As he ate Hermes came back in with a pile of messages.

"Reports from the Olympus Leaders, my lord," Hermes said, giving him a short bow.

Zeus chewed his loaf and looked out over the window. Here the mountain sloped away in a sheer jagged face, and far below he spotted a doe and a buck in a playful mating chase. "And what say the people of Olympus?"

"Such tales fascinate me as well," came a rich voice from the door. Zeus nearly dropped his bread. Demeter. Just what he needed right now.

Of course, his stupid body had opinions about that, too. He rearranged his trousers. He was finished with such nonsense. He'd made one stupid mistake, and he didn't intend to make it again.

Luckily for him, Eos and Helios came into the room too. "Oh good, you're back," Helios said to Hermes. "Tell us another Sherwood tale."

Sherwood tale? Zeus smiled broadly. Tales of his exploits as a child were surely starting to whip around Olympus.

But Hermes launched into some story about Hades and Harper Donovan, and defeating a giant monster that ended up being a Minotaur in disguise. Zeus recognized the seeds of truth in it — Hades and Harper had once tried an ambitious operation against Typhon, who had some Minotaur-like physical qualities. But their plan had failed miserably, and had resulted in the Outlaws being disbanded for a short time as everyone lay low and Typhon scourged the land, looking for culprits. No one ever wanted to know the real stories about the Golden Child. How Typhon had terrified half of Sherwood after that little incident, burned gardens and threatened to hang whoever he met. No, now it was a fancy adventure, cleansed of all the unsavory parts.

He stood abruptly. Hermes stopped in the middle of his tale. "If you can't gossip somewhere else, I'm going to go read in peace," he said irritably.

Hermes leaned back in surprise. "If you'd like us to stop —"

"You can do what you like," Zeus snapped. "Your nattering is giving me a headache."

He took his basket of bread and olives in one hand, the pile of missives in the other. He shouldn't really care, he knew. So what if people were spreading glorious lies about Hades and his young adventures? So what if Zeus' own stories weren't quite so widespread? It was petty to be angry about it.

This only served to make Zeus feel worse.

He went back to his suite and sat at his white marble table. He took a moment to savor the peace: a blessed lack of gossipy voices, with his only company the gentle music of thunder over his bed. Then he got to work.

The missives were boring. So boring they almost put him to sleep. But if he could finish them, then perhaps he could spend all morning in bed tomorrow, holding Hera, talking of their future.

It was still a terrifying prospect.

The door opened with a creak. "Is it you, my pet?" he called absently as he tried to parse out some of Merlin's incomprehensible babble. "If it's not, piss off."

"I'm not sure how to answer that," said the voice as golden as wheat.

Zeus clenched his teeth and let his head fall back. "When have I ever called you my pet?" he asked. "I'm busy. This is hard work."

"Hard work that's making you tense, I see." Demeter came around behind his chair. She was wearing a silk robe, so pale he could see the shape of her body beneath. Zeus swallowed. Her fingers pressed into his neck, working at the tense knots of his shoulder.

"You really…should go," he said, even as he sagged against

her. "This isn't happening again."

"Why not?" She sounded amused. The room filled with a faint scent of fresh hay and spring flowers.

"Hera's having twins," he said again.

"That didn't stop you last night."

"Things were...I wasn't..." Zeus stopped. He pushed her hands off his shoulders and stood. He didn't have to explain himself to her. "I'm loyal to Hera. There are rules."

He turned to face her, and wished he hadn't. She'd untied her robe and let it fall open, revealing her perfect body. As his eye traced over her form his body remembered every single place he'd touched, everywhere he'd kissed, and all the places she'd touched him in return. He was slammed by a desire so powerful he nearly fell back into the table.

Demeter laughed. "You are the king of the Gods. You make the rules, my lord. Where is it a rule that one man is tied to one woman?"

"Um. Olympus?"

"Olympus is down there." She waved a hand. "We are above that."

She stepped in. Her finger curled around the waistband of his trousers.

"Find another god," he gasped. "If all you want is a lover."

"That is not all I want." She stepped backward, pulling him by that finger at his waistband, and he was powerless to pull away. "Hephaestus is a bore. Eos and Helios are children. Hermes is flighty and gossipy and immature. I know my worth, and I would have a God who is worthy of me."

She'd reached his bed, and now she fell back. Thunder rumbled ominously. Zeus tumbled forward and brought his arms down to stop him from falling face first into Demeter. She wrapped her legs around his waist and pulled him closer. Her fingers moved up, pulling at the fabric of his shirt and trailing fire wherever they met his skin.

He pulled the shirt impatiently over his head. His body was taking over, now, reveling in the lithe form before him as some part of his mind screamed at him to think, to pull away from this. "I love her," he gasped as Demeter's hands went to his belt.

She paused and tilted her head to smile at him. Her hair was splayed out around her like a corona. "Go to her, then. But I think if she could satisfy your needs, you'd be with her now. I'd have opened the door on an empty suite."

Her calf curled around his thigh as his trousers fell to the floor. "It's your choice," she whispered.

He was a god. He had rules. He could do as he wished. He bore responsibilities to others.

He thought of what Poseidon would say. Then he thought of what Hades would say.

Then he clapped his hands, and thunder rolled, and all the doors in his room locked and disappeared, ensuring that no one would find them until he chose for them to be found.

CHAPTER SEVENTEEN: SEEDS OF JEALOUSY

"I'm pregnant." Demeter paced back and forth on the floor of Zeus' suite. Her wheat-gold hair was a tangle and her eyes were red-rimmed.

Zeus dropped his pen. He'd been trying to compose a letter when she came in, congratulating Merlin on some ingenious solution he'd had for a problem with excess rainwater in Lumina. "Impossible." This must be a ploy to get attention. As Hera's time with the twins neared, he was spending more and more effort on her, and Demeter must be getting jealous. He'd even begun merging their suites, complete with rooms for the children, a room for nursing, and a playroom.

For a long time, every day he'd resolved anew to spurn Demeter, to reject her next advance and tell her to find satisfaction with Hephaestus or some mortal man. And every night Hera had retired exhausted, leaving Zeus up and alone and bored. He was beginning to learn that being bored was very bad for him.

After a few months he'd given up on deceiving himself. Instead he'd built a separate office, one with a table and a shelf and a bed on which he could theoretically rest. The bed was used almost nightly, and never for rest.

His brother's reproving voices echoed in his mind. *What did you think would happen? This is what you get when you betray others' trust.* But was Demeter not also to blame? She knew he was in a relationship. And she'd been the one to tell him that as the King of the Gods, he should make the rules. Was she so wrong about that?

"How can you be sure?" he asked.

Demeter gave him a look that plainly said she thought him very stupid for asking. "I'm sure." She pressed her belly. "Soon everyone else will know, too. I suspect I'm eight or ten weeks along."

Zeus let his head fall back and put his hands over his face. "How did this happen?"

He felt her arms on either shoulder, forcing his hands apart. "You know exactly how this happened," she said grimly. He hated how excited his body got at the nearness of her. "I thought I was being careful, but…" She pushed off him and began to pace again.

"Well, claim a mortal father for the child," Zeus said.

"I can't. She'll clearly be born a God, and the child of Gods. Half-mortal children can't survive on Olympia."

"Go down to Olympus, then," he barked.

Demeter stopped. She looked at him, lip curling. "I have work to do here. And I will not abandon my child to be raised by strangers."

"What are your brilliant ideas, then?" he grated. "We agreed that Hera should know nothing of this."

"Believe me, I have no wish to incite her wrath. I don't see why it has to be anyone's business at all who the father is." Demeter tossed her golden head. "If anyone asks, tell them you don't know and you don't care. And I'll tell them to mind their own business."

"Fine." Zeus picked up his wine glass. "If that's all, you can go. I've work to do." Though he had little inclination to do it.

Demeter flounced out. Zeus squeezed the wine glass until it shattered, watching the shards of glass bite into his skin. He should really talk to his brothers. How long had it been since they'd met in the Chamber? *It's not your duty to call for them,* he reminded himself. He had aides and helpers galore, plenty of people to solve his problems thanks to Hades' meddling. If Hades or Poseidon struggled, nothing stopped them from calling a meeting themselves. Except, apparently, being perfect and never struggling at all.

He couldn't ask Poseidon for advice, considering how he'd ignored it last time. His brother would probably tell him that this was all his fault. Which it was, but that was the last thing Zeus wanted to hear right now. It also didn't solve the problem of how to get *out* of this situation.

Maybe he could send Demeter on a mission. If there were some sort of catastrophic crop failure — something that meant she had to be away for a long time — he could work on devising a more permanent solution to her little pregnancy. And who knew? Maybe she'd find love of her own on Olympus. Maybe she'd marry some strapping farmer and spend her nights pinning *him* to the bed —

Zeus shook off the jealousy that coiled like a snake in his belly, and started to pace. Yes, get her out of the way. Making a disaster of such caliber would take all of his power, and keeping it a secret from the gods would take all of his cunning. His blood began to race. It had been a while since he'd taken on a true challenge.

###

"I don't understand how this could have happened." Hermes' normally earnest face was crumpled in confusion as he set his satchel down on the table in the lesser chamber. "Mass crop failure over the whole planet?"

Thanks to an abundance of saltwater, carefully siphoned off the coast and out of tidepools and other places where Poseidon wouldn't notice. It had taken Zeus several weeks, working twelve or fourteen hours a day and under the cover of clouds, so that Selene and Helios wouldn't realize what he was up to. He was exhausted, but cheerful. Now he tried to let his exhausted side show as he started opening messages. They were one and the same: letters begging for aid, explaining the situation in heartbroken and confused terms. Words like *famine* and *disaster* liberally sprinkled the pages.

"There could be many reasons. Perhaps Poseidon allowed part of Olympus to flood while he was dealing with another one of his underwater tiffs. Or it could be that Hades was too busy acting the lover boy in the Underworld to ensure that volcanic eruptions gave us a continuous supply of fertile soil." He sighed. "Or a combination of the two."

"The people love Hades," Hermes objected, fiddling with the strap of his helmet.

"That's nice," Zeus replied shortly. "It doesn't mean he's doing his job."

He diligently opened every note. Then he shoved the pile into the middle of the table. The rest of the gods gathered as he worked; Hermes had called them all to discuss this state of emergency. Hera stood with her hands pressed to her back, her stomach sagging with the weight of her twins. Hephaestus was soot-streaked and sweaty from working his forge; he looked confused. Helios and Eos sat to either side of Hermes and even Selene had come down for the meeting, leaving the moon to wander alone for a few short hours.

And Demeter sat there, of course. With her hands folded over her belly, which had not yet begun to swell. Watching Zeus with narrowed eyes.

"Perhaps I could devise something to test the soil and determine the root of the problem," rumbled Hephaestus.

"Excellent plan. Do that. I will call my brothers to the Chamber and see if they have any possible explanation for this. Hera, do what you can to protect the families affected. Demeter, I need you on the ground. See what you can make grow from field to field. Even a single stalk of wheat is better than nothing."

"I am to be sent away?" she asked silkily.

"The fate of countless Olympians depends upon you," Zeus said.

She glared at him for a few long moments. She even opened her mouth, and he thought for a heart-wrenching second that she was going to reveal everything.

Instead, she stood. "I'd better not waste time." She glided toward the door of the Lesser Chamber.

Zeus wrapped up the meeting and headed for the Chamber, careful to walk with purpose until he was alone in the carved hallway that led to the Chamber itself. Then he allowed the spring back in his step. With any luck, Demeter would be gone for *months*.

###

"Push," he breathed, gripping Hera's hand tightly.

She opened her eyes long enough to fix him with a fiery glare. "Don't tell me what to do!"

Hephaestus put his hand between her legs and a moment later Zeus heard the raw squalling of a newborn. With care, Hephaestus swaddled the baby and handed it up to his father. "A boy," he said.

The boy had a thick head of light hair, like his father. His eyes were shut tight, his mouth wide open as he howled. A tremble took over Zeus' body.

The most perfect little boy.

"You…" He let his finger run along one soft cheek.

The girl followed soon after, as though her brother had shown her the way. Her hair was dark and fine like her mother's. Hephaestus put them both on a machine that measured their weight and length, then clipped their umbilical cords and presented them to Hera. She lay back against Zeus' bed, propped up by pillows of the softest cloud, and put one baby to each breast.

"They appear—" Hephaestus began.

"They're perfectly healthy," Hera replied. "I should know." She turned to look at Zeus, and her soft smile brought tears to his eyes. "And they're perfectly perfect, aren't they?"

"They're incredible," Zeus told her. He put his head on her

shoulder and looked down at the greedily sucking infants. "You're incredible."

He couldn't believe he'd almost ruined everything. He had to find some way to make it up to Hera, even though she didn't know. He had to find some way to prevent Demeter from ever coming back.

"What shall we call them?" he asked.

Hera stroked the boy's head. "Apollo." Then she traced the tiny shell of the girl's ear. "Nyx."

"Apollo and Nyx," Zeus repeated reverentially. Then, in a burst of joy, he hurled a ball of lightning up into the sky. It burst like fireworks, spreading across Olympus in a display that no one could miss. Thunder boomed. Electricity danced.

"Zeus." Hera smacked him. "You'll wake the babies." For they'd fallen asleep on her chest, milk dribbling from the corners of their mouths.

"Sorry," he whispered. But the children slept on, unbothered by the storm. It was their legacy, after all.

Zeus altered his rhythm to suit the twins. Each morning he received messages on the crop disaster, sorting through mail as Hermes told the others of the latest news. Often it included the most recent fictions of Hades' adventures on Olympus. Zeus didn't mind his brother's fame anymore, and even found himself chortling at the stories that were obviously untrue, or stories that Hades would be terribly embarrassed to hear.

Then he would go out, summoning storms and giving Olympus her rain. Sometimes he started a small wildfire, which had the double benefit of clearing the land and of giving Demeter more work to do. He ensured that they never crossed paths. This was exactly what he needed. A long break to forget her. When she returned he would be utterly immune to her charms. His new family gave him everything he needed — for after work he came home and played with the children while Hera got some rest. Apollo was endlessly curious. He learned to crawl first, and started to take everything off the table, delighting in the crash of fruit and bowls and cups on the floor. Nyx was a little more cautious. She watched her brother endlessly, and only ever copied his movements when he'd learned how to do something more precisely. They babbled unceasingly to each other, and to Zeus.

In the evenings Hera put them to bed while Zeus did a little evening storm-driving. He took any last-minute messages Hermes had for him, then joined his wife in bed, falling asleep to the gentle sounds of baby snores from the adjoining rooms of their suite.

It was too good to last.

Zeus was in the Lesser Chamber, going over the morning's mail with Hermes. Hermes looked up as the door opened behind Zeus. His mouth fell open.

Zeus turned. The golden glow at the edge of his vision told him everything he needed to know, and his heart sank into his knot-filled belly.

Demeter was even more golden than she'd been when she left, bolstered and revived through the prayers of reverential farmers. Her hair rippled in a fine sheet down her back. Her eyes were rich and cold. But what had caused Hermes' mouth to fall open was the child slung across her breast.

The child was light haired and blue eyed, staring at them with open curiosity. She sneezed. A tiny ball of lightning flew from her nose and set fire to the sling. Demeter, obviously used to such things, swatted it out.

She looked around the table. Selene, Eos and Hermes were frozen in shock. Zeus himself could barely dare to breathe.

"Well? I'm back."

###

"I can't *believe* you!" Zeus ducked as another pillow came his way. At least Hera hadn't yet resorted to throwing crockery, he thought as he dodged behind the bed.

"Hera, think of the children," he said.

"*I am*," she growled.

Things had only gone downhill since Demeter's return. Before Zeus had had the chance to spirit Demeter away somewhere, Hera had brought the children in for the morning meeting — only to see that Demeter's child, who she called Athena, looked more like Apollo than Nyx did. Helios, Hermes and Selene had quickly found somewhere else to be as the rage gathered around Hera.

Demeter, for her part, had been unflinching and unapologetic. "There's no point in denying it now," she'd said. "What's done is done, and the child is unquestionably yours. I won't go into voluntary exile to protect you. I finished my duties and now I have returned."

"It was but once," Zeus begged Hera now. "When you made me so angry with your little tete-a-tete with Hephaestus —"

"There was no tete-a-tete." Hera picked up a jug of water, as though considering throwing that at him too. Instead, she took a long drink, then smacked it back down on the table. "And that was long before she got pregnant. I'm not stupid, Zeus. I just had children of my own. Athena's not older than four months."

"Uh."

Hera stalked toward him. "How many times did you sleep with her while I carried your children?"

"Once, I promise," he tried again. "I must have gotten confused..."

"Try again," she said, falsely sweet.

"Once or twice, then. I was always working, I needed release and you were so tired from being pregnant..." He spread his hands. "I was trying to help?"

She seemed to shimmer with anger. No, she really *was* shimmering. Her fist came down on his bed, and there was such an enormous crack that he looked up to the clouds on the ceiling for the answer. They were nearly black, but silent. The bed, on the other hand, had cratered in the middle. Hera had broken it clean in two.

"*How dare you,*" she hissed. "How dare you betray me? And as if that wasn't bad enough, you can't even take responsibility for the child you brought into this world."

That stung. Zeus loved being a father, and despite the utter storm Demeter had stirred up when she'd returned, he'd wanted to sweep Athena into his arms the moment he'd seen her pudgy legs kicking out of the edges of her sling. "Listen, Demeter means nothing to me. But of course I care for Athena. We can adopt her.

She can grow up with our children — don't you think Apollo and Nyx would like having a playmate?"

"Apollo and Nyx will go nowhere near her," snarled Hera. "And you will go nowhere near them."

At this, Zeus stopped trying to cower behind the bed. Demeter's voice rang out in his mind. He was the King of the Gods. No one gave him orders. "I'm their father, and you will not stop me," he boomed, and the black cloud over the bed broke in a downpour. It plastered his hair to his forehead, dripped down the side of Hera's face and made her dress cling to her skin. "I will not be ordered about," he continued. Lightning lashed down to the floor next to Hera's feet. She jumped back, and he saw real fear flash in her eyes.

No. This wasn't the way. He couldn't intimidate her into loving him again. He took a deep breath and, with effort, pulled the rain back, making the clouds fluffy and pale blue, dispersing them to the edges of the room.

Hera was shaking. He moved toward her, and she didn't step away — but the look in her eyes told him that he would be wise not to touch her. "Think of the children," he said softly. "They need both their parents. And they need their parents united. I have messed up, Hera. I know." He had to stop and swallow his emotion. His voice was softer when he continued. "I'll do anything to make it up to you. I'll never talk to Demeter again, I'll never leave this *room* without you by my side. But the children love me, and they must stay with me."

A muscle in her lower jaw twitched. The children *did* love him, and he knew she was thinking about that. She knew they didn't deserve to suffer for their father's mistakes.

"I don't care what you do in your own rooms," she said finally. "The children will stay with me, in mine. My own *personal* suite. You may knock on my front door to request time with them."

She moved away and began to gather up her things. Zeus felt her rearranging the structure of the palace itself, separating the half of the suite that contained the children's rooms, a rocking chair in which she nursed them, a craft table and a loom and her own wardrobe. Zeus was struck, suddenly, by a terrible solitude. "You're tearing our life apart?" he said. "Just like that?" Leaving him with nothing but a table and a pool and a broken bed?

Hera paused to look at him. "You tore our life apart," she said. "Long before I had any choice in the matter. I'm merely accepting your decision."

She closed her eyes, and the wall came up between them.

###

Zeus knew that Hera wanted that to be the end of things. Luckily for him, she still had a purpose and a calling on Olympia, and the children *did* love their father. He knocked on her suite every morning to fetch them and let her rest, taking them out to play in a courtyard he'd built in anticipation of the times they'd be able to hold a sword or start wrestling. He usually stopped to pick up Athena on the way. The twins hadn't yet understood their mother's anger; Apollo greeted Athena with his usual curiosity and tried to eat her shoulder. Nyx watched them interact with her serious eyes, then gently pushed Athena back into Zeus' lap.

While the children played, Hermes read out the relevant messages to Zeus. He kept his tone professional, courteous and bland — the best way to ensure Zeus didn't know what he was thinking. In fact, all the other Gods spoke to him with this sort of disinterested blandness. It was unnerving and irritating, especially when he heard them talking to each other. Then they managed to speak of other things than business, or beg Hermes for more gossip or tall tales from Olympus. His tone always took on new life as he obliged, and the effect was more potent than the slamming of a door in Zeus' face.

He kept his head down and worked. Each evening he took the children again. Sometimes he wouldn't even see their mothers outside of the times he picked them up or handed them back. Demeter seemed to think the whole affair had been a grand adventure, but one best finished. Zeus considered knocking on her door a few nights, especially in those first lonely months when Hera didn't even speak with him. But, he came to realize, he'd hardly conducted their affair. Demeter had always instigated it, and he'd let it happen. All his effort had gone to ensuring they weren't caught. Now, without her making overtures, Zeus didn't know how to approach her. In his darker moments it made him feel even more like scum: he didn't have the courage to be honest about his desires and feelings, just as he hadn't had the courage to be truthful or strong-willed.

He should introduce his children to his brothers. They deserved good uncles to play with them, surely. Yet Zeus couldn't figure out how to do it. He couldn't have them meet Apollo and

Nyx without having them meet Athena, too, and then they'd ask questions, and scold him, and let him contend with even more judgment. And Zeus was getting enough of that. Hera judged him constantly. The other gods never talked to him unless it was related to the running of Olympus, and never in more than that plain, disinterested tone. As he prowled the halls of his grand, white palace, he often caught them conversing quietly. They always fell silent as he passed, too. The two things couldn't be unrelated. The real question was, what were they gossiping about? Were they dissecting his disastrous personal relationships? Finding failing with everything he did to protect and shepherd Olympus? Calling him weak?

He wouldn't know unless he found some secret way to listen in on their conversation.

He couldn't ask Hephaestus for some sort of device, for the boring smith-god was clearly on their side, blustering and fixing his eyes to the floor whenever he spoke to Zeus. Zeus could, perhaps, approach Merlin…but the old wizard might tell Hermes or Hephaestus that Zeus' gadget was ready, and then he'd be in the same position. Besides, he was a God. He didn't need to rely on mortals to solve his problems.

In the end he used the palace walls themselves as his ears. He built one invisible door that led directly to Selene's chambers, and one that led to Helios'. These doors were hollow, pricked with tiny dots that could let the sound through without giving away that someone was listening on the other side.

But he never heard them plotting. They discussed the work of the day, how hard it had been to move the sun or moon with some prevailing wind, or how a volcanic eruption made for a beautiful sight from above. Maybe they talked while he was out at work — the moon and the sun did share the sky at times, and it would be the perfect place to discuss things. Fear and anger gripped his heart whenever he thought about it. He *knew* his Olympians were on the verge of some kind of mutiny.

One day, as he sat in the courtyard and helped Athena with her walking, he was shaken from a rare enjoyable reverie by Hermes' joyous laugh.

"Tell us," urged Selene.

"Tell us." Helios rolled his shoulders.

"Tell us!" Eos bounced on his toes.

"All right, this one's from a new leaflet. I don't know who prints them, but they come out of Centennial City. They're promising a new issue monthly. This one is called, "The Plight of Persephone. Ready?"

They nodded.

Hermes cleared his throat and began to read. "'Persephone was bright and beloved by all who knew her. Her lips were as red as pomegranate seeds, and her hair was as dark as obsidian. Her skin was as pale as the white deer and her eyes were so deep with knowledge and kindness that even complete strangers were drawn to tell her of their woes. The first time Hades saw those eyes, he thought he could fall into them forever.

'But pretty eyes can be dangerous in the realm of Kronos the Tyrant." Hermes paused here as the other gods nudged each other. Satisfied that they were suitably enraptured, he continued. "There was one creature in the land who was legendary for her eyes, and that was the chimera Medusa, a foul beast with a fair face, designed through dark magics by the Tyrant's scientists and unleashed upon the world to torture innocents and bring suffering to all who valued freedom."

Zeus tried not to roll his eyes. They were laying it on thick, for people who had probably never seen Medusa.

"As more and more heard of the beautiful eyes of Persephone, Medusa was overcome by jealousy. She groveled before her master and begged for him to allow her to be dispatched to Sherwood Forest, where Persephone lived in a humble spice wagon with her mother. Medusa spun lies of a girl who was the very heart of the resistance to Kronos. Kronos wasted no time in sending her away. 'No mere mortal woman shall be the cause of my downfall,' he uttered."

"You're right about that," Zeus said under his breath.

Hermes apparently didn't hear him. "And so Medusa set out. She strolled into Sherwood by night, creeping along the stone paths, withering the plants that came into contact with her feet and hands and snapping birds out of the air with the rapacious snakes she wore instead of hair. She came upon the wagon, upon the woman and the girl inside it. Seizing Persephone by the shoulders, Medusa shook her awake. As the beautiful Persephone opened her eyes, Medusa hissed: "How dare you think you can outshine me. You will be punished for daring to be more beautiful than the most beautiful creation on Olympus!"

Persephone's scream died on her lips and she turned to stone, right there in her bed."

Zeus snorted, loud enough that the others looked over at him.

"But we know that's not how she died," Selene said. "She was…" Selene stopped and anger jolted through Zeus like lightning. So the people of Olympus spread plenty of lies about Hades that made him look good, but everyone knew how Zeus had failed his brother's wife. And, no doubt, they judged him for his impulsive mistake just as Hades did.

"I'm still reading the story. Shut up," Hermes took a drink of water, held up the pamphlet, and continued. "The next morning Persephone's mother found her in her bed. Her screams of anguish could be heard throughout all of Sherwood. And brave, bold Hades, walking the paths of the forest and thinking deep thoughts, recognized such pain in that voice at once. He ran toward the source of that cry, and when he came upon the little spice stall he understood at once what had happened. He fell to his knees, and tears of fire flowed down his face.

"When he found he had no more tears to give, Hades went into the little wagon. He took Persephone's mother's hand, and looked upon his beloved. They were not yet wed, mostly because Persephone's mother did not want to lose her daughter to a new home. But Hades took Persephone's cold marble face between his hands, and he kissed her one last time, to say goodbye.

"Medusa's curse was said to be unbreakable. Once stone, the people we love are no more than statues. But such was the power of Hades, such was *his* devotion, that his kiss warmed her lips and sent the flush of life through her skin. Her hair turned black, her eyes slowly blinked. She took his hand as she sat up. At that moment, overcome by joy and emotion, Hades asked her to marry him. Persephone agreed, and her mother joyously gave her assent. And thus they were joined in eternity."

Zeus laughed. He didn't like how it came out, bitter and angry, but he couldn't help himself. "What utter rubbish. Who's printing that?"

He reached for it, but Hermes twitched it out of the way. "Just some creative-minded people in Centennial City," he said defensively.

"It's not even close to being true. Medusa never cared about Persephone, never got jealous of her eyes, of all features. And I promise you, once that chimera killed someone, they *were* dead. No one could bring them back to life."

"The story's about the power of true love —" began Helios.

"True love? What did true love get my other brother, when his bride was turned to stone? Do you think he'd enjoy reading that?" Zeus flicked a lightning bolt and the pamphlet tore from Hermes' hand, igniting in the air and burning to ash like a sacrifice. "And why are you so obsessed with Hades, anyway? He didn't do half the things your stories claim he did."

"I…" Hermes looked between the other Olympians for support. "I thought it was a fun activity…"

"You're wrong. It's grating, it's boring and I won't hear it."

"You're just angry because everyone on Olympus is talking about Hades, and not you," snapped Helios.

Zeus froze. Then he gently untangled his other hand from Athena's, and stood. "Excuse me?" he said dangerously.

"You never want to hear them. You roll your eyes and scoff and tell us at length how untrue they are. But the most important parts are true. Like Hades' love for Persephone. No one's ever going to accuse *you* of loving someone so much you could bring them back from the dead."

The sky above them crashed with thunder, so abrupt and so loud that everyone in the courtyard jumped. Lightning snapped from cloud to cloud, then down into Zeus, playing over his fingers and turning his eyes into beacons of white fire.

Everyone stared at him for a moment.

Then Athena burst into tears.

Children first. Zeus breathed deep and dispersed the lightning, sending a long tongue of it across the courtyard toward Helios. He was gratified to see the young God jump back. Color was high in Helios' cheeks, his breath short. Zeus scooped up Athena and held out his arms to Apollo and Nyx, who came toddling over as fast as their little legs could carry them and threw themselves into his arms.

"Watch what you say," he told Helios softly. "You know nothing of the truth. You didn't even exist back then." And stories could be manipulated, *were* being manipulated, every day. Hermes' lying pamphlet was proof of that.

Speaking of — he turned to fix Hermes with his steely gaze. Hermes flinched. "We don't need such lies spreading across Olympus," he snapped. "Don't bring me any more stories of my brother and his so-called heroics. You can tell true stories, or no stories at all."

"But…" Hermes licked his lips. "Like you said, we didn't live through all these times…how am I supposed to know which stories about Hades are true?"

"Good point. Don't tell any of them," Zeus said.

He turned to take the children inside. They needed calm, and to be calm for them he needed to leave these prattling fools behind.

"You can't order us not to talk about something," Helios called after him.

"I'm the King of the Gods. Try me," Zeus snarled, and stalked away.

CHAPTER EIGHTEEN: SNAPPED

Late that night, as Zeus sat in his suite, he finally heard something worth listening to from Selene's room.

"I've just come home, and I'm tired," she groused, and Zeus checked his water clock. Was it truly so late? "What's so important?"

"You know what's so important. We can't ignore this anymore." Helios' muffled voice was agitated. "He's gone unhinged. Telling us we can't even listen to stories? And what about what Demeter said?"

Zeus felt his blood run cold. He snuck over to the door, pressing his ear against it.

"Demeter isn't innocent in all this. She could have some hidden agenda," said Selene.

"But her story makes sense. No one could figure out how famine could strike all of Olympus at once. Even Poseidon and Hades were completely flummoxed. But then Demeter says that there's seawater on everything…and Poseidon had nothing to do with that."

"So he says," said Selene.

"And do we have any reason not to believe him?"

"Zeus is the King of the Gods," Selene reminded him. Zeus heard a thud as she put something heavy down on the table. "His obligation is to take care of all the creatures of Olympus. To knowingly inflict famine upon them, just so he could send his lover away…"

"Would be a horrific breach of duty," finished Helios.

"Which would make it even more serious if it were true."

Heat began to boil up in Zeus. How dare they accuse him of such things? How dare Demeter betray him? She'd sworn not to tell Hera and then she'd flounced back to Olympia with a baby that was as damning a statement as saying it out loud — and now, nobody even saw his attempts to make it right? Everything he did, he did to protect Olympia, to ensure that Olympus could be properly governed. But it wasn't enough for them, was it? Nothing would ever be enough, because it would never live up to the nonsense legends of his brother.

Before he fully realized what he was doing, he'd stood and pushed open the door to Selene's chamber.

Selene's chamber was pale and cold, like the moon itself. A single, simple bed lay in the corner, and a pale table held a bowl of fruit and a jug of water. Selene glowed here like a star, and her brother's golden shine was more pronounced under a dark ceiling littered with pinpricks of light.

The two gods turned at the sound of the door. Selene's mouth fell open. Helios stumbled back.

"Instead of endlessly speculating, why don't you ask me any questions you have?" Zeus said. His voice was soft. Dangerous. Energy hummed through him, looking to ground on something.

Helios and Selene glanced at each other. Selene shook her head fractionally, but Helios squared his shoulders and turned back to Zeus. "Did you do it? Did you cause a famine on purpose, in order to send Demeter away?"

Zeus scoffed. "Of course not. Did she tell you that?"

Helios' lip curled. He obviously didn't believe Zeus. "But you sent her away to disguise her pregnancy."

"Demeter has a job to do, like the rest of you," Zeus reminded him. His tone was genial, casual. He spotted a spark of fear behind Helios' eyes, and it bolstered him. He was still in charge, and Helios knew it. "She's covering up her own failings by making up some story. And since you're all so eager to despise me, I guess it's an easy story to believe. Do you understand how difficult it would be to cause mass crop failure on the level we'd seen, if the crops were truly healthy? Is it not easier to believe that Demeter let her duties lapse, and then ran from the consequences?"

Selene looked at her brother. "Maybe," she said, and nudged him.

But Helios didn't want to back down. "No. I see Demeter walking the fields each day. She's always been dedicated to her job. But you're too busy chasing women around, then dealing with the children they bring you afterward."

Zeus' mirth evaporated. "Watch your tongue," he snarled, stepping forward. Lightning fizzled between his fingers.

"You have to be reminded to do everything. Hermes brings you messages, Hera tells you how to answer them. Eos brings the dawn, I bring the day and Selene brings the night. All you're in charge of is making sure it rains, and Demeter even tells you when you're supposed to do that! You like being called the King of the Gods, but what makes you king? I could be king if it were as little work as you make it out to be."

Zeus threw back his head and laughed. Here, at last, was the truth. It wasn't about safeguarding Olympus at all. "So you want to be king?" he said, his voice dropping to a low purr.

"I didn't say that." Helios took another step back. His eyes flickered nervously toward Selene, then to the table on his other side. Zeus wondered if he'd start throwing fruit in a moment. "I merely doubted that you earned the title."

"You little brat," growled Zeus. "I have worked harder and lost more than you can dream of. I earned this title through defeating the Tyrant."

"Three of you defeated the Tyrant," Helios scoffed. "How am I to know how big a part you played? Hades also —"

"Hades would never have been able to defeat Kronos without *me*," Zeus snarled. "If he had half my power, he'd be the one up here on Olympia." Rather than slinking around the Underworld, presiding over souls that needed nothing more than a few pretty trappings for their afterlife.

"If you had half his leadership, Olympus wouldn't be in complete disarray," Helios shouted. Suddenly he was in Zeus' face. He put his hands on Zeus' chest and shoved him back toward the door. "You can't even stop to think of the consequences of your actions, you're so busy running from them! Your famine *killed people,* all so that you could pretend you were faithful! Hades would never have done that."

Zeus shoved him right back, so hard that he flew into the table. Helios gasped as his back slammed against the edge. Selene covered her mouth, holding in a small scream. "If you love Hades so much, perhaps you should go down to the underworld and live with him," he said.

"Or maybe Hades should come up here and sort out your mess," Helios said as he staggered to his feet.

"Please," Selene tried. "Let's talk about this in the morning."

Helios shook his head. "I have nothing more to say to you. Tomorrow I will call upon the other Titans. I will beg an audience with them, and I'll see you unthroned."

"Unthroned?" Zeus laughed darkly, though there was nothing to laugh about. "This is my realm. You're here by my grace. I could end you in an instant." To prove his point he snapped his fingers, and all the doors out of the suite disappeared.

Selene looked around, eyes widening in terror. He could feel her pushing back, trying to make a door, but he was stronger than she was and could thwart her at every turn.

Helios' face twisted. "Let us out," he said.

Zeus laughed again. "No." *Now let's see who has the power here.*

"Please, Zeus, he didn't mean anything by it," Selene said.

"I did. I'm going to call the other Titans and tell them what a mess you've made of things."

"And how will you do that, when you can't even get out of this room?" Zeus mocked.

"You'll slip up eventually. You'll stop paying attention. You'll be so busy chasing some skirt or trying to get out of one of your other obligations, you'll forget about us. And then we'll be free."

Zeus snapped out, lightning-quick, and grabbed Selene. She shrieked. "Well, then," he said, pinning her wrists in one hand. "I'll simply have to make sure you can't get free."

"Let her go!" Helios raised a fist.

Zeus snorted and turned to the wall. Now, where would be

the best place to chain her?

He heard the scrape of Helios picking the jug up from the table. Zeus shoved Selene against the wall, hard, and turned in time to bring his arm up. The jug crashed against it, clay shattering over the floor. Pain sliced through his arm like the bite of a sword.

Red rage filled his vision. Lightning flickered over his eyes and thunder boomed outside. He dropped Selene and took one large step, wrapping his hand around Helios' throat. Lightning crackled along his arms, shivering over the sun god's body as he lifted Helios off the ground. "How dare you!" he howled. "How dare you defy me! How dare you threaten me!"

Helios kicked wildly. His fingernails clawed at Zeus' arm, leaving deep grooves in the skin. Zeus squeezed harder. "You will obey," he shouted, shaking Helios wildly. The god's body shook like a rag doll. His golden curls rose from his head to stick straight out. "You will obey!"

A tremendous bolt of lightning burst from his chest and struck Helios squarely. He spasmed, and the scent of burning hair filled the air. Then his feet went limp. His hands slid away from Zeus' arm. Zeus kept squeezing, though, as Helios turned paler and paler, from tan to white to blue. Zeus realized suddenly that his skin was ice-cold to the touch, and he no longer glowed with the gentle light of the sun.

Zeus forced his fingers to open. Helios fell, lifeless, to the floor.

No, he thought. *No, no.* Helios was supposed to obey him. He wasn't supposed to die.

There was a soft snuffling from behind.

Selene stood against the wall, hands over her mouth, struggling to breathe. She stared wide-eyed at her brother's body. Then at Zeus. Tears dripped from her eyes like fat pearls.

"No," she gasped.

Then she turned to run.

His anger turned on again, like flipping the switch on one of Merlin's infernal contraptions. He lunged for her — she couldn't get away, she couldn't reveal what she'd seen tonight — and his fingers tangled in her hair. He made a fist and yanked. Selene screamed as she fell backward, and Zeus released her so that she could hit the floor head first. Without thinking, Zeus brought his foot down on her throat.

Her eyes bugged almost comically. Then life fled them as well.

CHAPTER NINETEEN: THE WEIGHT OF DECEIT

For a long time Zeus sat in a room with no doors, staring at nothing.

Outside he heard the howl of the storm, the physical manifestation of the emotions that tore through his mind. But encasing all that was a feeling of numbness. Once more, he'd done something terrible, something he couldn't come back from. Once more, he had to figure out how to deal with it.

Seal up the room, he thought at first. He could leave and seal up the last door behind him. But someone clever might be able to make a door back in…

Focus. What had Ethan taught him about getting rid of tiresome cronies, back in the days of the Cross? Zeus had to stop for a moment as a fresh burst of pain, sharp as a knife, lanced through his heart. What would his father say to this? His lapses in judgment were understandable. His struggle to rule was more a matter of administration than moral failing. But murder?

No one could ever know.

The first step was to get rid of the bodies. Zeus took a few more breaths, listening to the wild wind howl. Then he turned to where Helios lay on the floor.

To where he *had* lain. For no body was there. Zeus' eyes widened in shock, and his heart thundered. Had someone already come in and discovered him? No, he would have heard it. Moving a body was never a quiet thing.

And Helios wasn't entirely gone. Instead of his body, a small pile of ash lay, slowly flaking away as if taking flight on some wind that only it could harness. Zeus knelt next to the pile. He took a bit of ash in his hands. It was soft, fine as dust.

Something glinted beneath the ash. Zeus scraped it away, revealing gold beneath the gray until he was able to pick up a small round stone that fit neatly in his closed fist. It was warm to the touch, like a rock that had spent all day in the sun, and glowed like the last light of the afternoon.

Selene had become a little pile of ashes, too. Hidden within was a pale pearl, as large as the sun stone, that radiated a light as cold as the moon.

They felt heavy in his hands. They felt...powerful. The essence of gods, captured in simple stones. He hefted them, and thought. Then he slipped them into his pocket. These stones would make a fitting present for his twins, his legitimate children and gods in their own right. And now all he had to do to get rid of the bodies was find a small broom and dustpan, and sweep up the ashes. A quick splash of water on the floor and even he couldn't tell where Helios and Selene had once lay. The only evidence of a fight was the broken water jug, and Zeus could easily dispose of that.

So you've gotten away with murder, he thought, and panic stabbed at him again. What was he supposed to do now? Where was he supposed to turn? More than anything he needed guidance, yet he could not seek it from anyone he knew.

Well, there was one person he should have trusted and confided in from the start. Zeus rubbed at his chin, feeling the prickle of stubble. Hera had the wisest counsel of all the gods. Surely she would not turn him away in his hour of deepest need.

###

"What are you doing here?" Hera sounded more confused than angry as Zeus stepped into her chambers. He hadn't knocked. "The children are fast asleep."

"I'm not here for the children. I need you." He sat on the edge of her bed. He'd forgotten how beautiful she was when rumpled from sleep, with her hair a tangle and her toga falling over one shoulder. He'd forgotten how she smelled of fresh bread and home.

She pulled it up self-consciously. "Zeus, you've been wonderful with the children. But our time together is over."

Don't say that, he wanted to beg. "I need your help with something else," he made himself say instead.

He confessed it plainly: how angry Helios and Selene had made him and how he'd tried to stop Helios from running to his brother. How he'd killed him instead, and then Selene. "I didn't mean to. You have to believe me."

Hera was pressed against the head of the bed. "I believe you," she said in a small voice, eyes wide.

"It was their fault for making me so angry. They were threatening to take it all away…and now, if Hades realizes what I've done, he *will* take it." Zeus' voice hardened as he fully understood. Had that been Helios' plan all along? Had he agreed to sacrifice himself, to entrap Zeus so that Hades had an excuse to take over? "What do I do?" he asked her, reaching for her hand.

She drew back. Zeus clenched his fist, snarling. "What must I do to make you *believe* me?"

"Nothing. I do believe you." Her breath was quick, and her fingers brushed over his knuckles, prying his fist apart. For a few long seconds they sat, joined loosely by the touch of their fingertips. When Zeus met her eyes, he saw that a war raged within them. She was still angry with him, yes, but she knew he relied upon her counsel. And when all of Olympus relied upon him…

"You must tell the truth, Zeus," she said gently.

"Impossible." He shoved away from the bed.

"One day it will come to light, and when it does —"

"Why?" Who's going to tell? Helios and Selene are gone, and the only other people who know about it are you and me." He started to pace. "Will you betray me?" The one person he thought he could rely on — could he not rely on her at all?

"Of course not." She slid out of the bed and came over to him, taking his arm. "But what if someone looks into it?"

"And what will they find? Nothing! There are no bodies, nothing but —" he stopped short of showing her the stones. "Anyway, there's nothing to be found. They could have gone anywhere. They could have run to the Underworld to be safe with Hades."

"We, too, can enter the Underworld," Hera reminded him. "It would be easy work to find that they are not there."

"Well, maybe they're not there because something else happened to them!" Zeus started to pace again. *Yes.* He could feel a desperate idea taking shape in his brain. "Someone else could have killed them, after all."

Hera let her head fall to the side. "Like who?" Her skepticism was evident in her voice.

Zeus stopped again. *Yes.* The plan fizzed in his gut. The way to take care of all his problems at once. "Like Hades."

Yes. People would stop hailing Hades as the great hero of Olympus if they knew what he was really capable of. And Zeus had no doubt he was capable of it — Hades had killed countless of Kronos' followers, far more than Zeus ever had. In fact, he wouldn't be surprised if they clamored to lock the gates of the Underworld and keep the Lord of the Dead out forever. And wouldn't that make sense? What need did Hades have of walking the world? Why did he need to act like he owned it?

Hera rubbed her lips together. Then she cautiously said, "You'll have a hard time convincing people that he's done it. And if Hades himself refutes you? Would it not be better to be honest now, rather than caught in dishonesty later?"

"*No.*" She still didn't understand. "That...we can find a solution for that. I know how to make doors and dismantle them—maybe I can do something to the entrance to the underworld. It's hardly safe, anyway, mortals can wander down and accidentally die any time they like."

If he could close the door, he could keep Hades from coming up again. It would be challenging, but there were many master wizards on Olympus that might be able to lend their skill to such an endeavor.

"Zeus..." Hera said.

He spun toward her. He didn't want to know what she was

going to say next. He couldn't bear it if she kicked him out now, or refused to abide by his plan. "Please come back to me." He seized her by the shoulders and she stiffened. "Hera, please. You're the only one I can trust. And you know you can trust me. Look at how I've been with the children. Am I not good to you? Would anyone else take care of you so well, if I were sent away? Do the children deserve to be without a father?"

"I..." Her tongue darted out over her lips. "You betrayed me, Zeus."

"And how many times must I pay for that?" he thundered suddenly, overcome by frustration. He shook her.

"Zeus, please," she whispered. A tear glistened at the corner of her eye.

No. He couldn't do this. "I'm sorry," he whispered, and drew her into an embrace. She didn't resist, but she was stiff against him, still untrusting. "Please, I didn't mean to frighten you. But how can I do this alone? You must help me." His grip tightened at the barest thought of losing her. "Please."

Slowly her arms came up to his back. She began to stroke it gently, reassuringly. She took a deep breath and said, "I'm here."

She was here. Zeus could cry in relief. Her body was soft against his, comforting, reminding him inexorably of the long nights they used to share.

He pushed her gently towards the bed, and she did not resist.

###

Zeus struggled to sleep. The weight of what he'd done bore

down on him, and he watched dawn break and the sun come up, as always. *Seems like your job wasn't so hard,* he thought sourly at Helios.

He sat up. Hera rustled next to him. They were both naked, having succumbed to their passions at last, and the sight of her filled him with new hope. This wasn't the end. It was a hurdle, a small misstep to be rectified before he could reclaim the life he deserved.

"I must make an early journey to Olympus today," he said, touching her shoulder. Her eyes fluttered open.

Her perfect mouth pursed. She looked like she was going to try to dissuade him again. Then she said, "What happened to your hair?"

Zeus slid out of bed. His face had itched and prickled all night, and now he felt a fuzz when he touched it with his hand.

He went over to Hera's wardrobe. A mirror was fixed to the inside, and he stared at his reflection for many long moments.

His beautiful ice-gold hair had turned completely white.

A beard had sprouted up to complete the look; easily a few weeks' growth condensed into the space of a night.

Fresh fear gripped him. This had to have something to do with those blasted gods. Well, there were all sorts of reasons his hair might have gone white. He'd figure out a plausible explanation later. For now, he needed to focus on one thing: tying up the loose ends of the murders.

"It's rather charming, don't you think?" he said, falsely jovial. "Now, I hope you'll be all right with the children until I return." He reached for his clothes. His shirt stank of sweat.

Without thinking he created a door between his suite and Hera's. She bit her lip, looking at it. But she didn't tell him to remove it. *Yes.* Something fizzed in his belly. She really was taking him back.

"I'll be back as soon as I can." He stopped only to claim her mouth with his, pressing in, hard. She resisted for a moment, then yielded to him, parting her lips and slipping her hand around his neck.

He broke away regretfully. "Soon," he promised, and she smiled. Soon they would begin the process of repairing their relationship.

He spared her one final glance before going through the door into his suite. She looked afraid, sitting naked on the edge of the bed, her hands curled around her belly.

###

Zeus had forgotten how wondrous it was to walk among the wilds of his own world. He took himself to the River of Life and wandered its banks for a little while, contemplating at the base of Mount Etna what he had to do. Great Dragons winged overhead, on the lookout for stray goats that could become their supper.

It stung, he realized, that Hera wanted him to turn himself in. Yet he understood now that she was merely misguided in her care for him, that she wouldn't force the father of her children away.

Merlin would notice the change in appearance, so at the banks of the River of Life he stooped and picked up some mud. He ran it through his hair, transforming it as he did so. It flushed over each hair, turning it the deep brown of the mud banks. Not exactly his natural color, but no matter. He did the same for his beard. Looking out over the fields of Solara at the riot of wildflowers, Zeus felt a sort of peace come over him for the first time since he'd stormed into Selene's quarters. Things had been done that could not be undone. Yet he would persevere. He just had to think of the right way to convince Merlin of Hades' guilt, without the wizard calling on Hades himself.

He sat among the purple and red wildflowers for an hour or two, smoothing out his plans. Then he made his way to Centennial.

The bustling city was far from Zeus' favorite place. He preferred the mountains, or the forests, or anywhere that didn't have infernal contraptions screeching down the streets, liable to run people over at any moment.

"Combustion engines," Merlin explained when Zeus appeared in his workshop, complaining. If the wizard was surprised to see him, he didn't show it. "The latest contraption on Olympus. It will revolutionize travel. To what do we owe the pleasure of your company?"

"I would speak with you in private," said Zeus, and guided Merlin toward his office.

"All right. Carry on," he shouted to his assistant, who'd been drawing something that looked technical and horrid.

Merlin's office was crowded with books and models of things that were in some stage of development or other — he showed a model of a combustion engine, then two or three more things that Zeus couldn't really comprehend. There were only two chairs in the office, and Merlin had to remove a stack of books from one of them before Zeus sat down.

"You've changed your hair," Merlin said.

"The rigors of ruling." Zeus waved a hand. "And ruling has not been easy. Hades has been...well, have you seen him on his walks around Olympus?"

"He always stops in," Merlin said, nodding.

"He loves this world, as do we all. But his love has taken a somewhat unfortunate turn of late. He would come to Mount Olympia unannounced, with grand plans for this or that —"

"Innovation, always a good thing." Merlin started clearing a space on his desk to take notes.

"It frustrated the other Olympians. No one likes being told how to do their job. I know Demeter found him quite irritating. And when she refused to do as he asked, he caused a mass famine to teach her a lesson."

Merlin stopped and looked up, aghast. "No."

"I'm sure you felt the effects," Zeus said.

Merlin folded his hands over his robe and looked out of his window. He could see the entire workshop floor from here, where his wizards and students constructed everything from new ways of digging a well to contraptions that could fly. "Some of us are still feeling the effects," he admitted quietly. "Grain became impossible to find. Fruit withered on the tree and bush. Food was so expensive, I had to nearly double the pay of everyone in the factory — and even then, most of them had to choose between food and a place to live. People lived eight or ten to a house. Which meant that sometimes, when plague came, everyone got sick."

Zeus refused to let guilt prickle at his belly. Things were done, and they could not be undone. Borrowing from Helios' reasoning, he said, "How could the land have done so well and then failed so completely? And who had the most to gain from such a venture? Hades must have welcomed many more souls to the underworld while Demeter fought to bring the famine under control. But no one had the power to create such an event. No one except the Titans."

Merlin's hands shook. "It hardly bears believing," he whispered.

"There's more." Zeus leaned forward. "Two of my own gods, the gods of the sun and moon, they've watched him walk the land for years. They confronted him about his actions and, in a rage, he struck them down."

"Struck them...?" Merlin's mouth fell open.

Zeus pulled the stones from his pocket. "There's nothing left of them now but these." He filled his voice with thick sorrow. It wasn't so hard to do — he was sorry, really. "I came upon him as he sat between their bodies, and he fled before I could stop him. He's back in the Underworld, licking his wounds. I grieve to say it, but I think he should stay there. He is too dangerous to Olympus as a free agent."

Merlin stared at the stones, seeing nothing. "It sounds impossible."

"Yet it must be true," Zeus pressed. "Why would I bring you such information, if I did not believe it wholeheartedly myself? Something has gone to Hades' head. Maybe he's being corrupted by Kronos in his prison cell. Or maybe the defeat of Kronos made him think that he's more than a God, more than a Titan. All I know is that Olympus must be kept safe from him."

His voice trembled. Perfect. He knew he had Merlin.

"This is quite, quite serious. And I regret to say, there has been no discussion surrounding how to contain a Titan — aside from Kronos himself."

"Surely we can close the door to the Underworld," Zeus said. "Prevent us from getting in, and him from getting out."

Merlin stroked the end of his long nose. "We could," he said, but as he looked at Zeus the line between his brows deepened. He wasn't convinced.

He couldn't be allowed to contact Hades himself. "I am, simply put, terrified that he'll do it again." Zeus dropped his voice. "Merlin, I have children to think of atop that mountain." He needed to push gently. Thunder rumbled outside, an ominous symbol.

"Perhaps this is something that can be worked out in mediation," Merlin suggested.

A flush of terror fizzed through Zeus. "Mediation? We're speaking of murder here." He raised his voice dramatically, then dropped it, as though his emotions had gotten the better of him and he'd only just remembered to keep his voice down. "When Kronos murdered, we didn't stand by and do nothing." Merlin nodded at that, and he pressed his luck. "Listen. If Hades truly repents, let him come to you for mediation. He can still get in touch with me, with Poseidon. We will welcome him when he comes to his senses."

He could feel the plan slipping out of his control. He

swallowed and clenched his fist. No, he could do this. He would simply have to sabotage Poseidon's messaging system for Hades when he paid his brother a visit.

Everything was still fine.

"I do understand your desire for speed," Merlin admitted. "But I am simply...I am simply not certain I have the power to lock up a god."

"By yourself, no." Zeus smiled. "But you also have me. If we go, and we go now, between my might and the element of surprise, we can stop the world from suffering another tyrant."

He urged the old man to his feet. Merlin still looked shocked by the revelations, but he managed to compose himself enough to fetch his satchel and his son Harry, and follow Zeus out into the bustling blaze of Centennial.

Zeus swept them up onto his cloud and whisked them over land and sea. Harry and Merlin clutched at each other. "I think I'm going to be sick," Harry grunted.

Zeus set them all down at the edge of Mount Etna. It was no work at all to summon the black crevice that marked the gate to the Underworld. Zeus strode toward it and the crevice unfurled, lengthened. Stairs appeared in a glittering spiral that went down and down. "Surely it's a matter of keeping it shut tight," he said.

"Oh, yes, no matter at all," scoffed Merlin. His old self was reappearing now that he had a problem to solve. "And how does one do that? Especially if we presume that Hades will, at some point, attempt to come up again?"

"What about some sort of great magical thread that could stitch the land together?" Zeus said.

"He could cut through a spell like that with ease," Merlin replied.

"Perhaps we could put some kind of weight on it, so he can't move it?" said Harry.

Like the weight of the world, Zeus thought with a sudden chill. That was how Kronos had killed Atlas. Surely it could stop Hades as well.

He touched the stones in his pocket. What about the weight of the moon? That would be a fitting way indeed to trap the god who'd killed Selene.

It wasn't easy to get a stone of the right size. Merlin had to go into Etna and negotiate with the Dragons who were, as ever, disinterested in the plights of men. In exchange for some of his technical knowledge, however, they consented to break off a chunk of an eyrie and roll it down the mountain. From there, Merlin and Harry trimmed it to size. Merlin set binding enchantments on the crust of Olympus all around it, frowning as he worked and muttering to Harry, who noted everything down in a little notebook.

When they weren't watching, Zeus put one hand on the stone, and the other hand on the pearl in his pocket. Strange power coursed through him. The power of the moon. He splayed his hand and let the surface of the stone ripple over with pale veins that shimmered weakly in the sunlight. It was a slight difference, visible only if he turned his head at the right angle. He could feel the stone take on extra weight. The ground around it cracked.

Merlin spent hours pacing the perimeter of the now-blocked entrance, making tests and dictating his notes to Harry. Zeus couldn't understand half of it. He took a seat on the slopes of Etna and watched the mound that marked the entrance to the Underworld. His emotions were a tangle of thread within. He would never see his brother again — Hades, who'd led a revolution, who'd always supported him. Hades, who'd always been better at everything, apparently even ruling over Olympus when he had his own realm to take care of. Hades, who would judge him so terribly for everything he'd done that Zeus could never look him in the eye again.

"We'll need to do more tests," Merlin told him at last. "I'm not certain Hades couldn't get out if he wanted to, and of course we must ensure that souls can still reach their ultimate destination."

Yet Zeus found relief welling up within him. Hades should look to his own realm, rather than trying to interfere in the realm above. The stone would remind him of that. And Zeus, with Hera back at his side, could return Olympus to its rightful glory. It would flourish under his rule. He just needed to sort a few things out first.

"I hesitate to involve myself in the business of the gods," Merlin said cautiously, and Zeus brought himself back to the present. "But have you discussed this with your brother, Poseidon? He must know if one of his brothers is breaching the agreement between you."

"There hasn't been time," Zeus said easily. It was true, after all. "I felt that action should be taken swiftly."

Merlin dipped his head and stroked his long white beard. "If you will trouble me to offer some advice: treat it as a matter of utmost urgency. If Hades has somehow been...corrupted by the influence of Kronos in his realm, it may be up to the two of you to stop him."

"Do you really think that's possible?" Zeus rubbed his arms against a sudden chill.

Merlin made a wide gesture with his hands. "I've never held a powerful Titan in stasis before. Who knows what might happen? Perhaps, on the other hand, the answer is as simple as your brother has been swayed by power into foolish actions. He wouldn't be the first to do so, nor to succumb to the stresses of ruling."

"A plan is a fine idea," agreed Zeus. Talking to Poseidon would also cement his word as the first, and most important. It would be far more difficult for Hades to contradict him if Poseidon had believed in the treachery for a long time.

He shook Merlin's hand and thanked him once more for the assistance. Then he began to walk.

This plan might be so much folly. Merlin had said himself that he couldn't guarantee their barricade would keep Hades out. Zeus tried to reassure himself. He was the most powerful Olympian, perhaps the most powerful Titan. But Hades' strength must have grown while everyone told gushing stories about him across the land.

Another reason for him to stay locked up, Zeus thought grimly. No one should have such power. This barricade would be a test, to see if he really could be kept in check, or if Zeus and Poseidon had something to worry about.

And if he got out, and managed to convince everyone that he

was innocent of Helios and Selene's deaths? Zeus felt in his pocket for the comforting warmth of the stones. There was still no evidence that could trace the deaths back to him. Only these stones, which he could conveniently 'find' in his travels and bring home as gifts for his eldest children.

He walked, and he thought, pausing in the evening to make sure that the moon was coming out as it should. He'd woven a delicate web of deception, he couldn't deny that. But it would bring peace to Olympus, and so it must be woven. The ends justified the means.

He walked for some time, lost in his thoughts. Eventually he looked up to discover that his feet had brought him to the bustling Market Place between Sherwood and Novaris, the very spot in which the trio of Titans had captured Tom Ambrose and come up with their plan to defeat Kronos. He smiled at this, remembering the disguises he'd so carefully donned each day in order to follow Tom without being spotted. Now he pulled his cloak over his head, letting his darkened beard conceal the lower half of his face while the hood concealed his electric eyes.

Either Merlin had made some kind of announcement, or one of his assistants had been eavesdropping. Zeus heard whispers everywhere: "Helios and Selene, yes. By Hades himself," said a woman in hushed tones as she loaded a bag up with apples.

"Impossible," said the woman across from her, who was examining basil leaves with a frown. "Why in the world would he do such a thing?"

"No one knows. He's capable of great power, but no one's ever accused him of uncontrolled violence before," said the woman with the apples.

"They must have done something," said the woman with the basil.

Zeus ducked his head so that no one could see him scowling. Why were they so quick to give Hades a chance? A chance he never would have gotten?

The two women weren't the only ones. As he walked through the marketplace everybody was wondering *why*, and coming up with all sorts of excuses. Perhaps Helios and Selene were the violent ones, and Hades was defending himself. Perhaps he had a grander plan. Perhaps it was nothing more than rumor — after all, did the sun not shine?

That was me, Zeus wanted to scream. He kicked a wall to vent his frustration.

As he passed a blacksmith's stall, the smith tried to engage a youth who was looking at knives in conversation. "Do you really think he could have done it?"

The young man, a light brown fellow with broad shoulders and bright blue eyes, flipped the knife up, watching it spin up and then down before catching it. The muscles on his arms and legs were well-defined, and he smiled with an easy charm. "What does it matter?" he said. "The best we can hope for, from any Titan, is to be used and abandoned. Why should I care what Hades did or didn't do?"

"That's blasphemy there," the smith said, shocked.

Zeus was inclined to agree. But something about the boy held his attention. He looked self-assured and easy-going, despite his words. He shrugged, grinned and flipped the blacksmith a coin.

"What do you intend to hunt with that?" the blacksmith asked, skeptical.

The boy grinned at him. "Something that'll give me a challenge."

He set off. Zeus couldn't say why, but something about the boy told him to follow. As though it was his destiny. He kept his hood up to disguise his electric eyes and stayed at a distance.

It wasn't hard to follow the young man; he was half a head taller than most people in the market, and the crowd parted around him with a sort of deferential friendliness. He stopped on several occasions to talk to this old lady or that man, consent to getting his high cheeks pinched or to trying a piece of fruit from a stall. More than one young woman looked longingly after him, too.

He was chatting with a man at a skin stall when a voice made him look up.

A voice straight from Zeus' past.

"Hercules!" The voice's owner strode toward him. She was tall, too, with the boy's same high cheekbones. Her skin was much darker, though, and her eyes a deep brown that Zeus knew all too well. She'd braided and coiled her hair atop her head like a crown. Then again, she'd always borne herself like a queen.

Like his queen.

The queen he'd walked away from.

"The day draws on, Hercules," Leda said. "Let's go."

And, with no indication that she was aware of Zeus at all, she took their son by the hand and led him away.

TO BE CONTINUED.

About The Author

Joseph Bell hails from the quaint town of Pittsfield, Maine, where he grew up amidst the playful chaos of four younger brothers. Such an environment, rich with adventures and mischief, nurtured in him an expansive imagination that only deepened over the years, particularly as he transitioned into the roles of husband and father.

Today, Joseph is the proud parent of two wonderful children, Ethan and Livia. The whimsical stories he spun for his son, inspired by the intricate artwork tattooed on his arm, became the seed for the captivating narrative you hold in your hands. As he navigated the joys and challenges of parenthood, Joseph recognized the profound impact of childhood memories. From beloved stuffed animals to bedtime tales, these moments shape who we become. It's this nostalgia and desire to craft a lasting memory for his own children that spurred him to put pen to paper.

In "The Cosmic World of Olympus: Battle for the Throne", Joseph has woven together the threads of his personal experiences, his children's wonder, and the tales behind his tattoos. He invites you into this world with the hope that you'll find as much joy in reading his story as he found in writing it.

Acknowledgments

To my dad, Matt Breslin:
Thank you for being the role model I needed as I grew up. Your hard work and love have shaped who I am today in more ways than I can count. Every step of this journey has been inspired by your dedication and support. I love you.

To my uncles Timmy and Toby, and my aunts Tracy and Terri-Jean:
You are the best and tightest group of loved ones I know. I love each of you so much; there aren't enough pages or time to express how much you mean to me. Thank you for everything.

Made in the USA
Coppell, TX
19 January 2026

68612362R00164